SIN

AND

REDEMPTION

THE PINK ELEPHANT
CONNECTION

(BASED ON A TRUE STORY)

James E. McCarthy

Sin and Redemption: The Pink Elephant Connection

by James E. McCarthy

© 2016 by James E. McCarthy

ISBN: 978-1-944136-00-0

Ashanti Victoria Publishing
109 Ambersweet Way
Suite 313
Davenport, FL 33897

jamese_mccarthy@yahoo.com
www.jamesemccarthy.com

Disclaimer: This book is a work of fiction molded and adapted by the author's life experiences. All characters are fictional and while some locations are specific, their use as a setting is in a fictional manner in this book. Any similarities between characters and live people are purely coincidental. The author is in no way making any moral, ethical, or legal judgements or evaluations for the activities described in this book.

Permissions:

Stock Photography: Anna Baburkina |Dreamstime.com, Couperfield |Dreamstime.com, David Taylor |Dreamstime.com, Denis Aglichev |Dreamstime.com, Eldadcarin |Dreamstime.com, Elmirex2009 |Dreamstime.com, Laroslav Horbunov |Dreamstime.com, Kavida27 |Dreamstime.com, Paulus Rusyanto |Dreamstime.com, Pavel Chernobrivets |Dreamstime.com, Roman Hraska |Dreamstime.com, Sinisa Botas |Dreamstime.com, Tinamou |Dreamstime.com, Zim235 |Dreamstime.com

Newspaper articles / Court Documents: Supplied by the author.
Freehand Drawings: Supplied by the author.

Additional photography: Public domain from government sources.

Book Cover Design: Rik Feeney / www.RickFeeney.com

Dedication

This book is dedicated to those who have inspired me to be all I can be by never giving up on my dream and always finish what I start.

To my dearly departed wife Helen Ann Robinson McCarthy who constantly showed me love and kindness and always believed in my dreams by supporting everything or adventure aspired to achieve. She never said "NO! You can't do that".

To my darling daughter, Dominique' D. McCarthy who spent endless hours helping me edits and re-edit the manuscript to this book and stuck with me to the bitter end while missing her mother love who she cherished and was so close to.

To my little dear sweetheart daughter Ashanti Victoria McCarthy: She makes my day every day, when she wake up every morning giving me kisses and telling me how much she loves me with her innocent smile showing me how important I am in her life.

To my mother Katie M Baker who called me every night asking me "You finished the book yet? You mean, you still working on it? How many years now? You don't give up do you?" which had me laughing every step of the way.

To my closest friends who are my brothers, Johnnie and Darius McCarthy who may have doubted me ever completing this book never show it, nor made me feel that I was wasting my time.

To my Darling wife Phuc "Missy Mae" McCarthy, who's think I walk on water and always say to me "You're always busy, it gives me headache" which makes laugh because I know she fully supports every move I make without doubt or question. Thanks girl for believing in me unconditionally.

To my sisters: Ruthie Mae Murphy and Willie Pearl Calhoun thanks so much my big sisters for always expressing interest in me and always being so concern about my next move with genuine concern with nothing but hope for the best for me because you all knew I was always the dreamer and was never afraid of trouble.

To my darling daughters: Tracy T. McCarthy and Yolanda Bailey who never said it but I could always read their thoughts that screamed out at me saying: "Dawn daddy you're been working on that book a long time!" Are you ever going to get it published?!

Acknowledgments

To Rik Feeney my mentor, my friend, my agent and soon to be best bud. My respect for you touches the sky and cannot be put into words. He really understands me and truly know now where I come from as well as, trying to go. He <u>never</u> and I mean <u>never</u> said "no" and always showed me another way to get it done, until we got it done.

To my closest friends Gary, Jessica, Sandra and Brenda Jackson and to Glenn Corbett who were instrumental in helping me with a fresh new start by introducing me to my current wife to give my life new meaning after Helen died, many, many, thank for Lord know I did a lot of crying and Sandra and Brenda kept holding me all the way to Vietnam and back. What they did for me can't be put into words.

To my click whom I eternally lean on for positive stroking and unwavering support: Omayra Rodriguez, Maria Borges, Yvonne Delvalle, Veronica Narine, Mildred Diaz and Nicole Rodriguez. All who help me get through the day to day grind of life when we are at our best or worst. Thank you all for being there for me.

To my dearest and sweet friend Brittney McCleave and her mother who committed the ultimate sacrifice to help me write and rewrite the manuscript to add a woman's prospective to the book. Many, many, many thanks because I couldn't have done it without them.

To my friends and artists who did the art drawings: Ronnie Belsar and Indhira Hernandez good job. I solute you and hope your careers prosper.

And for those friends I didn't mention such as Joseph Watts and Ulissys Chisholm a special thanks for just being a life time friend and just being there for me through my ups and down especially when I went to prison seemingly to never get out but they stood by me.

Jessie and Glenda Dozier a big, big shout out!!

To Belvin Perry, Chief Judge for the 9th Judicial Circuit for Orange and Seminole county Florida; my close personal friend sense we were little boys playing together. You never looked down on me and to this day you supported by bid for a Presidential Pardon with a letter of recommendation thru the Bush and Obama Administration. Brother they don't make them like you anymore. Sir I salute you and your loving family and it also hurt me deeply when your father died too. He was a good cop and made us feel safe every time we walked out the door at mom's house.

To Edward L. DuBois, III owner of Investigators, Inc.; You knew about my past illicit life but you still supported me in allowing me to become Agency Manager at the Orlando Office, Fidelifacts, Inc., and to this day you've continued to allow me to be license as a Private Investigator through your agency. Sir this brings me to tears because I've never met anyone with a heart as big as yours and if there's anything I can do for you just name itttttttttt!!!

To Steven "Woody" Igou, Attorney at Law; you treated me like your own son when my father turned his back on me labeling me a "dope head" and not to be trusted. You knew better and supported me financially, spiritually and morally. God knows I wouldn't even be where I am today if it wasn't for you. And as far as I am concern you are my father. And as far as I'm concern Anita Caruana is the best damn secretary/paralegal I've ever met. So you make damn sure you keep her.

To Attorney Michael Maher one of the best dressed lawyers I've ever had the pleasure to know; Sir you dressed and cloth me with the finest suits, shirts and ties which instill me with pride and dignity and made me feel like one of the best dressed men in America and my mother Katie and I thank you from the bottom of our heart.

To Attorneys Victor Mead, Daniel Mazar, Edward Casoria, Jr., Hernan Castro, Peter A. Shapiro and the Law firm of Morgan and Morgan; you guys worked the hell out of me as your independent Investigator and Process Server which sustain my career for years, and for this I thank you all, for good hard work don't hurt anybody, it just makes one a better human being.

Table of Contents

Introduction
– page 11

Chapter 1: Prime Target
– page 13

Chapter 2: Trouble in Paradise
– page 29

Chapter 3: The Rock
– page 38

Chapter 4: Pink Elephant
– page 95

Chapter 5: Nothing to Declare
– page 142

Chapter 6: Fire aboard Flight 502
– page 160

Chapter 7: The Golden Triangle
– page 180

Chapter 8: The Snitch
– page 210

Chapter 9: Pleading for Presidential Pardon
– page 250

Appendix A: Corroborating Documents
– page 255

Appendix B: Character Descriptions
– page 263

About the Author
– page 273

Ordering Information
– page 275

Introduction

For more than a century, Heroin has increasingly plagued our society. But it wasn't until just a few years ago, that the Chinese Mafia imported heroin to the U.S. with their interesting Trademark Seal (the Pink Elephant) and the pink heroin- the most deadly opiate-type narcotic sold on the black market today.

On the cover of this book is a replica of the Seal or "Trademark" presently being used by the Chinese Mafia; it represents the world wide existence of their "Loose-knit Heroin Network." The Seal is mass produced in Hong Kong, Bangkok, Singapore, Thailand and Mainland China; then shipped to nearby clandestine laboratories and safe houses for product labeling.

The huge prehistoric mammoth, with its bulging bloodshot red eyes is an expression of rage, symbolizing the very strength, which has given pink heroin its lucrative value. More secretive and aggressive than the United States Italian Mafia, the Chinese Mafia supplied the heroin that has given the world its massive addiction problem.

CHAPTER 1

"Prime Target"

Orlando, Florida 1967; 3:00 p.m.

A hot wind dripping with midsummer humidity is blowing in from the east but Joe Stegner is sweating for an altogether different reason. He is no closer to paying off his gambling debt than when he made the first payment.

The telephone rings. Joe is frightened. He receives a final warning: "Make the rendezvous." He wonders whether to obey the order or leave town. He had two reasons for disobedience: one personal, one professional. The personal reason: he didn't want to die. The professional reason: he couldn't be seen gambling while his debt remained unpaid, his debt of $20,000.

Joe didn't want to risk his life without a good reason. He was torn between responsibility to his family and his gambling debt with the mob. He was supposed to go to the doorway of a condemned building between Fashion Square Mall and E. Robinson Street to meet his contact. Each would carry a Bible. If certain they weren't being followed, they would agree that "John, Chapter 3: Verse 16" was "most inspiring." Otherwise, one would say, "I'm afraid I haven't read it yet."

The building might not be there anymore, but that wasn't what troubled Joe. His gut instinct told him they might be setting him up for a hit since the Mafia threw professionalism to the wind back in those heady days when Blackburn, Lanetti, and Gambino seemed to take over. Joe hadn't trusted them since.

Against all logic, he wanted to make the prearranged meeting. It was a foolish risk, but the simple reason was… he had become unspeakably bored and tired of running. It had been 10-years since he experienced anything remotely close to "action." Yes, he would make the rendezvous, but not in the way they expected.

Joe Stegner took his Bible and gun and stuffed them into his coat pocket. It was dark and damp outside, so he carried an umbrella. The rendezvous was set for some time between ten and eleven p.m. that night. He arrived at the condemned building at nine minutes past ten. The contact was in the doorway with a black-bound Bible under his arm. Joe hurried past; his head down. The man was a young Italian, of medium height, broad shoulders and a black mustache. He was chewing gum, preoccupied; waiting for the phone to ring from a nearby pay phone.

When Joe walked by the second time on the opposite side of the street, he spotted the tail (hit man). However, if the contact in the doorway couldn't get Joe out in the open, the tail in the alley would take over. Joe assumed the worst, then thought of a way to deal with it. There was a telephone booth in the parking lot next to the mall. He went inside and memorized the number. He then found "John…. 3:16," in the Bible, tore out the page, and scribbled in the margin: "Go to the phone booth near the mall." Joe walked around the back street until he found an old drunk sitting on a doorstep.

Joe said, "Say fellow! Do you know the condemned building near here?"

The drunk's eyes rolled skyward. "Yeah..," he mumbled as he staggered to his feet. "What's it to ya?" He fell into Joe's arms. Joe frowned, as a foul smell lingered in the air. He straightened the old man to his feet. Reaching into his pocket, he gave the drunk a fist full of money.

"You like money, old man?" he asked, waving the money in the drunks face.

"Why hell-yeah…!" the drunk replied forcefully with slurred speech, spit and all. "Whadda-ya want me to do for it-t-t?" The drunk lost his balance and fell into Joe's arms once again.

Joe helped him to his feet, handed him the torn Bible page and pointed him in the direction of the condemned building. "There's a man in the doorway, give this page to him and keep your mouth shut." He shoved a fifty dollar bill in the man's dirt ridden coat pocket.

The man staggered off, Joe following in the distance. As he approached the contact, Joe ducked into the doorway of another building. Watching from afar; observing the tail lurking in the dark shadows of the alley. Joe stood just outside a door pretending to be struggling with an umbrella to block him from the tails view. Both he and the tail watched as the drunk exchanged the message with the contact and walked off. Joe ended his charade with the umbrella and walked in the opposite direction. He looked back briefly to see the tail run after the vanished contact.

Joe decided to stop at the nearest telephone and dial the number to the telephone booth near the Mall.

Ring… ring… "Hello?" a deep voice answered.

"What's with the special rendezvous?" Joe asked.

"John… 3:16," the contact responded.

"Most inspiring," Joe confirmed.

"Yes, isn't it?"

***

This fool has no idea of the trouble he's in, the contact thought to himself. "I must see you," insisted the contact. "My orders come from high up… do you understand?"

Joe pretended to comply. "All right… I'll meet you," he said. "But in two days, bottom of the I-4 overpass at the 33rd Street Exit at eight a.m."

"Can't you make it sooner?" the contact uttered with urgency.

"No," Joe replied, hanging up the phone, quickly leaving the booth. He walked two blocks and came in sight of the telephone booth near the Mall. He saw the contact walking toward E. Robinson Street. No signs of the tail. He decided to follow the contact until he got to his car and drove away.

Joe decided to head home, thinking he outsmarted the contact, as he whistled a tune to his success. He strolled through a succession of residential streets, feeling at ease in his 'hood,' never looking over his shoulder even once.

On the way home Joe ducked into a rundown stash house; a second place away from home. The grass hadn't been mowed in months and the paint was dried and flaky from years of neglect. There was a wooden fence; broken where a tree rotted and fell to the ground. The house had a dormer window in the roof; that would be a room, high up for better observation.

***

The hit man scanned the house from the opposite side of the street. Walking past Joe's house he turned the corner, walking to the next parallel street and counting the houses. Almost directly behind the house Joe had entered was a vacant house. *Good*, he thought to himself. His heart beat a shade faster. The game was on!

Dressed in a black woolen hat, leather flight jacket, and rubber-soled shoes, Nick the hit man would be almost invisible in the night's shadows.

After midnight, Nick drove through the quiet street; parking a quarter mile from his destination. He walked, not to Joe's house, but to the vacant house on the next street. It was dark, only a dim light from the neighboring houses and the cloud covered moon. Dogs barked in the distance. He entered the doorway and went through the house to the rear.

Nick jumped over a fence and walked to the kitchen window of Joe's house. He removed a small scoop-shaped blade from his pocket to remove the brittle putty around the glass. This was his way in. After some time, Nick was able to remove a pane of glass from the window and lay it down. Slowly he reached around and opened the latch to raise the window, and climbed inside.

The house smelled of moths and disinfectant. Nick unlocked the back door, a precaution for a fast exit before entering the hall. He shined his pencil flashlight on and off quickly. He observed a small table with one plastic lawn chair, a disheveled couch with the springs exposed and a pile of tattered clothes next to the staircase. Silently the hit man climbed the uncarpeted wooden stairs. Halfway up he noticed a light coming from under the door at the top of the stairs, followed by an asthmatic cough and the sound of a toilet flushing.

He froze against the wall as the door opened, flooding the stairs with light. An old man came out the bathroom and turned to walk into the dark bedroom to the left. Suddenly the old man stopped. He must see me, the hit man thought to himself as he pulled a dagger from his sleeve. The man, whose eyes were half open, turned back to the bathroom to turn off the light and grunted before stumbling back to bed.

The hit man crept to the door on the right. He gently tried to turn the handle. The door was locked. He removed a slim black case from his pocket which carried his tools of the trade and picked the lock. Once the door was open he slowly edged inside. From the opposite corner of the room came the sound of deep, heavy breathing. He walked along the wall until he reached the bed where Joe slept.

He grabbed Joe tightly by the throat and quickly straddled his chest. In his raspy smokers voice he whispered, "2nd

Kings….1/12." Joe struggled against the hit man, lack of air causing his eyes to water and bulge. The hit man loosened his grip and brought his dagger to Joe's neck.

"You gonna let me up or what?" Joe asked demandingly.

"Why didn't you cooperate? You were watched at the Mall." The hit man said.

In a moment of desperation, Joe replied, "I... I had to be sure you all weren't out to kill me!"

The hit man looked at him. Tightened his grip and said, "I think your right," with a sly grin on his face. He placed his left hand on Joe's chest firmly, with his right hand he thrust the dagger in just under the ribs and stabbed upward to the heart. Joe's body convulsed as blood flowed onto the bed.

***

Going under the assumed name of Nick MaChinso, the "hit man" had been paid $25k to do the job. He'd traveled from upstate New York leaving dozens of unsolved murders in his wake. He opened the closet and dresser drawers and tried to think like a burglar. He leaned over Joe's body and pulled the rings off his fingers then quickly, but quietly ransacked the room.

Nick washed his hands and sat down to think of anything he may have missed. It had been the perfect 'hit,' evidence free until he remembered the old man. Then Nick made his way gently towards the old man's room and suffocated him with a pillow, making sure no witness would be left behind.

Nick would have to spend the rest of the night in the open, and then shift to his second identity, still needing a new job, papers, passport, license, and social security card. With little fear of being caught by the police, the flashy, vulgar, commercial traveler who occupied the master suite at the Langford Hotel in nearby Winter Park looked rather different from the shabby, parcel clerk who had killed Leo's father. Machinso took a last look around and walked off into the night.

***

A week later, the landlord discovered the bodies of the old man and Joe Stegner. The police notified Stella, Joe's wife shortly after.

Stella was momentarily paralyzed at the news. She fought down the panic and tried to think rationally as her life shuddered to a halt. Joe had been murdered, leaving her alone with the kids and mounting bills. What would she do now? Whom could she call for help?

That night she called her father Lester over to the house to ask for guidance. Her soft voice flooded with tears, "What am I going to tell the children?"

"You'll know then; I suppose," her father replied; unsure what to say himself. Lester took Stella into his arms. Her eyes shut tight as she wept. "Don't... you can't let this thing get the best of you," he whispered.

Lester and Stella talked quietly throughout the night making plans for the funeral and her family's future.

***

The next morning Stella told her children as calmly as she could that their father had been murdered.

"Who murdered him?" Robert, Joe's oldest son, asked.

"We don't know, honey. Probably the people he gambled with." Stella said.

"Does that mean he went to heaven?" Doris asked; she was Joe's youngest daughter.

"Yes, I think so." Stella replied, holding back her tears.

Leo; Joe's youngest, son sat quietly and stared at his mother; as if he knew the answer to every question.

Days later Joe was buried on the west end of town, in the Washington Park Cemetery off of Bruton Boulevard. Two hundred or so members of the Mount Siani Seventh Day Adventist church came to offer condolences to the family. A bald preacher conducted the brief service, the pages of his Bible rippled by the gusty winds.

Leo stood away from the others, his head to one side, picking at his eye as if the wind had blown some speck in it. The way Joe was killed bothered 17-year-old Leo almost as bad as the times when Joe made the three of them stand in a belt line and recite all the books of the bible; from the Old Testament to the New Testament by heart. Leo remembered the night Robert missed one of the books of the bible and Joe had beat Robert's ass as hard as he could with an extension cord, which was repeated nightly until they learned them. Leo would have to become a man now and help Robert defend their family. This would be the beginning of a new way of life for Leo.

Despite the beatings, Leo loved his father. He didn't always like the way his father treated him, but he did love him and whoever had murdered him now had a serious problem named Leo Stegner.

Leo looked forward to the summer. He'd just graduated from high school and begun his search for a job. Most of the permanent jobs had been filled, and Leo didn't score high enough on the entrance exam to get into college. Being a native to a less than wealthy lifestyle, he would have to come up with other ways to make a living. Nevertheless, Leo was determined not to let that limit his options. Easily influenced by his peers, and out of desperation from not finding work, Leo joined a group of thugs called the "Ring-Eye Gang."

Ted Morgan was the leader of the gang. He was the meanest looking 'black-mother-fucker' Leo had ever seen in his life. He was only 24 but stood about 6'2, 240lbs. His nose had been broken once or twice, all gnarled up. He had a sinus issue that caused him to constantly sniffle and a multitude of old scars on his face. His mammoth hands were swollen and bent out of shape from whaling on numerous past opponents.

He led a gang of professional car thieves; one of the best in Florida at the time. Their reputation and specialty were as well known by the police as it was to Leo Stegner. They stole as many as ten cars a week. Most of the gang had been arrested, but never proven guilty let alone done any time.

They had become experts, never leaving fingerprints or evidence that could lead to their identities. So clever, they avoided committing a theft in the presence of unreliable people who might stand as witnesses in the case of a prosecution. They stole vehicles from car lots, hotels, malls, and restaurants. Places they were sure the owners would not return in less than an hour.

Ted Morgan wouldn't allow a member of the gang to keep any of the cars they stole. He had each car unloaded an hour after they were stolen.

If a car was locked and the Ring-Eye Gang wanted it, they would have it started within twenty-seconds from the time they spotted it. If a car had a hidden burglar alarm, the alarm would be disabled before it even went off. The secret was teamwork and know how. They specialized in Corvettes, Mercedes, Jaguars and Cadillac's. Their tactics were conducted in a military fashion, sometimes risky, but well sequenced.

Leo Stegner and his pals had become so popular that other gangs soon infiltrated the state. There were stories in the press, almost daily, about "gangs of thieving youths; a swelling army of young criminals."

The holiday season had already started when Ted Morgan went to pull his next job. Basically, he was a loner, but he was having more trouble than usual since every officer in the state knew him by face. He was driving the officer's nuts and they wanted him bad. On Thanksgiving Day, Detective Hood spotted Ted in a Mustang.

Det. Sergeant William H. Hood was a 54-year-old, short, stubby man and one of the Orlando Police Department's finest officers. He'd been with the department for nineteen years. Ted, as slippery a snake was determined not to let Hood ruin his glamour as the leader of the Ring-Eye Gang. He led Det. Hood on a high-speed chase throughout the city. The funny part of the chase was when Hood lost his composure and forgot to follow official police codes and procedures.

He shouted over the noise of the siren and chase, "Damn-it! I can't catch that son-of-a-bitch! Set up road blocks! Send out APB's! And let's force that motherfucker onto Interstate 4." He paused for a quick second, to spit tobacco out the window and proceeded. "That son-of-a-bitch is driving a Shelby Cobra and he's flying!"

***

Ted had stolen the Cobra with a 427 engine that had a L88 cam, headers, with a two four-barrel cross ram carburetor set up; from a car lot off East Hwy 50, intending to strip it for parts. As the chase continued, he knew they couldn't catch him. After all, it was the fastest street car ever built at the time.

***

Almost instantly, a soft, sweet voice replied over the radio, "Copy Det. Hood, and will respond." The OPD blocked off all exits leading out of Orlando, forcing Ted to take I-4 East bound, which runs high over the city in and around the downtown area.

Both Ted and Det. Hood could view the approaching roadblock ahead.

"I've got your ass now Morgan!" Det. Hood said smugly.

Ted Morgan had other ideas. Under a hail of bullets, Ted gassed the Shelby Cobra up to 120 miles per hour as he went into an "S" curve. Ted lost control of the car, jumping the guardrail and plunging some 300 feet to his death. The explosion on impact lit up Lake Ivanhoe like the Fourth of July.

Det. Hood was angry as hell, until he got to the sight of impact and found Morgan's body had been thrown clear of the wreckage. He scurried across the slippery green grass embankment then dove into Lake Ivanhoe and retrieved Ted's body. Hood was after Morgan's address book and he found it.

***

When Leo Stegner saw the shocking report on television his mouth snapped closed. He knew Ted carried a list of names and addresses in a little black address book in his pocket and the police would be closing in to round up the names listed for questioning. Leo couldn't sleep at all that night. He was stressed and by morning had decided to leave town.

Leo was spotted trying to board a Greyhound bus bound for New York City by two policemen who stopped him to ask for his identification.

"What's in the suitcase?" one officer asked.

"Just some personal stuff," Leo snapped back.

"Then open it!" The other officer demanded, hastily grabbing the suitcase from Stegner's hands. Upon peering inside the officer shook his head suggesting to his partner they had stumbled on the mother lode.

"Tools of a burglar's trade; lots of money in small bills, a pistol, ammunition, and papers that says he's an unemployed high school graduate. Let's take him down for questioning, but first we better read him his rights."

Several hours later, Det. Hood arrived at the police station and met with the two officers. "Let's have a look at him." They went down the corridor to the cells.

"This one," said the turn-key cell guard. He opened the door and Det. Hood followed him in.

Leo sat on his bunk with his legs stretched out and his back against the wall.

"So this is one of the thugs in the Ring-Eye Gang, huh?" grunted Hood to the guard.

"It's hard to be certain," the guard muttered back.

"What's your street name?" Hood demanded.

"Leo Stegner."

"You don't have a nickname?" Hood replied.

"No! Just Leo Stegner! And nothing else!" Leo said somewhat irate.

"I see we have us a smart ass," Det. Hood commented. "Why were you carrying a gun?"

"Protection!" Leo fired back, "New York ain't no picnic!"

"Where did you get it?" Hood insisted.

Leo sighed. "My father, he left it to me when he died."

The guard glanced at Det. Hood, who shrugged, then said, "Your story sounds silly! You better start telling the truth!" Leo sat up in his bunk, and got loud.

"I am! You fool… you think I wanna be here?" Stegner yelled.

Hood's face turned red as a fire engine. He turned toward the guard, took all the loose change out of his pocket and tied it in his handkerchief, saying nothing, swinging the little bundle in his left hand.

"Whaddaya know about the Ring-Eye Gang?" Hood shouted.

"Leo sighed, shook his head from side to side, "Nothing!" he replied.

"Nothing?" Hood fired back, "On your feet!" he demanded sharply, and then came forward and struck Stegner with the weighted handkerchief in one swift motion. The blow caught Leo on the bridge of the nose. Leo cried out. His hands went to his face.

"Stand at attention!" Hood insisted forcefully, "Now! Tell Me!"

Leo stood upright, frightened, then let his hands fall to his sides. "I don't know what you're talking about! And I demand to see my lawyer," he shouted.

Detective Hood struck him again in exactly the same place. This time Leo went down on one knee and his eyes watered.

"You know something!" Hood insisted, "I'll be damned if I don't make you talk!" Hood pulled Stegner to his feet and punched him in the stomach. "Why were you carrying a gun? And tell me about Ted Morgan! You do know him!"

Leo shouted angrily, "But that's about all, I just know him!"

Hood wasn't satisfied; he punched Leo again, this time harder. Stegner fell to his bunk.

"That's enough!" the guard shouted. He grabbed Hood's arm just as he got ready to punch Leo again. "This is my station and I can turn a blind eye only so long."

Hood rounded on the guard. "We're not dealing with some punk kid! This son-of-a-bitch is involved in grand theft auto," he shouted, outraged. "And I'll do whatever I have to get a conviction." Hood turned back to Stegner pointing; "And if that means the prisoner gets hurt, then I'll just have to take that responsibility."

"Not on this floor you won't," the guard responded. With pain written all over his face, Stegner took the opportunity to interrupt.

"Man-nn! What is this shit! A setup?" Leo yelled out.

Hood hauled him to his feet. "Aren't you Leo Stegner, born November of 1950, here in Orlando?" Leo nodded. "And, wasn't your father killed by some mobsters over a gambling debt?" Stegner nodded again. "Well… your name was found in Morgan's address book the night he went off the bridge. And—"

Leo became brave. He snatched away from Det. Hood, interrupting him, then said, "That doesn't mean I steal cars! You can't just pin something on me just because of that! Besides, I haven't even been identified yet!"

Hood looked at the guard, angry. "He hasn't been identified," the guard stated.

"But his name," Hood insisted.

"Yes, I know," the guard said, "But he could be telling the truth. And isn't that for us to decide?"

Hood felt cheated. He stood silent for a moment, and then walked out.

"What's his badge number?" Stegner demanded. "I'm gonna press charges against his fat ass!"

The guard turned toward Leo, then said, "If I were you, I'd just leave town and forget about what just happened."

Leo Stegner turned his back to the closing cell door. He was hurting. He shut his eyes, closed his mouth and dropped his arms. Exhausted, he slid down the door and fell to the floor. The thought of leaving town sounded like a great idea, until moments later when flashbacks of Joe's death began to hunt him. "Oh hell no," Leo shouted out loud. "Somebody killed my motherfucking father and I'm not going anywhere. VENGEANCE IS MINE SAID THE LORD and somebody is going to pay." Leo pulled himself to his feet, pacing back and forth in his cell. Thinking, thinking and thinking his next move.

CHAPTER 2

"Trouble in Paradise"

Ted Morgan's death had given Leo a wake-up call. He was determined to get on the straight and narrow. In reading the classifieds, Leo discovered a legitimate career opportunity as a mail courier at the Kennedy Space Center. He believed this might be his way out of the hood and a way to hide in plain sight while he put together his plan to avenge his father's murder. He pursued the career with NASA ostensibly seeking a path to a better life; far away from struggles of poverty, drugs, crime, and the stigma of being a black man in America in the 60's.

Atlanta was the heartland of the South, but Orlando was becoming the pulsating center of tourist attractions. Orlando, Florida had been named the "City Beautiful," however; Cape Kennedy Space Center held in its hands the fate of future space exploration. And he, Leo Stegner, was going to be part of it.

The physical presence of war and space technology was everywhere. If it came to war, such as the "Cuban Missile Crisis," under President John K. Kennedy, Florida could've been the first possible hit.

Leo was bewildered by the presence of military uniforms that filled the streets of Orlando: Navy, Air Force and the Army Reserve. For the first time, he began to feel the grim possibility of war as something real.

Leo moved into a second floor walk-up apartment, with a fair-sized sunken living room. The apartment was perfect. It had an adjoining bedroom and a spacious kitchen. He spent the entire spring decorating his apartment and took enormous pleasure in doing it… in everything from the painting and plastering to the selection of each and every object he acquired. The interior had been cleaned and aired and there were thick rugs on the stone floors. Leo had become independent of his brothers and sisters.

The pressure within Leo had lifted like vapor, leaving him empty with happiness. He saw this as an opportunity to get clear of the surrounding ghetto's and become the man his father never was. For Joe had instilled deep religious values in Leo and his siblings. Joe conducted himself as though he was a man of God going to church every Saturday never missing a day. He even went door to door soliciting; selling bible books, speaking to those about God as though he was God, but in reality Joe was a sinner in disguise.

***

Leo was delighted when he received word that he had been hired as a mail courier by TWA, a subcontractor within NASA's giant conglomerate.

Leo enjoyed working for TWA and the Space Program and had become comfortable and confident with his co-workers. It was the only decent job Leo could get and he decided he actually liked doing it.

As the months went by, he was less intimidated working around astronauts and NASA's Director, Werner Von Braun.

Leo's fresh outlook on life had given him values and goals to shoot for and real hope for a successful future. He still went to work every day concealing from the world and his coworkers that burning need for vengeance against the man that is responsible for his father's death.

He worked on the first floor of the Headquarters Building, a thirty-story, twentieth-century sky scraper, carved from marble and stone. His job was one of awesome responsibility, with emphasis placed on the handling of top secret and confidential documents.

Alfred Nelson, a fat, jolly sort of fellow was Leo's supervisor. He was clean-cut, intelligent and well-dressed for his size. Nelson appeared to be efficient in his work and showed no prejudice towards him. In fact, they got along extremely well.

In the meantime; the J.F.K. Space Center was on "Full Alert" status making ready for the "First Three-Man Apollo" flight into orbit. Air force Officer's Virgil "Gus" Grissom, age 40; Lt. Col. Edward Higgins White II, age 36; and Lt. Commander Roger B. Chaffee, age 31 were in gravity "G" force training in the M.O.S. Building, when word came from Mission Control (NASA), acknowledging their appointment for the mission. The M.O.S. was a multipurpose building where many advances in space

exploration took place under strict security. Training maneuvers had become a part of the astronaut's daily routine. Such as weightlessness, flight simulations, scuba diving and "G" force gravity training.

Later that January, word from Mission Control for "All Systems Go" was announced; the countdown to commence at 10 am. Weather balloons floated majestically in the blue skies. It was the coldest winter in fifty-years with temperatures reaching 18 degrees. The media had been notified to move into position, while crowds of people parked their cars along the embankment of the Cocoa Beach/Titusville shoreline.

The V.A.B. (Vehicle Assembly Building) was one of the largest and tallest buildings in the world. It was made of grey stone and slate, the color of the sea. It stood at the mouth of the Atlantic on the Northeastern end of Cape Kennedy. It was a multipurpose building, where advances in technology took place. It included tracking stations, backup systems, ground-to-air communications, deep space scanners, monitoring devices, chemical propulsion labs and computers; and the rocket stages and boosters were assembled there as well.

The three-man Apollo mission had been moved to Launch Pad 9 where high propulsion fuel had been pumped into its fuel tanks. Staff and employees were on standby and had been evacuated from the back blast areas to the V.A.B. while astronauts Grissom, White, and Chaffee were being strapped into the Apollo Capsule.

***

Communication documents vital to the launch had to be delivered, however, Leo had not completed his mail route yet. He was on route from Patrick Air Force Base, roughly sixteen miles Southeast of Cape Kennedy.

The tires on the Dodge van he drove were badly worn, but Leo drove fast just the same. He had climbed a steep Pineda Causeway and just cleared the top when the right rear tire blew. The down side of the hill was steep and slippery. He could hear the distant roar of an approaching truck. The courier van's tires squealed as he skidded around the bends.

Damn he thought, "This bitch is going too fast." The back of the van skidded on a left curve. Leo down-shifted afraid to brake in case he skidded again. There was a sharp right-hand curve and he lost traction on the back of the van. The curve seemed to go on forever. The van slid sideways and turned one hundred and eighty degrees, so it was going backward, then continued to spin in the same direction. "My God!" he screamed. He heard a loud horn, and then saw the truck. It was struggling up the hill on the other side of the two-lane causeway at a snail's pace. Leo glimpsed the driver's face; the guy's mouth was hanging wide-open, he appeared to be standing up straight as he stomped on his brakes.

There was just enough room to pass the truck if he could regain control. He heaved the steering wheel over and touched the accelerator. The two vehicles nearly collided head on.

Leo was miles from the nearest telephone, and he could not afford to abandon the courier van, with top secret documents aboard.

Meanwhile Alfred Nelson, the mailroom supervisor, had become frantic with worry. He was pissed and at a loss for words. He rushed out of his office and headed to the mailroom floor, then yelled out aloud, "Where in the hell is Leo Stegner? Where can he be?" Alfred pointed his index finger shaking it up and down at one of the mail couriers sitting at a nearby desk and then said, "Grab a telephone. Dial Wackenhut Security and ask them to search all roads leading from the air force base, and to get Leo back at all costs! The Director of NASA is threatening to delay the countdown if Leo did not arrive with the weather reports."

Nelson raced back to his office and placed several calls in a desperate attempt to get a fix on his location. The weatherman at Patrick's Air Force Base had verified his departure nearly twenty -minutes ago, and the Bendix's people confirmed the same. Every department involved in the launch program was conducted in a classified manner and given a classified status. For that was the nature of the space program.

Leo had just finished changing the tire and lit a cigarette when security drove up. They jumped out of their cars with their hands on their guns and approached him with extreme caution.

"What the fuck!" Leo said. "Are you going to shoot me for smoking a motherfucking cigarette?"

"Are you Leo Stegner?"

"That's right," he replied. "What's going on?"

"That's what we want to know?" one officer said, craning his neck, looking right and left. "Everyone is looking for you!" His voice was angry, then alarmed. "You're delaying the launch and got the astronauts mad, and the Director is threatening to fire you."

Leo frowned "Well I don't give a damn! I almost lost my damn life fucking with this rush delivery shit, and I just finished changing a tire that blew out! Besides, I was given specific orders not to abandon the mail under any circumstance."

"Well, we can understand your position, but you can explain all of that when you get to Mission Control. Now let's get out of here. We will escort you!" another officer demanded.

Leo jumped into the van and they sped to the V.A.B. reaching speeds up to one hundred miles per hour. It seemed like hours before the V.A.B. building came into view. Leo steered toward it. There was a figure standing in the doorway, looking out at them. It was Nelson, who'd been worried about Leo's whereabouts, ran out into the street to meet them as they came to a screeching halt in front of the building. Nelson rushed to the van and snatched the door open. He noticed that Leo was inside, his hands and face, were filthy and dripping with sweat.

Nelson threw his arms up in the air. "What happened...what happened to you?" Nelson pleaded.

"I couldn't call... had a flat on the way back," Leo replied.

"Inside and get those reports to the tenth floor. Hurry! Hurry!! Hurry!!! Our careers are at stake here," Nelson shouted in a sharp tone.

Leo ran into the building and took the elevator to the tenth floor. When the doors opened, Leo; who was sweating like a race horse, hurried to find the ranking NASA official at his huge semicircular desk, in his smart new suit, tapping his pencil on the paper blotter, looking annoyed.

Leo rushed into the office anxious and out of breath, not knowing what to expect. He threw up his hands and said, "I'm sorry I'm so late, I blew a tire. I got here as soon as I could!" He surrendered the documents and sat down. He began thinking about the near miss with the truck, and almost causing the halt to the three-man Apollo test launch. He could visualize the newspaper headline reading: "COURIER HALTS APOLLO LAUNCH/ FLAT TIRE."

The countdown was to resume just in time. Over the loud speaker he heard; "T-minus ten, minutes and counting." The "test" launch would commence, with hundreds of people and media affiliates watching seven miles off base. The on lookers had a view from every conceivable angle. The sky was crystal clear up and down range.

Nine minutes and several seconds later, the voice crackled over the loud speaker again. "Please stand by, please stand by… it is now T-minus eleven seconds and counting…Ten! Nine! Eight! Seven! Six! Five! Four! Three! Two! One! We have ignition… we have lift off!!

The crowd of reporters, family members and employees applauded as the giant three-manned Apollo space craft roared into high gear as a simulated launch rehearsal.

All of a sudden, without warning, all hell broke loose. "There's a fire in the cockpit…there's a fire in the cockpit!" We're on Fire, we're on fire!!! The astronauts yelled. "HELP, HELP….Aahhhhhh!"

The giant Apollo space craft had become a towering inferno. Leo stood there utterly paralyzed while shock swept over the crowd watching the launch. In that instant, astronauts, Grissom, White and Chaffee were dead; there was nothing anyone could do to help them. The fire alarm echoed in the distance.

Though the fire had been the fault of an electrical shortage (causing sparks to ignite, and fire to rapidly spread) the fire had left its undeniable mark on Leo and triggered a new stage of depression in him.

Leo was dejected, unable to eat, and felt condemned that President Johnson had ordered a massive cutback of NASA's employees and all was forever lost. His misfortunes seemed to have been divinely planned one disaster after another, from his father's death to the Ring Eye Gang, now this.

Leo console himself by taking a prostitute out on the town and getting drunk. Distracting himself of his grief, he suddenly became aware of his obsession with prostitutes and liked it because it didn't require him to have developed skills and intellect.

CHAPTER 3

"The Rock"

March 1970 - 4:30 A.M. - Fort Jackson, Columbia, S.C.

All hell broke loose that cold miserable morning when Drill Sergeant Daniels came crashing into the barracks of Company E-10-2, shouting as though he was stark raving mad, and swinging his Billy club; cracking it like a whip, against the lockers and bunks.

"Get out of the rack; get out of the goddamned rack! Move, move, move it, you're in boot camp!! And it's time to train."

A new wave of recruits had arrived on "Tank Hill" to meet their doom with six months of AIT (aptitude intelligence training) and BT (basic training). Leo had witnessed a quarter million men training to kill using skills like: bayonet training, demolition, target practice, and hand to hand combat.

***

The city of Columbia didn't look like the capital of a nation at war but there were many signs, and Leo noted them all. He was considerably more observant than the average recruit. He monitored the movement of troops around Columbia's Jet port.

He knew the significance of workers pouring into factories, where only months previously, there were hardly enough positions available; now jobs were plentiful.

In May of 1970, Leo rubber-stamped a batch of forms that led him to believe a new evacuation force was to be gathered.

Leo was fairly sure the force would have a company of about one hundred thousand soldiers, who orders stated that they would be sent off to fight in Europe and Vietnam.

He knew of no reason why he wouldn't be sent off to war, nor did he feel any sentiment about running from it, but trying to relax at Fort Jackson was like sitting in a dry bed of sandy spurs. Leo volunteered to join the army because he was hell bent on becoming a trained killer and eventually return home to seek vengeance on his father's killers.

Guyda Henderson, Leo's steady girlfriend at the time, had come to Columbia to visit him for the weekend. They first met at a small house party back in Orlando and had been introduced by Thomas Scalli, Guyda's cousin and a friend of Leo's from the hood. Leo had grown fond of her. He needed a woman to smarten him up, there was no doubt about that and Guyda needed a man to keep her company and to love. Leo rented a second floor room at the Lake Shore Motel, half a mile from the Post.

Leo and Guyda were drinking on the terrace in the afternoon shade when Leo told Guyda that he had scored well on his exams and had been considered for officer training at the OCS (Officer Candidate School). Leo, with a boyish enthusiasm, wanted to be a fighter pilot and war correspondent, if time permitted.

"They say this war will be won or lost in the air, you know," said Leo.

"Aren't you afraid?" Guyda asked softly.

"Not a bit!" Then he looked at her and said, "Yes, I am." Guyda thought he was very brave and held his hand.

Later, they put on swim suits and went down to the lake. "Are you a good swimmer?" Leo asked Guyda.

"Better than you!" she replied.

"All right, race you to the sandbar?" Leo suggested.

The sandbar was a small patch of trees about two hundred yards from shore. Guyda struck out in a fast freestyle motion. Leo won, of course, with his powerful arms and legs. Forty yards from the island, Guyda had to roll onto her back and float. Leo was already on shore and jumped back into the water and swam to meet her, he angled himself behind her as if to perform a lifesaving maneuver and pulled her slowly to shore.

"I'm enjoying this!" he said, as she giggled.

A few moments later he smiled and said; "I suppose I might as well tell you, the lake is only four feet deep!"

"What?" as she squirmed out of his arms, splashing and laughing until she could find her footing and stand up straight. He took her hand and led her out of the water to a clearing, completely surrounded by bushes. He sat beside her, kissed her and then pushed her gently down to lay flat. He stroked her hips and kissed her neck in an erotic fashion.

Guyda, who was shy said, "No! Not here!" Leo buried his face in the hollow of her shoulder. "Guyda, please this may be our last chance to have some fun and excitement together!" She rolled from under him and stood up. With one swift movement she took off her suit. The guilty pleasure made the memory more pleasant. Even if it had been a well-planned seduction, she was a willing victim.

June 1970, 1:45 P.M. Frankfurt, West Germany

Every large country has a distinctive image, but Germany was different. The East and West territories were restless, crude and without direction. The United States Army sent Leo on a plane with many other recruits including a Colonel, a Captain, and a Master Sergeant to the 3rd Armored Division at Drake Edwards Kaserne in Frankfurt, West Germany. They gave him uniforms and ran him through additional basic training for a few weeks. From there, he was sent to Kirchgoens, West Germany to work at Ayers Kaserne 'The Rock'.

'The Rock' was a detachment of the 3/36th Infantry Division which housed G.I.'s who defended the Russian Front. They called it 'The Rock' because words like cold and dismal were invented in regions such as this. Here, drug abuse was five times higher than that of civilian life, and as a result, most officers ran the military outpost like a concentration camp. They didn't care if the recruits had housing for their families and restricted all 30-day leaves to the States. Additional rations had been regarded as a sin and personal vehicles were strictly taboo. Civilian clothing had been outlawed and any man late for company formation was to be court-martialed.

Colonel Bob Bronson, the commander of the 3rd Armored, 3/36th Infantry Division was pleased to be in control. He knew the strength and morale of the military division under his command lay squarely on his shoulders. So, he used the privileges that were afforded the troops to keep them under control. Bronson overlooked the fact the troops were young, inexperienced men and his ragging them, along with his lack of respect for them, was what caused the tension and massive drug problem in the first place.

***

Hundreds of Soviet paratrooper forces had just landed in Central E. Germany deep inside enemy territory as part of their war games under the WARSAW Pact agreement. The troops jumped from planes that flew from separate locations inside the Soviet Union. Other planes dropped tanks and armored personnel carriers for the troops. Their landings were softened by retrorockets fired just before impact; a device and technique that were new to the military.

As a show of force in the region, the Pentagon ordered an unscheduled alert (war games) of its own. Col. Bob Bronson and other division commanders alike had 36-hours to get prepared; the war games were scheduled to last approximately fourteen days. In less than forty-eight hours, eight hundred troops from the 82nd Airborne Brigade would jump from the modern 'C-121 Starlifter' transport planes. Their eight-hour trip and one-thousand-foot drop would bring the paratroopers down on a German farmer's field in front of an admiring cluster of Generals. The 82nd Airborne's new long-range capability, flying nonstop from the U.S., not only brought reinforcements to Europe, but it also had been ordered to take a quick reactionary force to Vietnam and Leo Stegner was now a part of it.

Col. Bob Bronson and other division commanders expressed concern about the United States' ability to defend the Russian Front. They knew there would be limits to the maneuvers because a large number of their soldiers dreaded going to war and as a result, had resorted to alcohol, acid, speed, hashish and heroin to keep their nerves in check. They also knew that the WARSAW PACT was widening the military gap, mostly in the range of conventional strategic nuclear missiles.

Headquarters - H.Q. Company 3/36th Infantry Division - 9:45 a.m.

The man behind the desk was sandy-haired and tall. He had an ugly face and a crushing handshake. Col. Bob Bronson was a combat intelligence officer who had served seven tours of duty in Vietnam during the 60's, then reunited with the army to voluntarily share his expertise in torture, intelligence gathering, and human interrogation; only someone had forgotten to tell Col. Bronson that his troops weren't the "gooks."

"Private Leo Stegner reporting for duty. Sir!" Leo saluted.

"You don't salute an officer inside, Private! You Married?" Bronson questioned.

"No Sir! But there's a special girl in my life back home," said Leo.

"It's tough you had to leave her. My wife died in 65' and we never had a child," muttered Col. Bronson.

"I'm sorry to hear that Sir! We're not having any. Not with the hellish state the world is currently in. There's too much child and sexual abuse going on. You agree, Sir?" asked Leo.

"Oh absolutely," Bronson agreed.

Leo stood at attention in front of the square desk. Colonel Bronson was touched by his circumstances, and found himself thinking of his late wife Rose Mary. That was unusual; he had been immune to sentiment for some years.

"Your orders say you had some leadership schooling and qualified to go into O.C.S. (Officer's Candidate School) is that right, Private?"

"That's right, Sir. All the way!" Leo replied.

"That's all well and good, Private. But you should have straightened all that out before you got here," Bronson said.

"What do you mean, Sir?" Leo asked.

"May I be frank, Private?" Bronson asked.

"Yes sir, go for it," Leo responded.

"Once you're sent to the 'Russian Front' Private, there isn't a snowball's chance in hell of getting to O.C.S. from here. Don't get me wrong, soldier, it has been done, but you might as well prepare to be with us for a while. Is that clear?"

Leo frowned in dismay and then replied as though he had a frog in his throat, "Crystal clear, Sir!"

"Can you type?" Bronson asked.

Leo responded with displeasure. "Sir! Yes, sir! I can type."

"How many soldier?"

"75-words a minute, Sir" he replied.

Col. Bronson snapped to in his chair, "Then I'll tell you what, Private. I'm going to bring you aboard. But if you can't hack it, I'll have to ship your ass to Nam! Agreed?"

Leo frowned again. "I agree sir," he responded. Leo couldn't believe how unpredictable Bronson could be.

"Good! Then we'll consider your future at a later date." Bronson looked at his watch. "Now, I want you to meet a very bright member of my staff. His name is Paul Underwagger, a first lieutenant we pinched from the Pentagon." Bronson smiled.

Leo sighed. "Ah, I see."

"Yes!" Bronson said, clapping his hands together. "He's a narcotic intelligence officer with the D.E.A."

"A what, sir?" Leo pondered. "What do they do, sir?"

"A bloodhound, Private! He investigates those goddamn 'dope heads' around here!"

"Must be a real problem…, sir?" Stegner responded.

"A pain in the ass to be more like it," Bronson replied.

"Wow! I've never been involved, sir!" Stegner replied.

"Well… see that you don't, soldier. Any man I catch… his ass belongs to me!" Bronson reassured him.

They left the room, rounded a couple of corners and entered a small office. A Playboy centerfold of a pretty girl hung on the wall.

"Paul Underwagger, meet Leo Stegner, our new replacement clerk."

"Well, well," the lieutenant said, "Let's get you checked in, Private."

"Tell you what Paul, I was just going home for an early lunch, so I'll leave you to it." Bronson said.

Lt. Paul Underwagger was blonde and tall. He had an oval face and sweaty palms. He showed Leo where he would be working. It was a lousy setup; Leo had a fourteen-year-old typewriter and a termite-infested desk in a 5x7 area of the room.

There were about 200,000 U.S. soldiers on the Russian Front. The racial percentage was 60 percent White, 30 percent Black, and 10 percent Hispanic: 150 men to a barrack, and 15 soldiers to a room. Approximately 8,000 of them were on 'The Rock.' They were a real division… or was it a detachment?

"So Sir, what's it like to be a drug enforcement agent?" Leo asked. The Lieutenant paused as though he was surprised Leo had popped him with the question.

"That's confidential, Private."

"You mean you're undercover, Sir?"

"I mean.... You'll be court-martialed, Private," he said, "If word of this gets out!"

Leo threw up his hands. "Not a word, sir, not a word," he said, "I only mention it because Colonel Bronson confided in me, but why the D.E.A., sir?"

"We have to face facts, Private. National security is at risk. Massive drug abuse along with isolated incidents of assault against the officers has broken out like wildfire... and this is something," pounding his fist on the desk repeatedly in a fit of rage," that the Generals at the Pentagon just won't tolerate!"

"G.I.'s attacking officers to support their addiction, sir?" Stegner asked.

"That's right, Private. Those goddamn heroin addicts are assaulting off duty officers dressed in their 'civi's' in town, to make it look like a mugging."

"That's terrible, Sir, "he replied, "I hope you bring it under control."

"It won't be easy, Private. But we'll do whatever's necessary to stop them. Your brilliant Colonel Bronson never figured they would attack his officers. That's why I had to be called in."

Leo nodded. "Oh, I see, but do you have any idea who they are yet, Sir?"

"No, but we're working on it, soldier," the Lieutenant replied. Fear was never far from the surface of Underwagger's emotions. He understood in that vague way in which one sometimes understands the most fundamental things about oneself that his own insecurity was the reason he chose the military profession; it was the only way of life permitting him to kill or punish those who posed a threat.

Several Months Later

Weekends, off duty personnel would pile into taxis and head for a place called 'The Playboy Discotheque' located in Butzbach, West Germany. It was a large bar with 30 or so apartment flats, lots of girls and unlimited music to boogie by. Military police accompanied the recruits on some of the outings to make sure they didn't fuck-up and do something stupid. One of the MP's responsibilities was to cover the whole town, both sides of the tracks, so to speak... making certain to keep the peace.

***

Leo had joined the Army hoping to be sent to Officer's Candidate School and a warmer climate, but it wasn't happening. He spent his entire tour-of-duty at a Post called Ayers Kaserne (The Rock). He visited Frankfurt, Germany often on weekend passes, and spent most of his time dancing at "The Playboy Discotheque." The best dancer he had ever known in his life was PFC Darwud Shaw, his roommate in the Army. Leo would make sure to be in his company when they visited the Playboy because that way he was in line for all of Darwud rejects and there were plenty of women he tossed to the side.

PFC Shaw was a handsome, smooth talking guy who had good hair and danced the "Robot" as if he'd invented it. On the way into the city (Frankfurt), in the taxi, this tall, graceful, virile roommate of his would give him lessons in how to make out with the girls. When they reached the Playboy, Leo followed Shaw's instructions and from time to time would hit the jackpot. The only place Leo would see Shaw in the city would be the Playboy, because Shaw would always hook-up with some young lady and be gone until time to return to the post.

Leo returned to the barracks past midnight. Nearly the entire Post of Ayers Kaserne (The Rock) was vacant that Friday night.

Most of the officers were at home with their wives, while the troops were scattered about Germany, pursuing sex for money. Private Ricky Dicks and Darwud Shaw were waiting for him. They sat side by side drinking Russian Vodka and smoking from a hash pipe, debating the issue of Soviet sponsored terrorist attacks throughout Germany and how everything about the Russian front stunk. The Baader-Meinhof Gang (A.K.A. the RAF) annoyed the fuck out of them by bombing the U.S. Army V Corps headquarters and the Terrace Club in Frankfurt am Main, killing a US Army Lieutenant and wounding 13 other soldiers. Dicks and Shaw had finally figured out a way to strike back and

all they needed now was Leo to complete the mission.

The Baader-Meinhof Gang was a communist and anti-imperialist urban guerilla group who engaged in armed resistance against what they deemed to be a fascist state.

Leo was fond of Shaw, but strangely enough the way Leo came to know Shaw was the night they solidified their plan to attack the Russian Embassy in Bonn, West Germany.

PFC Shaw said, "Everything is all set," and told them the plan. Dicks was excited; Leo looked tense, however gamed. Leo saw this as a perfect opportunity to see if he had what it took to go on the offensive and kill if he had to. He had been raised in a Seventh Day Adventist family who constantly preached the Ten Commandments, with one of them being "Thou shall not kill," but after what happened to his father, all bets were off. Not to mention, Leo was already madder than hell that he hadn't been sent to Vietnam because learning how to kill was his primary reason for joining the army. Trial by fire, he knew he needed to have the same mind set when going after Joe's killer because he didn't have the financial means to get the job done.

They dressed in their green fatigues; put their two-way radio and night light (infrared) binoculars, explosives (C-4 and dynamite) and fuses, batteries, and a couple of yards of wire into a shoulder bag. They were ready. Dicks worked in the supply room, so he had taken all the goodies from there, while Darwud Shaw hotwired a Sergeant's car and had hidden it behind the barracks.

"Are you guys sure we can pull this off?" Leo asked, in control, but with concern.

"Sure!" Shaw whispered. "We're about to make one giant step for mankind."…they laughed and Shaw continued.

"Dicks and I checked it out the day we applied for a passport."

"Man!" Dicks interrupted. "If you are looking for adventure Bonn, West Germany is the place. That's one clean city."

"Well alright then, let's go dirty it up!" Leo said aggressively.

They drove for nearly an hour until they came to Waldstrasse 42. The twelve-foot high iron Embassy gate was coiled with barbed wire at the top. They backtracked into a dense growth of trees and climbed the tallest. They had done this sort of climbing at boot camp before.

There were two levels of security, stationary Sentries at the Embassy and a foot patrol around the inner perimeter.

Private Leo Stegner, PFC Darwud Shaw, and Private Ricky Dicks climbed down the trees and concealed themselves behind the bushes inside the embassy property. They had to know when the foot patrol passed this point. If they were lucky, the patrol would be by shortly. Soon they heard the sound of marching feet. There were four men marching by smoking cigarettes. Five minutes later they were inside the gate. They ran north, they kept close to the building and avoided open space where they might be silhouetted by the moonlight. It was 12:45 a.m. when they came across the first indication of Soviet activity.

Several yards ahead Shaw and his crew saw a row of one-story garages at the rear of the Embassy. They dropped to the ground immediately, doubting the reality of what they saw; there were bright lights and noise. They lay still for a few minutes, but nothing happened except for two mechanics, perhaps three, working on Consular General Vladimir Femyomor's limousines. Leo and Shaw crawled forward, inching closer. They realized that it might not be as easy as originally planned.

"Those fucking bastards!" Shaw whispered. "They would be working in the middle of the night."

"Stop worrying… by the time we finish," Leo stated with a show of confidence, "they won't have a damn thing to work on." They all grinned.

The sound of a man's chuckle startled them. A cigarette lighter flared briefly and died, leaving three glowing red lights flickering in one of the garages. Leo, Shaw, and Dicks decided they had learned all they needed to know and crawled back. They had revenge in mind and allowed approximately one hundred feet between the garage and where they placed the explosives. The mechanics would have no time to get the hell out of there when the Embassy blew. Leo and his friends had enough explosives to win a small war. Somebody was going to die.

Leo's mind was reeling at the implication of what they were about to do, but Russian sponsored terrorist attacks had already taken the lives of over 20 American soldiers over the past 12 months and that was all they could think about.

"Are you sure we should be doing this shit Shaw?" Leo asked.

"Hell fucking yeah," Shaw fired back, insulted that Leo asked the question. "The first RAF terrorist strike occurred when a tiger tank skidded out of control, overturned, and exploded killing six. They had just finished field maneuvers in Wildflecken, Germany when a vehicle came speeding out of nowhere tossing dynamite. Another attack happened on the way to Fulda, Germany at another war game site when the steering section of an APC went out after explosives planted along their route the night before detonated. The armored personnel carrier went into a wild spin and rammed into one of "Comrade's" $160,000.00 home. Hell! The APC was filled with white phosphorus ammunition, killing 10; including Comrade (nickname for German allies). Not to mention, the last terrorist attack that occurred in Grafenrheinfeld, Germany; another "third world" war game site when a fucking helicopter pilot and his crew died instantly as they were in flight. The dust cover area underneath the chopper had been filled with Nitroglycerin causing the helicopter to explode while in flight. So let's get these motherfuckers, NOW!" Shaw demanded.

Leo had learned the term; "Fill the Gap," with regards to the United States military war game maneuvers held in the cities of Wildflecken, Fulda, and Grafenrheinfeld, West Germany. Three key cities that held the first line of defense if a strategic war between the U.S. and the Soviet Union broke out.

At 12:55 a.m. Leo, Shaw and Dicks exited the Embassy grounds. Their timing was good. The moon had begun to glow brighter as they came in sight of the gate. Leo saw movement from the corner of his eye. Two guards emerged from around the corner, conversing and looking around.

Dicks, Leo, and Shaw stooped down and ran. Dicks led the way and Leo and Shaw followed close behind, unwinding the spool of wire. They hurried. They were terribly conspicuous, carrying a handful of equipment that time of night, scampering across the open yard of a restricted area. As they climbed over the gate several minutes later, Leo felt an enormous release of tension. The period of greatest risk was over. Leo ran hard and slid behind the bush. He was scared. He knew once the explosion went off they would have to get far away from the Embassy area fast.

Leo nervously wrapped the wires around the 12-volt battery poles and was about to set off the explosives when a man in uniform stepped out from a patch of trees several yards away, and in German said, "Who goes there? What do you think you're doing?"

Leo, Shaw, and Dicks froze, letting instinct come into play. The intruder wore the uniform of a Russian officer in the Guard unit. He had a Luger, a German semi-automatic pistol, in a holster with a buttoned flap. He was tall and rangy and looked to be in his early thirties. He made no move to draw his gun.

"You're interrupting our stakeout. We should be asking who you are." Shaw said in German.

"Lieutenant Karl Rukeyser!" he said. "Officer of the Guard!"

"Ru—who?" Leo said. Leo laughed. They stayed half-hidden in the bush so they could not be easily recognized.

"We're frog hunting," Shaw said.

"To eat the legs!" Dicks added, in German as well.

"This time of the night? Cover them Kolloff." A youngish man appeared on Leo's right carrying an AK-47 automatic weapon; there was a third man behind him. "From which direction did they come Sergeant Krouse?" the Russian officer called.

The reply came from several yards away. "From the Embassy area, Sir."

Dicks, Shaw, and Leo were calculating odds. Three to two until Sergeant Vladimir Krouse came into view. They had four weapons: two AK-47's, the Lieutenant's Luger and a Truncheon.

"Embassy?" Shaw said. "All we saw was a bit of gate!"

"Nobody goes frog hunting in the dark," Officer Rukeyser replied.

"Sure they do," Shaw insisted. "If you hide away in the dark, you're concealed by the time they wake up. It's the accepted way to do it," he added before he was interrupted.

"Now look!" Rukeyser said, looking doubtful. "You'd better come with me. What do you have there?"

"Binoculars, a camera, and a reference book," Shaw called out.

"Kolloff," the Lieutenant said. "Check them out!"

"Raise your hands," Kolloff said. Leo and his companions raised their hands, each man keeping his right hand close to his left sleeve. Leo and his friends were profoundly aware that there must be no gunfire for it would unleash holy hell upon them.

Corporal Kolloff came up on Leo's right side, pointed the AK-47 at him and then opened the flap of the shoulder bag. Leo drew the standard issued bayonet from his sleeve and brought the knife up to Kolloff's neck. Leo's other hand twisted the AK-47 out of the young man's grasp, while Shaw's thumbs gouged at Kolloff's eyes, who screamed in pain and tried to push Shaw's hands aside. Shaw turned vicious and knocked him out with a clubbing right hand. The other guard on the slope moved toward them and Lieutenant Rukeyser crashed through the bushes.

Leo released Kolloff's neck as he collapsed. The Lieutenant was fumbling at the flap of his holster when Dicks leaped into the air with a single leg drop kick, sending the Lieutenant staggering. Dicks struck at him with his knife, but Rukeyser was too far away for an accurate thrust. Instead, the point caught him in the collar of his shirt and jerked up slashing his chin. His hand came away from the holster to clutch the wound. Dicks moved toward him, kneed him in the balls and then knocked him out with a vicious right hand.

Shaw, the handsome one with a pointed nose, whipped around to face the slope. The soldier leaped toward him. Shaw stepped aside, watching as he flew past. The impact with the ground knocked some air out of him. Rukeyser body convulsed, then he jumped back up and resumed his attack. This time Krouse held an MP's Truncheon. He brought it down hard. Shaw shifted to the right causing the blow to miss his head and catch his right shoulder. His right arm went numb. He struck Krouse's neck with the side of his hand, a powerful, accurate blow. Amazingly, Krouse survived and brought his billy club up for a second swipe. Shaw closed in groaning in pain as the feeling returned to his right arm. Shaw took the soldier's head in both of his hands and pushed, twisted and pushed again. At the same instant, the billy club landed again; this time on Leo's head. Leo reeled away, dazed. Shaw and Dicks closed in. They struck the soldier with several clubbing blows across the forehead sending him to the ground. Leo came up to Krouse and turned him over. Krouse was out cold.

Leo leaned against a tree hurting. Shaw threw up while Dicks considered whether he should drag the three guards into the bushes. It would take between three to five minutes; Dicks estimated, during which time the three of them might get caught. Dicks weighed the risk against the precious minutes they might gain by delaying the discovery of the bruised bodies. The three men would be missed very soon. The searchers first move would be to send a runner to cover the patrol's route. If the bodies were left as they were, the patrol would see them and raise the alarm.

The alarm would be raised by the explosion anyhow, Dicks reasoned. He decided not to risk the few minutes; he set off the explosives: "Voooom! Woommmm!" They could hear the sound of breaking glass, then another explosion like an incendiary bomb, "Vhoomh Whoomph" The sky lit up as the Embassy

exploded into the air, much like the latest military explosion like that of a small "Daisy Cutter" (fuse used to convert conventional bombs into defoliant and anti-personnel weapons).

"Holy shit!" Dicks said. "We better get the hell out of here!"

Leo and his companions left no sign of their presence. They left the guards' bodies where they laid and brushed the ground around them with loose foliage. They hadn't been recognized because it was dark; they were soldiers and their faces were covered with mud. They got out of the area as fast and inconspicuously as possible. Private Ricky Dicks would hightail it to the second half of the Janice Joplin and Earth, Wind, and Fire concert in Frankfurt. PFC Darwud Shaw and Leo would keep the stolen car long enough to race carelessly to the Playboy Discotheque. Leo could hear the German Police sirens echoing in the background from the direction of the Soviet Embassy and they could hear the tires of the high performance Volkswagen squeal whenever it leaned into the curves. Each turn took them deeper through the narrow residential areas of Bonn, Germany. An hour later they arrived at the Playboy where Leo mingled with the crowd until it was time for him to leave. Leo made sure everyone saw him and Shaw.

The next morning there was a wakeup bugle call and Colonel Bob Bronson was on the parade field, madder than hell. The C.I.A. (Central Intelligence Agency) was there too.

"Everybody out! I mean everybody!" the Colonel demanded over the public announcement system.

Leo got up and out to the parade field along with eight thousand other grunts, the guys who set the explosion and brawled with the embassy guards, and the guys who didn't.

The Colonel said, "Who in the hell blew up the Russian Embassy? There's been extensive damage and there will be repercussions. It is my understanding that some of you were there. I don't want to punish people who weren't involved, so I would like all those who were at the Embassy last night to take one step forward." Nobody moved. The Colonel fumed. "So it's gonna be like that, ha? Well, all right!" he said, "Everyone is restricted to post! There will be no leaves whatsoever, for the next six-months."

One of the guys in Leo's company was a lawyer and said, "That's not legal, Sir! You can't do that!"

The Colonel said, "I know I can only put you on for one month, but I'm going to put you on for one month and take you off, and then put you on and take you off, and put you on and take you off, and you won't get off this post for six-months... until somebody tells me what went on last night. We're going to have investigators coming from the Pentagon to get to the bottom of this and those of you involved are going to be court-martialed!"

Nobody spoke. The investigators came from Washington, D.C., and still no one talked. The investigators never got to the bottom of it. They never knew who was involved. They never knew anything about it. The entire post was put on restriction, which remained enforced for a period of three months.

On the first weekend following the lifting of the restrictions, Dicks, Shaw, and Leo were at it again. This time the threesome became more aggressive. Leo felt good since their first mission was so successful, but he wanted more. He was already pissed because he had volunteered to be sent to Vietnam, but was sent to Germany instead, so Leo knew he needed to prime himself by sharpening his killing skills so he would be ready for Joe's killers.

Leo and Shaw thought of themselves as highly developed pieces of machinery, designed solely to make trouble against the Soviet Union and to kill anyone who tried to interfere with their plans for revenge. Leo with the help of Dicks had programmed themselves like machines. They creeped around in hostile darkness, seeking to destroy Communism and blow up ammunition dumps, while Shaw sabotaged a power plant in East Berlin, ambushed a truck convoy, demolished a Soviet radar installation, and booby-trapped an East German foreign diplomat headquarters.

Darwud Shaw was like an animal and gave a pretty good account of himself when trouble started. He was smart too, and knew a lot about many things.

Ricky Dicks was just as corrupt but not a very smart man. He had a bad habit of getting innocent bystanders injured when he went around misbehaving. It was just a matter of time before he got caught doing something stupid or corrupt, and then something reckless trying to get out of it. Private Ricky Dicks had done reckless things before, and at least one of them involved a bayonet. Darwud Shaw and Leo Stegner warned each other that it wasn't wise to tinker with any particular enterprise in which Ricky Dicks was involved.

A month later, Dicks was caught trying to blow up the East Berlin wall by two communist guards pulling duty. Dicks had drawn his government issued bayonet, upset because they left him no way out. He killed one of the Soviet guards, breaking the blade of the bayonet in the guy's chest, and made his getaway. Dicks was apprehended several weeks later; trying to sneak across the Dutch border.

Leo worked as a company clerk. He was privy to any and all secret information that came down the pike involving sweeping changes and troop morale. Leo had just read a teletype communication announcing the unexpected arrival of Four Star General Alexander Haig. Leo put the word out quickly across "The Rock" (Ayers Kaserne).

***

Leo watched the news reports intently in his small office space. General Haig's visit was of great interest to him and his buddies. He told his buddies what he learned from the media on the general's visit.

The huge Supersonic Concord transport plane with British emblems on the wings, skidded to a halt on the wet runway at Rhein-Main Air Force Base, in the West German forest. A hefty man with a large, pointed nose disembarked and walked quickly down the ramp to a waiting limousine. After a thirty-minute drive, the limo arrived in Bonn, the capital of the German Federal Republic. It carried the Commander In Chief for NATO: Four Star General, Alexander Haig, along with the increasingly neurotic circle of Generals surrounding him.

General Haig had scheduled several high-level conferences to meet with all the division commanders first: for them to come to terms with the increased decline in troop morale. The General put on his cap and got out of the car. Lieutenant Colonel Alex Hernandez, Officer of the Guard, wordlessly saluted; then held out his hand to receive his.

The conferences were held at the American Embassy headquarters in Bonn, West Germany. There were two dozen or so commanders already there including: Colonel Bronson,

1971

Al Haig, the baggage carrier

In South Viet Nam

with NATO in Brussels

Colonel Wade, Lieutenant Colonel Wallace, and General Davis. They all stood when Haig entered, wearing his Military Dress Greens. Lieutenant Colonel Hernandez observed Haig was upset as he walked straight to the podium and spoke without preparation. He had been sent to reveal the State Department's new views on military morals, as a result of thousands of complaints filed by both the inductees, regarding civil rights violations, and the commanding officers, regarding massive drug abuse and insubordination. "Gentlemen! I'm in charge!" General Haig said. "There is still great dissatisfaction on the part of the State Department; there is no change in the attitude of the enlisted men. The troops contend that they are denied the protection and awards that ordinarily result from good behavior and proper performance of duty. They contend that they receive nothing but hostility from community officers and the community officers contend they and German civilians are being victimized by a worthless bunch of G.I. addicts to support their filthy drug habits. The community officers in uniform are expected by the War Department to develop high troop morale in a community that offers them nothing but humiliation and mistreatment. Gentlemen! Officials of the War Department and General Staff have sent me here to take action to eliminate these obstacles."

The Army, by its direction, and by the actions of General Alexander Haig, introduced the "Monthly Efficiency Report," both at home and abroad where it had not hitherto been practiced. The Monthly Efficiency Report was used to rate each soldier on individual merit and to determine if the solider should be promoted to a higher rank. Leo, as well as all the company clerks in each battalion primary responsibility was to prepare the monthly efficiency reports and forward them to Battalion Command for review.

Leo and his crew considered the implications of the general's statements with regard to their plans and future in the military. For the time being, it seemed best to let things cool off.

Several months later:

Leo came to really know Darwud Shaw on a cool fall Saturday morning. Leo sat on his bunk contemplating the next course of action in their "private war" against Russian sponsored terrorism when Leo smelled a weird, stink-ass odor, drifting across the room.

"Something is burning!" Leo said out loud, and then jumped to his feet to check it out, only to find himself in the middle of a dope party, right there in the barracks. Leo cleared his throat and waited for the guys to notice him. Leo recognized PFC Shaw, then Benjamin Striker, a black guy in his early to mid-twenties, with round shoulders and a powerfully strong handshake, wearing a three-piece tweed suit. Ben motioned with his left hand for Leo to sit down and then a big smile spread across his face.

"What's the matter?" Striker said. "Don't you smoke?"

"Yeah, I smoke cigarettes!" Leo responded, with a suspicious look on his face. The guys laughed. "What's up?" Leo insisted as he gave everybody the power (handshake) before he sat down. "And what's that foul smell?"

Shaw grinned "Hashish! man, hash!" Striker said, giving Leo one of those "man you must be lame" looks. "Haven't you heard of it?"

"Yes, as a matter of fact I have," Leo replied. "But I've never smoked it."

"You mean you've never gotten high! You're a square?" Striker said.

Leo nodded. He was sort of embarrassed from the daring put down.

"Lock the door," Striker demanded, "We don't want the pigs waltzing in on us." He shoved the pipe toward Leo's chest. "Here, take a hit. The shit won't bite ya."

"My friend, there is no way in the world I'll do anything illegal in this place." Leo fired back.

"Hey!" Striker said. "There's nothing to worry about. Everybody here is cool. Here! Check it out, we won't let anything happen to ya."

Leo felt like he was being 'Pearl Harbored,' but he hit the hash pipe anyway. He choked from the smoke in his lungs.

"You better have a seat," Shaw suggested.

"Jesus Christ," Leo said. "I've hit the pipe and now you want me to take a seat. What's next?"

Striker and the others grinned. "You'll see," another guy said, "You'll see."

Minutes later, Leo felt limp, defeated, and ill. His efforts to regain self-control had become super human.

"Man, what's in this shit?" Leo said "Poison?" He tried to restore his sense of alertness and balance but couldn't. Now he was angry for letting himself be conned.

Striker shook him. "Stegner!" he said. "Are you all right?"

Leo nodded and rose slowly to his feet. He could barely stand. Striker looped Leo's arm over his shoulders and began to walk him. The others continued to laugh.

"I'll help you get him to his bunk," Shaw said. They led Stegner through the barracks to his small cornered off living quarters. "I started to warn you that hash will do you like that," Shaw said. "But I figured you could handle it."

"Yeah, next time let me do the figuring," Leo said, "And where did you get that shit from, anyway?"

Shaw grinned, "I'll have to get back to you on that one." He paused briefly, "There's some questions you just shouldn't ask."

Leo shouted. "What!" He threw up his hands. "After all we've been through?"

Shaw looked serious. "But this is different!" he said. "I know we've done some heavy things together, but I gave my word." He paused again. Leo looked at him intently. Shaw continued, this time sounding melodramatic. "Why you want to put me on the spot?" He smiled. "If all you want is a little something to smoke, I can get you all you want right here on Post. See, the people I do business with only sell Kilos."

Stegner looked at Striker, who nodded. He resented not being told everything, but he also knew, in a strange sort of way, that Sergeant Striker had something to do with it, so he just sort of wavered back and forth between being pissed at Shaw and being cool.

"You mean you handle that shit in quantity?" Leo asked.

Shaw laughed, then pushed out his hands, palms up, and said, "Does Saint Nick ride a sleigh?" All three of them laughed.

"Hell I think I'd be better off if I just left the shit alone. I don't need Colonel Bronson and those fucking D.E.A. agents on my case. Not now! I have too much to lose," Leo sighed.

Leo's statement surprised Striker and Shaw. Up to now, Sergeant Striker had just laid back taking it all in. Now he had a suspicious look on his face.

"The D.E.A.! What in the hell are they doing on the Russian Front?" Striker asked.

Leo lay back on his bunk, both hands clutched behind his head in a relaxed position. "The way Colonel Bronson tells it, they're here to put a halt to all the drug abuse around here," he said.

Striker's head snapped up. "Come on! Are you serious?" he asked.

"Sure, why would I kid about something like that?" Stegner replied.

"Well, who are they? Who are they after? Is it anybody we know?" Striker asked, seemingly over-concerned.

"I'm not at liberty to say," Leo said.

"The Colonel confided in me with the strictest of confidence, and I don't think it's wise to betray him."

Shaw laughed. "You've got to be shitting me! You mean you're not gonna tell us?"

Leo laughed, this time. "I can't! I gave my word. Remember?"

"Ok! Ok! I see your point," Shaw said softly. "But you wouldn't just leave us hanging like this, would you?"

Leo smiled. He sensed Sergeant Striker felt nervous as Striker's hands began to tremble, but Striker couldn't help himself. Leo knew Striker now realized how valuable he could be to Striker's military drug organization.

"Ok, I'll tell you what," Striker said. "If you look out for us, we'll look out for you."

Leo sat up in his bunk. He looked at them intently, with a suspicious look on his face. "Alright, but just what am I supposed to be looking out for?" he asked.

Striker frowned and then looked at his watch. "I can't go into it right now I have to go," he said. "I have a meeting with the first Sergeant." He turned and shook Leo's hand. "Meet me at the Playboy later. We'll talk then."

Leo looked at him and half smiled. "All right... I'll be there."

***

Sergeant Benjamin Striker was a drug pusher who never married and made very few close friends. He was one of the best weaponry soldiers in the Battalion. Many GI's envied him while others wished him harm, but he was a lady's man, and as flamboyant as they came.

Striker was well connected and a disc jockey who fit in. His drug outlet stretched from Frankfurt to Bonn, from Munich to Berlin, and places in between. Since World War II, the U.S. Army built more than 30 armed infantry bases throughout West Germany. Each base had the capacity of housing up to 8,000 troops, and geographically, they were only 20 to 30 miles apart. Striker had recruited six G.I. pushers from each Post. He had a total of 180 soldiers on his payroll, each netting approximately $800.00 per day, with a 60/40 split of everything they sold. His profits were as large as his ego.

They Playboy Discotheque was a popular place and neatly tailored to its customers. It stood high up on a hill overlooking Germany. It was an ideal place from which drugs were sold: hashish, heroin, and raw opium.

The Playboy's spectacular A-frame design included two balconies; one was accessible from the rotating bar with elegant mirrors on the wall. The second balcony was accessed via the upper level, which led to the upstairs flats. Its impressive upper level and exterior were designed English Tudor style. The grand foyer formed the primary entrance and directed traffic into all parts of the discotheque. Straight ahead was the dance floor, where a cluster of lights hung from a cathedral ceiling. Moreover, it had a game room, cushioned booths and chairs, and featured a see-through fireplace.

Prostitution was legal. While the ladies of the night took their "G.I. John's" upstairs, the G.I. pimps mingled throughout the Playboy soliciting more business. Nobody tried to stop them. Not even the MP's.

***

Leo was calm. The feeling had crept over him gradually. He was momentarily paralyzed by the thought he was sharing a barrack with drug peddlers. He was possessed by a cool-headed watchfulness that surprised even him. As he went about his daily routine, he wondered if Sgt. Striker had noticed the change. Striker didn't miss much, and there had been a definite wariness in that confrontation over hash and Leo's first experience at getting high.

Leo met Striker in front of the Playboy. A pleasant-looking "Fraulein" (young German woman) in a low-cut, sexy dress stood talking to Striker, Leo's breath quickened. Leo wanted to meet her. The Playboy was filled with people high on hash, or with brains buzzing on heroin looking for sex and adventure. Leo felt good. After being introduced, Striker led Leo to a side door and they stepped inside. Leo found himself in a small foyer. There were potted plants in the corners and a calendar on the wall with the dates superimposed over a photograph of a woman's nude body. Leo wanted to see Striker's place. Striker's three -bedroom flat was on the third floor. It was a bachelor's pad that looked like a psychedelic haven that set the right mood for every occasion. It was spacious and it overlooked the Playboy and all its glory.

Leo cleared his throat, uncertain of what he should say. "I've heard of mood-lighting, but is it usually this dark?" Leo asked.

Striker flipped on the light switch, but the lights on the second and third floor landings didn't come on. "No" he said. "The bulbs are probably blown... I'll look and see if I have some." Striker had not given it a serious thought until he and Leo spotted the figure of a man at the top of the third floor landing, standing in front of Striker's door with some sort of screw driver in his hand. The overhead emergency exit lights had provided just enough light for them to notice the intruder.

The intruder had an intense look on his face. He tapped on the door and tried the doorknob gently, but it was locked. He seemed unaware of their presence, as he jimmied the lock and forced his way in.

When the Vietnam War broke out, Leo and Striker had volunteered. The army had trained them in wireless transmission, codes, sabotage, and silent killing. Leo and Striker considered themselves licensed to kill. Striker led the way.

Striker had intended to step over the stairs that creaked, but he stumbled and tripped on them kind of hard. The intruder was so busy stealing hashish, heroin, money, passports, ration cards, and a couple of weapons; he didn't hear the minor disturbance.

Striker and Leo made their way to the third floor landing and considered whether they should make the first move. Striker knocked on the door and spoke out.

"Hey Striker!" Striker said. "May I have a word with you?" His voice sounded neutral, not angry nor hostile. He wanted the intruder to believe that Leo and Striker thought he was 'Striker,' thus preventing the intruder from panicking. "We need to discuss some business with you!" Can you spare a few minutes?"

Leo smiled and gently cracked the door open in anticipation of the intruder's response. He saw the intruder hesitate, while writhing around in the chair and fishing in his pockets. "I'm busy!" he said. "Come back later!" He stuffed a fistful of currency and hashish, which had been buried for a while in sacks. He filled the sacks and piled them up, his frown showing his concentration, his lips moving as he made visual inventory.

"Ok!" Leo said. "We will catch you in the Playboy later! All right?"

"Okay!" the intruder replied. "Down in the Playboy later!" He laughed. He thought he had gotten one over on them and that's all that mattered.

Leo and Striker stomped their feet as though they were heading downstairs; then tip-toed back to the door and unlocked it. In one swift motion they stormed the flat catching the thief on his way out. The intruder looked like he might try to break and run, but before he could react Leo, then Striker grabbed him.

Striker recognized him. It was Andre' Cooper, a tall, dark-haired white joker who got his kicks by stealing from homes and getting involved in sex crimes.

Cooper, now a G.I. convict had lied about his age to join the Army. He had escaped from Mannheim Stockade planning to leave the country. Every policeman in West Germany had a copy of Cooper's 'mug,' and half of them were engaged full-time in the search.

They were checking hotels and guest houses, railway stations and bus terminals, empty cottages and ruined castles. They showed the photograph to ticket clerks, patrol station staff, ferry hands, and toll collectors. All ports and airfields were covered, with the picture at every passport control desk.

Cooper refused to give in. He struggled in a rage of anger to be free. "Turn me loose!" he shouted. "Turn me loose! You fucking bastards!"

Leo and Striker rushed Cooper over to the edge of the third-floor landing and dangled him on the end of it.

"Do you mean that figuratively or literally?" Leo said with a devilish grin. Cooper struggled harder. He was real mad now.

"Why I believe he meant it literally," Striker commented.

"Then we better accommodate the gentleman," Leo suggested. They looked at each other, and then pushed Cooper as hard as they could down the stairs. It was quite funny when Cooper, eyes stretched wide, let out a high-pitched yell while snow-balling down the stairs.

Striker stashed the drugs while Leo cleaned up all signs of struggle. The cover-up had already taken shape in their minds. Leo went over to the sink in the corner of the room and washed his hands and face. He looked at himself in the shaving mirror and thought about how shrewd he had become, then picked up the nearest telephone and placed an anonymous tip to the military police.

***

"Well, well, well," the military police sergeant said heartily. "I think we have a warrant for this one." He stood with the landlord and several beautiful young German tenants in the corridor of the second floor. "There appears to be signs of a struggle," then he paused. "You touched anything, Buddy?"

"No! We found him just lying here." The landlord was a middle-aged Black American from Fayetteville, North Carolina. "And the name's Mr. Prentice."

The military police ignored this and went over to the stairs. Cooper's pale face was free of pain. He couldn't feel anything and his hands were clasped over his chest.

"I'd say heart attack, if he wasn't so young. He must have been on a mission to attack one of the ladies but slipped and missed a step," another military policeman assumed.

"He was hanging around here earlier," the landlord said. "I should have known he was up to no good."

"Well," the military police sergeant observed, "If he was as sane as he looked, he'd still be in the Army."

The tenant's edged closer. "He's the rapist who escaped from Mannheim!" one tenant said. "Isn't he?"

"Yep; but don't touch his body!" one military police noted. The Sergeant gingerly turned Cooper's face. It revealed a small trickle of dried blood. "He is bleeding, but he's still breathing," he said. "Where are those damn medics? Where is the nearest telephone?"

One of the tenants said, "This way Sergeant!"

The medics arrived around the same time the MP Sergeant got back. He showed them where Cooper lay.

"Who is he?" the medic asked.

"Andre Cooper, an escaped convict from Mannheim," the Sergeant told him. "We have reason to believe that Cooper came here earlier tonight to rob and molest the ladies, but tripped down the stairs.

The medic looked at the bruises on Cooper's neck, arms, and back, and then checked his vital signs. "We'll take it from here, Sergeant" the medic said.

"All right... but he's a clever, ruthless, bastard!" the Sergeant warned. "That's why we've never caught him."

"I'm sure we can handle him, Sergeant," the medic said reassuringly.

"Well you just remember," the Sergeant warned. "You're responsible for him."

The medic frowned. "Right, let's get him out of here."

Cooper had hit his head against the wall going down the stairs, and snapped a couple of vertebrae in his spine. The last

Leo and Striker heard Cooper had been paralyzed from the neck down and could only move his eyes.

***

Kinds of Hashish	Europe & Middle-East Prices			United States Prices		
	Retail Sales Per Ounce	Retail Sales Per Gram	Wholesale Per Kilo or 2.2 lbs.	Retail Sales Per Ounce	Retail Sales Per Gram	Wholesale Per Kilo or 2.2 lbs.
Turkish Green	$15.00	$ 1.00	$ 300.00 - 800.00	$60.00	$10.00	$4,000.00
Black Afghan	30.00	1.00	850.00 - 1500.00	85.00	10.00	8,000.00
Pakistan Black	30.00	1.00	850.00 - 1500.00	85.00	10.00	8,000.00
Choking Red	25.00	1.00	700.00 - 1350.00	80.00	10.00	8,000.00
Red Lebanese	20.00	1.00	300.00 - 800.00	75.00	10.00	6,500.00
Green Lebanese	20.00	1.00	300.00 - 600.00	65.00	10.00	5,500.00
Blond	15.00	1.00	450.00 - 600.00	65.00	10.00	4,500.00
Spaghetti Black	35.00	1.00	1200.00 - 2000.00	100.00	10.00	9,500.00
Moroccan Black	35.00	1.00	1200.00 - 1800.00	100.00	10.00	8,500.00

* All Purchases over a Ton Sell for $35.00 per Kilo *

"You want a beer?" Striker asked.

"Sure," Leo said. "I'm still a bit tense."

"Don't be hard on yourself," Striker suggested, with a spirited look on his face. "The joker deserved it! He shouldn't have gotten caught. Right?"

"Yeah, suppose you're right," Leo said hesitantly.

"Then come on! Sit down and unwind. We have a lot to talk about," Striker said.

Andre Cooper had discovered Striker's secrets. Therefore, his cover was not perfect. Striker had made careless mistakes. He should have put a dead bolt lock on the door. That was the surface error; the deep flaw was that he had become too well known as a drug peddler. Striker thought about this with irritation, not conceit.

Leo had not realized the trust Striker placed in him. He handed him a sheet of paper, stacked the hashish on the huge living room table and said, "A kilo of hash is equivalent to a thousand grams or 2.2 lbs. You see, once it's smuggled from one country to another the price automatically quadruples."

Leo took the paper and read aloud: "Profile of the Different Kinds of Hashish Prices"

"As you can see," Striker said, "There are roughly nine kinds of hashish. The most popular brands are: Black Afghan, Pakistani Black, and Choking Red. Moroccan and Spaghetti Black are popular too, but they're harder to come by, so…" Striker gestured grandly at the piece of paper.

"What do you think?"

"I'm absolutely amazed!" Leo replied. "Hell, it's cheaper here than it is in the United States; especially their Kilo's."

Striker smiled. "Yes sir!" he said exaggeratedly. "That's why it's such a precious commodity. The only problem now is cutting the odds. Shit, the chances of getting busted are fifty-fifty!"

"Damn!" Leo uttered. He was making mental notes when he realized Striker was silent. "Yep, cutting the odds is the most logical thing to do, considering the circumstances."

Striker laughed. "You're not worried are you?"

"No, No," Leo said. "I can deal with the D.E.A. situation, but when I don't know more than a tenth of what's going on, and I'm involved in that kind of situation, I get nervous."

Striker laughed again. "I don't like you nervous," he said.

Leo frowned. "I don't like me nervous either. So why don't you enlighten me?"

Striker looked Leo straight in the eye. "Over here, I get the job done any damned way I can. There are risks. We're not school teachers or shoe salesmen. What you may regard as a battle of wits back at 'The Rock' is war out here." Striker said, and then continued. "Shit! If you ask me, I think I'm luckier than hell to have a hundred and eighty guys selling this fuckin shit." Suddenly Striker seemed angry, though not at Leo. "I'm thinking about the planning, the care, the money, and the manpower, that went into the creation of my own military drug outlet. Now the whole thing is in jeopardy because of that fucking thief, Andre

Cooper who's just bright enough to know he's really stupid. Cooper reminds me of a guy I knew back in high school."

Striker handed Leo another sheet of paper. "This is a hash identification chart I put together; part of my memoirs." Leo smiled. Striker continued, "Study it carefully, it may be of some use to you later on."

Kinds of Hashish	Rank of Potency	Country Origin	Major Characteristics
Spaghetti Black	#1	Iran	Approx. 2cm in circumference, 4 inches long, gummy, moist, & loosely compressed. Black in color with white strips of opium embedded.
Pakistanian Black	#2	Pakistan	Approx. 1mm thick, has gold 101 seal stamped on it. Black in color, gummy, moist, loosely compressed, 3 inches wide, 8 inches long, and wrapped in beige canvas.
Black Afghan	#3	Afghanistan	Approx. 1 cm thick, 4 inches wide, 7 inches long, black in color, grainy, hard, slightly moist, tightly compressed, and wrapped in canvas.
Moroccan Black	#4	Africa	Approx. 1cm thick, black in color, dry, hard, well compressed, 8 inch long, easy to burn, five inches wide, heavy in weight, grainy, & wrapped in canvas.
Choking Red	#5	Lebanon	Approx. 2cm thick, 4-8 inches wide 10 inches long, grainy but gummy, moist, brownish-red in color, comes in 100 to 300 gram slabs, heavy, & wrapped in canvas.
Red Lebanese	#6	Lebanon	Approx. 1cm thick, 4 inches wide, 6 inches long, grainy, slightly moist, light brownish-red in color tightly compressed, hard, & wrapped in canvas.
Green Lebanese	#7	Lebanon	Approx. 1mm thick, 3 inches wide, 6 inches long, dry, hard, grainy, light weight, hard to burn, tightly compressed, & light lime green in color.
Blond	#8	Lebanon	Approx. 1cm thick, 3 inches wide, 5 inches long, dry, grainy, tightly compressed, hard to burn, light in weight, & blondish brown in color.
Turkish Green	#9	Turkey	Approx. 1/2 - 1mm thick, 3 inches wide, up to 5 inches long, extra dry, light weight, hard, grainy, easy to break, hard to burn, dark green in color, & tightly compressed & harsh taste.

Leo took the paper. He shook his head from side to side, and then said, "You've got to be the most meticulous person I've ever met."

Striker grinned, then walked to the other side of the room and turned on an electrical fan to stir the hash and tobacco smoke in the air.

Leo read.

Striker waited patiently and tried to read Leo's expression. Leo sat in silence, staring wide-eyed, not saying anything. It was as if the world was strange and unpredictable, again.

"You mean to tell me that Iran, Afghanistan, and all these countries are responsible for the world's hashish supply? " Leo asked.

"Hell yes!" Striker assured him. "That's why so much shit is going on over there." He laughed. Leo was trying to figure out what was so amusing. Striker continued, "You see, they're competing for the American dollar."

"But what's so special about American money Sarge?"

"Well, it's like this," Striker said. "The more drugs they sell, the more arms and ammunition they can purchase on the open market; for the Revolution, they say. But in any case, the value of the American dollar is supposed to be worth more on the international exchange."

"Is it?" Leo asked out of curiosity.

"You better believe it," Striker replied. "Why you think I'm so willing to jeopardize my military career? I'm going for the gusto, pal, and I'm not letting nothing or nobody get in my way. There's too much money to be made. You know what I mean?

Leo nodded. "But don't you feel a little guilty, selling it to the other soldiers?"

Striker laughed. "Shit no!" he said. "If I didn't do it, somebody else would. Besides, those motherfuckers are begging for the shit. They don't care if it's hash or heroin, as long as they can get something to make this time on the 'Russian Front' go faster."

Leo frowned. "Jesus Christ!" he said. "What a fucking racket. I go for months clipping my little military pay and here I am right where the money is and didn't even know it!"

"Don't worry," Striker said. "Before you leave 'The Rock' my man, you'll know who's a diesel freak and who's a dope head."

Leo laughed. "A diesel freak! What in the hell is that?"

Striker laughed this time. "An alcoholic!" he said. "Comprende?"

"Oh! I see," Leo replied. "I think I might actually enjoy it here after all."

Striker placed both hands on Leo shoulders and then opened up. "Man, if you can just keep those fucking D.E.A. dudes off our backs until we rotate, I'll leave the entire operation in your hands."

Leo swallowed. "You mean…?"

Striker nodded, and then gestured around the room. "I'll even let you take my D.J. gig and my flat to boot."

Leo blinked. "You've got to be shitting me, Sarge?"

Striker shook his head from side to side. He walked over to the edge of the terrace and peered over, then walked back. "If I'm shitting you, you can turn me in yourself." He paused, "I'm getting old, and I've got to leave this thing with somebody." He paused again. "What, you don't want it?"

Leo frowned. "Hey! Wait a minute, Sarge. I'm not saying that. It's just this is all happening so fast and I want to give this some thought."

Striker smiled. "Ok," he said. "Then you have exactly five seconds to make up your mind." He looked at his watch. Then began counting backwards. "Five…four….three….two…"

Leo frowned again, and then interrupted the count. "Ok! Ok! Sarge! I'll take it!"

Striker wore a broad smile. He pounded Leo on both shoulders. "Good!" he said. "Then it's all settled. Meanwhile, I'll teach you the ropes and see what we can do about putting some bucks in your pocket."

Leo was excited. "Damn, Sarge! You're all right!" he said. "You go ahead and continue doing your thing. Anything comes up, I'll let you know."

Striker had to smile. Leo took a deep breath, and then Striker removed several more documents from his desk drawer feeling suddenly good about himself. "You're a hell of a soldier yourself Stegner," Striker said and then continued, "I must admit, working for Bronson and knowing those D.E.A. dudes, gives us a tremendous edge."

Leo smiled. "Yep! But I'll have to get back to you on those names. The only agent I know of right now is Lieutenant Underwagger."

"Underwagger? Why, that slimy son of a bitch!" Striker said. "He's in our company! You take your time and find out about the rest of them. But make sure you get back to me."

"Don't worry, Sarge. It's all taken care of. Remember, I have a stake in this now too." Leo said.

Striker smiled.

"What's that? Some sort of map?"

"Oh yeah!" Striker replied, "Here!" He paused. Leo took the document and began to study it.

"That's a map of West Germany," Striker gestured. "The areas shaded are places where American bases are located."

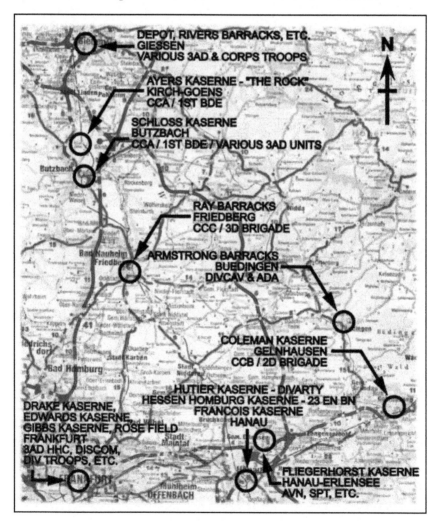

Leo ran his fingertips down along his jaw. "That's over thirty U.S. outposts, Sarge! This is an awful lot of territory to cover. How often do you see your people?"

Striker smiled. "Every two weeks!" he boasted. "Every two weeks they come and re-up. Put your money on enough pushers and if just half of that many manage to stay out of trouble, then it's worth it."

"Ah," Leo said. "Exactly, the greater the numbers the greater the chances some of them will remain in business. We can't control time and circumstance." He sneezed, and then sipped the German beer. "Sarge! What does it cost to fund such an operation?"

Striker scratched his head. "Well, let's put it this way," he said, "What I can't afford, I get fronted."

Leo looked surprised. "What? You're that well connected, Sarge?"

Striker laughed. "Actually, I've been involved in two rather complex clandestine operations in this part of the world. That's too damned much. The hashish, I get locally. But the heroin has to be smuggled in from Amsterdam, Holland. Rocky, the China-man I do business with has to check your bona-fides before he will have anything to do with you. When Rocky puts his ass on the line, he wants to know what he's getting into. Rocky types have their own underground heroin networks, and he thinks with security in mind at all times. If Rocky had the slightest hint of the D.E.A.'s penetration on our bases, the question then becomes, who wants to get rid of us more; the D.E.A. or Rocky? The word on Rocky is that he does only one deal at a time. In the past, he's worked for himself smuggling guns or heroin. Now, his loyalty is to his employer, the Chinese Mafia. That's how he stays in business."

"I can't believe I'm about to get involved in something this heavy," Leo said. "I never had this in mind."

Striker laughed. "Smuggling heroin is what I would call one of my 'esoteric professions.' It's a matter of on-the-job training, Leo. Despite the impressions you may have gained from the movies, there's precious damned few people who actually do it. Speaking of people, why don't we tidy up and get out of here, pick up some ladies, and have a little fun?" Striker suggested; around a cigarette.

"Well all right!" Leo responded. "Our own contribution to the war effort, huh?"

Striker grinned. "Why not… I'm getting too old to fight," he said.

Leo had never liked the nudging, contemptuous way some men talked about women, but Striker wasn't like that; he was cool.

They entered the Playboy Discotheque and were greeted in the lobby by Jerry Prentice, the landlord. Leo shook his hand when Striker introduced them. Prentice was a fat figure of a man, short, heavy around the neck, shoulders, and stomach. He wore a black eye-patch over his left eye. He had lost half his sight in an auto accident… one hazy, thick, foggy night, on his way home from the Playboy. Germans seldom had accidents, but when they did, hundred car pile ups weren't uncommon.

Prentice didn't smoke, but he drank and spent most of his evenings at the Playboy placing orders for new songs he heard on the radio. The American forces broadcasting network was his favorite station. It was located high up, overlooking Luxemburg. It was a good place from which to broadcast. Casey Kasem and Wolfman Jack had transmitted from there as a part of their epic contribution to the Vietnam War effort.

The layout of the Playboy Discotheque was nearly identical to Studio 54 in New York, but the atmosphere was different. It was exciting, energizing, and physically stimulating. A wide variety of nationalities were there; Whites, Germans, Blacks, Swedes, Hispanic, and Jews. They were loyal season members of the club who traveled from all over Europe to be there. They were mostly friends of Jerry Prentice and Sgt. Ben Striker. However, Striker muttered about the fact that they were more Jerry's friends than his. But when Leo asked who had the most finesse with the ladies, Striker finally admitted, grudgingly, that he was the man.

Everyone for the most part danced the Hustle, the Robot, and the Bump, but once in a while some of their own latest cultural dances. The Playboy was crowded enough so Leo didn't feel self-conscious about his presence, and he was loose from a few tokes of the hash pipe.

Prentice, a veteran of World War II, led the way into his office where a handful of ladies sat by the wood burning fireplace, smoking hash and sipping Germany's best white wine. The Fraulein's were plenty sexy and very well dressed. They wore sleek, silky dresses with low necklines.

Jerry Prentice was forty-nine, although he lied about it. He was shallow and appeared dishonest about most things. He was a black marketer, a pimp, and a former heroin distributor. The building in which he lived was one of the most expensive in Germany, and that was why he chose to live there. And, the fact that Prentice and other discotheque owner's allowed their customers to indulge in hash and other opiate type drugs on their premises baffled Leo.

"Striker!" one young German Fraulein yelled. She was high and excited to see him again. "Who's the handsome stud with you?"

Striker smiled, and then put one arm around Leo's shoulders. "Ladies," he said, "This is a personal and professional friend of mine, Leo Stegner."

Leo nodded, not knowing what to say. He was handsome in an almost pretty way, smooth faced, with curly soft black afro that fluffed over his face. He was unprepared for the scene that greeted him when they arrived. At first he was amused... he was so happy and high, kissing each of them on the cheek.

"Hi ladies," he said cheerfully.

"Umm," Elfi said. "Fantastic partner Striker; is he married?"

Eva giggled, and said "I hope not."

"No," Leo said, "As a matter of fact, I'm not."

"Marvelous," Bagetta said, "A toast to the partnership!"

They drank more wine and smoked. In Leo's mind, he realized he was getting too stoned around people he didn't really know and he must not forget that he's an American soldier with his uniform still on and what he was doing was a court-martial offense under military law. Not to mention how uncomfortable he had suddenly become over being so visible.

He fought back the paranoia, and then found himself reminiscing the event in Florida several years back. He and Ted Morgan were having a drink one night, at one of Jack Holloway's ABC Liquor Lounges, when some guys snuck out and smoked some pot in the restroom that left an awful smell in the air. All of a sudden, a platoon of pot sniffing dogs, narcotic agents, a SWAT team, and a half dozen or so plainclothes detectives stormed in from every direction yelling "This is a raid," literally demolishing Holloway's place and damned near arrested everybody there. They only had a joint Leo thought. He came back to reality when Striker nudged him to take the hash pipe again.

"Wow! Sarge," Leo said. "It's not like this back home."

Striker grinned. "Yeah, I know," he said. "It hasn't always been this way. The German polizi have pulled some pretty wicked raids themselves, but now that the Palestine Liberation Organization and the Baader Meinhof gang have increased their violent acts of terrorism, the polizi had to regroup, and shift their priority from crack downs on drug usage in the discos to protecting their national security."

Leo swallowed. "Then it's safe to smoke here, Sarge?"

Striker guffawed. "Sure. It's safe. You don't see Prentice worried, do ya?" Prentice was smiling. "Someone has to take over when I'm gone," he added.

"That's right!" Hillery said. "Somebody has to take care of us good little pussycats."

"Umm," Leo said. "Good pussy?" As if he had very casually announced his attendance for an orgy.

"Good pussy!" Hillery repeated. She felt wonderful to be with other people who felt wonderful, altogether. She smiled happily at Leo, who smiled back at her.

"I have an announcement to make," Leo said. "I didn't want to go on Post tonight." They all smiled. Leo was beaming at them in general but it seemed to Hillery that he was talking to her. Hillery thought his features were fine and Leo looked even more handsome now that he'd loosened up.

Leo took his jacket off and sat next to Hillery at the fireplace, grinning broadly, and she wanted very badly to touch Leo.

"You have beautiful hands" Hillery said to Leo. "Looks as though Michelangelo chisel them." Leo smiled.

"Dig that, Lady," Prentice said. "That's the first nice thing I ever heard her say to a man."

"Here," Leo said. "Take them, they're yours." Leo held out his hands and she took them, examining them, self-conscious but not embarrassed. It was funny, but it was all right.

At Hillery's end of the fireplace, Elfi was rolling more hash joints. Elfi passed Hillery a joint which she dragged on, then passed it to Leo by placing it between his fingers. Leo tapped Eva's arm and gave it to her, Eva dragged on it and then gave it to Prentice.

"Why don't we go up to my place?" Striker suggested.

"Marvelous idea," Bagetta said. "I'm getting jealous of Hillery." She moved around the others so she was closer to Leo too... Hillery began singing with the music from the disco.

"Shh," Elfi said, "the music is so beautiful." The guitar was still playing but now there was another instrument accompanying it. The music was quite beautiful.

"Your eyes," Leo said, "are more beautiful than my hands."

Elfi smiled. "Why thank you!" She replied. "If I was a fortuneteller, I'd tell your fortune from the top of your hand, not your palm."

"Go ahead," Leo encouraged. "Tell me what dark secrets lie in my future?"

"Hmm... It says... you may be attacked tonight." They all laughed as though it was the funniest thing anyone had ever said.

"And me? Elfi," Hillery asked. "Will I finish college? Will I have lots of babies?"

"I can't tell about babies from hands," Elfi said. "I have to see your feet." They all laughed again.

Walking back to Ben Striker's flat, Leo felt tense. He had accepted Striker's offer without a doubt, but the thought of a huge D.J. gig in front of an audience was a bit unnerving.

Striker lit the candles; he didn't want the overhead lights to ruin their mood. Leo sipped more wine, took off his shoes, and considered whether he ought to make the first move, but before he could overcome his obvious shyness, Elfi, the blonde fraulein with an oval face, had turned on the stereo and joined Hillery, Eva, and Bagetta who were dancing around the room, taking off their silky garments, doing their 'ooh let's get it on' sounds from Marvin Gaye music in the background; moving their arms and shoulders widely, bending at the waist sometimes but moving their hips and taking tiny steps with their feet. They stopped to sip their wine and kept watching him; anxious and excited, then went back to their dancing.

"Too hot in here," Leo said. He took off his shirt. He was sweating, but he used any opportunity to display his torso, which the frauleins admired.

"Aren't your pants too warm?" Hillery teased. Leo blinked, then slowly took them off and folded them neatly over the chair back. They were army pants; he never wore jeans, which he associated with the hippies he despised, but grew to admire after Striker informed him that hippies, in that part of the hemisphere, were primarily responsible for hashish being smuggled from Iran, Afghanistan, Pakistan, Turkey, Lebanon, and South Africa; then cleverly buried in thick wooded forests on the outskirts of small towns all over Germany; a method practiced by American pot growers.

Hillery was getting more and more excited as she watched Leo, but she didn't let him know she was most turned on when Leo was least interested in her. Leo put down the glass of wine and closed his eyes. His legs were slightly hairy and very muscular.

Leo had an erection. At first the frauleins didn't seem to notice, they just kept dancing. He peeked at them through almost closed lids. The ladies dancing excited Leo just as much as it excited them. Leo closed his eyes again, trying to look relaxed although his heart was pounding. After a moment, he went into the guest bedroom. Hillery and Bagetta followed. He lay down and they came over and stood up on the bed, Bagetta on one side and Hillery on the other side of his body, so that when they nudged him with their feet and he opened his eyes, he was looking at their vaginas.

"Mmm…," he murmured, closing his eyes again. "I'm so sleepy."

Hillery and Bagetta jostled Leo with their feet so he'd opened his eyes again.

"What have you been doin' that you're so tired?" Bagetta asked jokingly.

"Oh, nothing really," Leo responded, "Just the hash… you know."

This time Hillery kicked him and he grabbed both of them and soon they were tussling and they went down on him. He was fighting hard because he knew it only turned them on more. Hillery started kissing his chest and continued down his body. He knew what she was up to, but he couldn't stop her. Her hands slid between his legs and her cool tongue touched his swollen penis. It seemed like everything inside him turned loose.

Moments later, Leo and Bagetta made love. It was the way it had been at the beginning, the music and the moaning sounds and the changing of positions, until he touched her hot spots that made her moan and then he whispered with a kind of vengeful satisfaction, "You like that, huh?" Leo asked.

She reached her climax and when Leo was getting his again, he wanted to stop; but couldn't. They climaxed over and over, again and again, without stopping.

Striker, Elfi, and Eva occupied the master bedroom. Lord only knows what happened there!

Private Leo Stegner and Platoon Sergeant Benjamin Striker got back to 'The Rock' early that Monday morning, where they had just reported for company formation. Leo was awake, his body needed sleep, but his mind was hyperactive, thinking about drugs, women, and the new D.J. gig at the Playboy. Now that Striker was close to getting out, Leo daydreamed about things back home. He thought of things like big juicy hamburgers and fries, American cars on the right-hand side of the road, and of his own language. Normally, he did not permit himself this indulgence of sentiment. Now, though he was so close to financial independence, he felt free. Not free to relax his vigilance, but free to fantasize a little.

Guyda, Scalli's cousin back in Florida, came into his thoughts in vivid images he could not quite control. He fell out of formation and gave an exasperated sigh. He had let her affect him too much. It was undisciplined since his tour of duty was only halfway over, and his heavy involvement with hard drugs meant anything could happen. He thought of the situations he had already come through: the hit on his father, Detective Hood's obsession in capturing the Ring-Eye Gang, and the bombing of key Soviet installations in and around Europe; Leo felt he was sitting pretty.

***

Several months later, Leo had changed. He had become a heavy hash smoker, but handled the drug well. He learned to speak German and how to use his job as leverage among his peers. He looked sharp and walked with confidence and grace. He was respected without being ill at ease in the company of superior officers. His habit of talking to superior officers as if they were equals came to be accepted as pardonable. He boldly monitored the covert movements of the D.E.A., by eavesdropping whenever the opportunity presented itself. He cleverly intercepted early warning reports that alerted the D.E.A. of known drug activity.

Leo engaged in informal chats with Colonel Bronson and First Lieutenant Paul Underwagger, the D.E.A. Director for that area, and relayed the information gathered back to platoon Sergeant Striker, who passed the information on to all 180 G.I. pushers working for them. Leo obtained an American passport and felt a sense of freedom and greater flexibility to travel at a moment's notice. He went to Dillenburg, West Germany and registered to become a German citizen. Jerry Prentice provided proof of employment and an established place of residence since dual citizenship was rarely granted on the word of one man. Prentice always took care of his D.J.'s. Stegner also went to the Department of Highway Safety and Motor Vehicle in downtown Freiburg, West Germany, and obtained an International Driver's License so he could travel across any border anywhere in the world by automobile with less chance of being harassed by border police. Then Leo went to Frankfurt, West Germany and purchased warm winter clothing and a used Porsche.

Leo felt well established. He was determined things were going to be different now between Germany and himself by becoming less vulnerable to winter and considerably more streetwise. He was going to bring to the relationship with

Germany a hint of the tough, self-reliant maturity he so strongly admired in platoon Sergeant Benjamin Striker, who seemed to be in control of his life. Leo vowed Germany and the D.E.A. would not be dealing with some dead unknown gambler's kid from Florida. They were going to be dealing with "Mr. Leo Stegner." Man to man!

Leo arrived at Striker's flat above the Playboy. He telephoned Striker then said, "Hey man come outside. I got something to show you."

Moments later, Striker trotted downstairs to find Leo leaning against his newly purchased canary yellow 911 T Targa Porsche with a removable roof.

"What the HELL!!!" Striker said grinning. "This is nice! And on that note I have a surprise for you as well. I'm delighted to inform you that I've chosen you as my successor and would like for you to take over my outlet."

"Oh my God! Are you for real?" Leo replied waving his arms in the air.

"As real as real can get my man. I have every confidence that you can handle it," Striker replied.

Leo wanted to be closer to Striker and he was surprised and delighted Striker named him successor to his military hashish/heroin outlet, and not since his high school days had he really had a close friend. Someone he could talk too easily, and not just in a time of crisis, but confide in daily and say whatever came into his mind. Of all the men he'd come into contact with and worked with, Striker was the closest. Yet even with Striker, Leo had never really let down his guard. In fact, he had a much better sense of Striker's life than Striker had of his own.

Striker questioned Leo about his past and Leo had responded with a laugh and reassured him that his past held no meaningful significance, just bad memories too painful to talk about. Leo had told him a little about his mother, but nothing about the rest of his life. Leo often implied to Striker that the main reason he's become so radical was because he could never accept the way his father died.

No more than five months after the lucrative partnership began (making drug drops, money pick-ups, sex orgies, enjoying fine cuisine, and the D.J. gig at the Playboy) the time had come for Striker to leave (rotate back to the United States). Leo regretted seeing him go, for he had become attached to Striker and respected him immensely. Striker had given Leo something no ordinary man would have done, and all Striker expected in return was for Leo to continue the tradition that had been handed him.

Leo had learned many lessons from Striker. The principal lesson was on the question of some men being better than other men. Striker helped Leo to understand that he was surrounded by a society perpetually hostile to pushers so Leo assumed a position and a pose designed to say: "I am NOT going to let you roll-over-me, hostile world." Leo discovered that his psychological guard was constantly up, sometimes unnecessarily.

Striker the neurotic degenerate platoon Sergeant had left Leo, a three hundred thousand a month retail military drug outlet. Leo wasn't satisfied. He decided to get out of the Army in the cleverest way he could think of. Leo heard a great deal of talk about guys who smuggled drugs through Fort Dix, New Jersey, while being discharged. He also heard about dozens and dozens of other guys who had tried it, and when it didn't work for them they wound up being court martialed and going to jail. Leo had said to himself, "Well, I have to do it, and I have to do it right." He devised an approach, and once it was settled in his mind that it was the correct approach, he rehearsed it thoroughly before setting it in motion.

The differences between Striker and Leo were few, but the one difference that stood out the most was that Leo loved Germany and trafficking drugs enough to come back to Europe; Striker didn't. Striker just wanted to return to the U.S. with the 4 Million he'd earned from the drug outlet and never be heard from again, which is exactly what he did. Leo decided he'd study the feasibility of converting the military drug outlet into a heroin distribution network. He reasoned that on the Russian Front the demand for heroin surpassed the demands for hashish and the conversion could be a worthwhile adventure. Plus the application of such a network could have some far reaching effects, possibly heroin smuggling into the United States.

Leo believed he was luckier than Striker. Striker had given him Eva, Elfi, Bagetta, and Hillery; four of the best female courier smugglers in all of Europe. Some said in the entire world. Jerry Prentice had trained them himself nearly ten years ago. Leo was able to see it all now. He believed that Germany had been given him a second chance. He had been reborn at a crossroad: a place that mattered, a place that could change things, a place where vows might be met and destinies fulfilled. There would be those who would call it madness, he knew. But they were wrong. The truth was simple enough if people could only see it as he saw it. There were times when he thought about his father Joe, and there were old scores to be settled, lots of them.

Leo remembered the Florida mobsters the best. His father had owned a ten-acre estate; which he sold in order to finance his gambling habit. Then when Joe couldn't pay his I.O.U.'s they roughed him up, and made him grovel on his stomach in front of his house, groaning for more time to pay. Leo remembered Joe's feet on one occasion; they were crusty, broken hunks of meat.

The mobsters had broken several of his toes to keep him from running. That's why he became a radical and now an International Heroin Smuggler because he needed the money to make sure Joe's killers would die.

Of course Leo knew that was a copout. As far as Leo was concerned you were with him or against him; there was no middle ground. To Leo, being a radical was like being a saint and those who disagreed with him were by definition hard-hearted and seemingly believed in a perfect world.

Leo knew he had become emotionally defective, even though the Army released him with an honorable discharge. He told himself he wasn't crazy, but was living through temporary insanity due to early exposure to a dangerous society. From the moment his father died, Leo entered this strange, new, complex, crazy society. After it became apparent the authorities couldn't find Joe's killer, that fact did weird things to Leo's head emotionally. Leo had become terribly disoriented and easily lured into the Ring-Eye Gang.

A few months later, Leo collected his belongings. His orders stated that he would be sent to Fort Dix, New Jersey, from where, after one week of processing, he would be mustered out of the United States Army.

The huge 747 Boeing aircraft touched down at the airport in Fort Dix, New Jersey. Leo hustled his way through the terminals, and then waited for his luggage to appear on the roundabout. Leo noticed that most of the transatlantic passengers were monitored closely, but since he was under military orders, customs seemed totally unaware of his existence.

CHAPTER 4

"Pink Elephant"

August 1972

After Leo's year and eleven months of service he became a civilian again returning to the streets of Orlando, Florida, three months before his twenty-second birthday. He received the customary mustering-out pay, but had it taken out in the form of allotments for his mother. He had illegally earned in excess of $100,000 so he really didn't need the allotments. He rented a room and generally re-established himself again in the city, fully confident this time he would be able to manage, armed as he was with an additional 2 years of experience, several thousand dollars in his pocket, and a frighteningly fresh memory of what the city and the summer had done to a bewildered 17-year old boy. This time they would be faced off against a 22-year old man who knew the score.

Leo knew that if he were to attempt vengeance for his father's death he would need a plan not only to enact the retribution but to prepare a quick departure from the area. That would take lots of time, money, and planning. He couldn't just walk up to the man who killed his father and blow him away.

There were too many consequences from the man's associates and local law enforcement. It dawned on him that what he had learned about the drug trade while serving in Germany could be put to good use to achieve his goals.

From his $250.00 a week room on International Drive he wandered around for a while, looking at all sides of his potentially brilliant plan for smuggling heroin into the United States of America, rerunning his options over and over in his mind, weighing the merits against the flaws, each time convinced that it could indeed be a brilliant plan - but there were flaws. First, the heroin would have to be stored in special containers to cover its powerful odor. The infrequently used dope-sniffing police dogs at U.S. Customs could easily detect the scent. Secondly, he was a civilian, and civilians were monitored closer than military personnel. Third, Leo had limited resources. He hadn't established the connections it took to bring him into the United States by way of indirect flight or sea routes that most courier/smugglers used. Because of this, he was limited to routes of the airlines; Germany to London to New York, then Florida, 3 of the toughest custom and immigration check points. (He didn't have to get off the plane in London; it was only a pickup and departure stop.) Fourth, routine routes would make him vulnerable and potentially tagged as a smuggler. He knew he wouldn't be able to justify his many trips to the United States carrying large commercial goods, of sorts, to conceal several Kilos' of heroin. The fifth and last flaw in his potentially brilliant plan was that he didn't have an established wholesale drug outlet here in the United States. It would have taken him more time than he was willing to spend establishing one.

***

A month later, Leo was ready to return to Germany. His confidence and resilience had begun to erode. Leo's old drug dealing friends from the hood tried to work him over. They tried to con him and break him at the hand-to-mouth level by asking Leo to front the drugs, but when it came time for Leo to collect they didn't have all the money due.

Leo decided to be patient. His ultimate goal of seeking out and disposing of his father's killer would have to wait until he was fully prepared, so Leo called his travel agent and made reservations, and then prepared for the 9-hour flight back to West Germany.

Leo wondered about Guyda, the girl he'd left back in Florida. Last he heard she went off to College and had begun a relationship with a boy she met. Leo had daydreamed a lot about the kind of relationship that fit him and thought Guyda might be that girl, but he really missed all the girls he'd gotten to know during his tour of active duty in Germany.

Leo's departure from Florida was a major step that could net him major dividends that wouldn't mature, of course, until a full month later. He had scheduled to meet with Jerry Prentice at the Playboy, which was sure to be encouraging. Then it would be a matter of following his previous plans. Get the couriers together, re-establish himself on the Russian Front, and visit Rocky in Amsterdam, Holland.

***

The Playboy Discotheque was empty, barely lit, and noisy with the bangs and booms from the sound track. Prentice was already seated in the empty back row, a short, fat figure slouching in his usual unobtrusive way. No one within listening distance, even with any hearing device… the noise of the soundtrack would take care of that. Leo slipped into an adjacent seat. He sat in silence for several minutes, making sure he hadn't been followed. But no one entered the discotheque, giving them the chance to talk.

"Rocky has agreed to meet with you," Prentice said. "He's impressed with the way you handled the outlet."

Leo's quiet smile lightened his calm face "Fantastic!" he said. "When do we meet?"

Prentice looked at his watch, "Within the hour."

Leo was excited. "You mean tonight!" he said. "Shit, he doesn't waste any time, does he?"

"Well, since he was here in Germany on business, he thought it would be good to talk to you before he left for Holland," Prentice said. "Now, how soon can you be ready to leave?"

Leo smiled, "Immediately!" he said. "I've wanted to see him ever since Striker told me about him."

"Good! You'll be in for a treat," Prentice said. He reached in his coat pocket, and pulled out a map. "Here, you'll probably need this. I circled the borders you should become familiar with, so study them carefully! Your life may depend on how well you get to know them."

Leo smiled. "Thanks!" I will," he said. He took the map and reviewed it briefly:

"Kassel!" Leo said, and wondered. "Who do we know in Kassel, Germany?"

Prentice laughed. "No one person in particular. This is some of Striker's doing. He asked me to give you this address and key if you returned."

Leo's smile was broad. "You've got to be kidding?" he said.

Prentice smiled this time. "No, would I kid about a thing like that? Striker leased the summer cottage for a whole year, but he never took time out to use it. There's an option to buy it if you want it, because he was only going to use it as a safe house."

"Damn, the Sarge was all right, wasn't he?" Leo asked.

Prentice sighed. "Yep, he was one of the best."

"But what about the girls?" Leo said. "Will…"

Prentice threw up both hands. "Don't worry, they'll be here," he said reassuringly. "Elfi and Bagetta were needed in London, but they'll be flying in tonight… Hillery is still in Brussels, she won't get back until tomorrow. You look tired. Why don't you go on up and get a few minutes rest before you leave."

Leo gestured upward, "My room?"

Prentice interrupted again. "Still there. You have your key?"

Leo nodded. "But what about Eva?" he asked. "Can't I use her too?"

"I'm not sure, yet." Prentice said, and wondered. "She makes herself too visible. She could be a danger… to herself, and to you."

"You notice everything, don't you?"

Prentice smiled and shook his head from side to side, then said, "Not everything… but, you shouldn't use her unless you have too. I've used her in the past, but she won't keep her papers (passport, immunization records, and visa) in order."

"And the others?" Leo asked.

Prentice became serious. "Oh they're reliable, you can trust them with your life," he said. "In fact, you couldn't be in better hands. Hell! You don't have to worry about language barriers at the borders. Elfi speaks 3 languages, herself. And Hillery, that bitch knows even more… not well, but enough. Bagetta and Eva know French. Bagetta was born in France. "So you see," Prentice gestured with his hand, "You have a well-arranged travel group."

Leo sighed. "I see," he said. He kept his voice casual, amused. "I just hope they'll know what they're doing."

"Hold on," Prentice said, with a frown on his face. He sensed some reservation on Leo's part. "You'll be safe," he reassured him. "I know the D.E.A. has made their presence felt around here and with the way things are going it might not be so easy nowadays, but just keep out of the trouble spots, and the girls will take care of the rest."

"Okay," Leo said. "Now what about my cover?" The border police are bound to ask questions."

"You're a disc jockey and a musician," Prentice said. "That's all you've got to say."

Leo laughed. "Just that simple, huh?" He expected Prentice to join in his amusement. He didn't.

"Let me put it this way," Prentice said. "If you're not thinking optimistically in this business, you'll find yourself locked away in some German dungeon and those Nazi bastards don't play. They'll beat your ass, and starve you until you talk."

"Ok, I see your point," Leo conceded. "It's just that Striker never told me how the heroin was being smuggled; only that the girls were involved, and that I should get in contact with them if I wanted to purchase some. But I didn't know enough about the drug to deal with it, so I never asked them and they never volunteered to talk about it. But don't the border police check everything?"

"Not everything," Prentice said. Leo raised his brows. "They're not allowed to body-frisk women. They can only pass their hands over their clothes or through their pockets, but no real body contact," Prentice added.

"Well I'll be damned! I wasn't aware of that," Leo said spiritedly. "And if I know those girls like you apparently do, they don't take kindly to being harassed."

Prentice grinned. "That's one of the reasons why I can trust them," he said. "They know the laws, they know how to handle themselves, they know all the back roads and small borders, they know Rocky, and most of all, they know how to smuggle. Hell, they've smuggled for me since they were 17-years old."

"Say what!" Leo said, surprised. "No wonder you talk about them with so much confidence. You really know them, don't you?"

Prentice laughed. "Hell, I should," he replied. "We've smuggled from here to Timbuktu. And, now that you're back, I'm making up my mind about a change. Advancing years, you know." Prentice's smile was infectious.

"What will you do Jerry?" Leo insisted making sure he tucked away the map as they headed toward the door. There, Prentice shook his hand with a firm grip. Leo winced slightly.

"You're to meet Rocky at the Ventura House near the Bahnhof (train station), Room 302, in 45 minutes, so don't be late." Prentice said.

Leo slackened his pace slightly, caught Prentices' arm and pulled him alongside. He winced, too. "Can't you talk about your new ideas?" Leo asked.

"Well-l... I'm still undecided," Prentice replied. "I'm not sure if I want to get involved in an oil company in Iran or and import/export business here in Germany."

"Oil brings an awful lot of money nowadays," Leo said reflectively. "But, the import/export business will offer you lots of opportunity for travel. I think I'd settle for Iran."

Prentice looked at Leo, shook his head, and then laughed. "I'd better let you go. It's getting late," he said. "You'd better hurry... And be careful!"

"I will," Leo replied. "I'll talk to you later, ok?" Prentice nodded. Leo walked to the nearest taxi stop, to catch a quick but safe route to the Ventura House. Precautions, precautions... they seemed comic, an unnecessary waste of time, Leo thought to himself until reality took over again and he remembered that drug enforcement agents could be monitoring his moves, with well-disguised, highly sophisticated equipment. The smile was wiped from his face. "The Bahnhof," he told the taxi driver, "By way of Bahnhofstrasse." And having established the fact that he knew his way around he relaxed and didn't worry about the meter, which gave him a chance to relax and reminisce about his upcoming plan meeting with the girls, then Rocky. Suddenly, Leo's mind was jolted out of the neatly planned prospects, just as the taxi arrived at the Ventura. He began wrestling with more practical matters such as counting out the dollars and calculating a sizable tip.

***

Leo would soon learn that Rocky Congo Lee was a quiet, self-effacing man who had dodged suspicions of the authorities about his highly secretive work for nearly 10 years. He would soon learn that Rocky was linked to General Chung Che Fu, ruler of the Golden Triangle province, and that the quiet intensive briefing on the quality of heroin available, its cost, and a discussion of tactics was all he could be told for the time being, for discretion was the key to safety for everyone involved. Strategy would come later when Leo had gathered the information he needed to put the heroin smuggling operation into motion.

There was also a possibility Rocky would have Leo under surveillance that could last until the reports on his movements demonstrated competence and skill in the drug trade. Leo's return trip to Germany to organize a major military heroin network would be a very tricky period indeed. This was not the time for him to draw Rocky to anyone's attention, much less himself.

The following week, Leo, Elfi, Bagetta and Hillery were heading for Kassel, West Germany, up into the highlands for a visit to the summer cottage on Lake Catherine to convert it into a safe house. There were scattered farms, groves of oranges, groves of sugarcane, and maple trees at the beginning of spring. There were browsing deer by day, bobcats screaming over the hills by night, raccoons dodging under woodpiles, and an occasional bear wandering down from the Russian border.

A week or so later, Leo and the girls traveled to Amsterdam, Holland, in the Netherlands, for a few days stay at the Sheraton-Schiphol (airport) Inn, to visit Rocky. The Inn provided tennis and scuba diving, saunas, Jacuzzi, flowers for all seasons, and people from everywhere.

After that Leo is scheduled to travel to the mountains of the Russian Front for a week of heroin drops throughout the military drug network; then returned to the Playboy Discotheque. February would be almost over.

Rocky had reserved several suites for the benefit of his traveling clients and his own private meetings. His room was on the third floor, but the fire escape staircase near it had easy access, as Rocky believed in limited visibility of his coming and going.

8:30 p.m. exactly, the door to Rocky Congo Lee's suite opened, upon Leo Stegner's arrival.

"You look well," Leo told him, studying Rocky's lean and trim, suntanned body, as he closed the door. Rocky gave Leo a warm handshake and then a quick embrace with two hefty pats on Leo's shoulders.

"Good to see you Leo. Pick a chair," Rocky said. "Sorry about the décor. I take what the hotel offers, but my partner from South America seems to like it."

"It's my kind of place." Leo told him as he chose one corner of a spindle-legged sofa. He glanced around the green and gold room, while Rocky studied him, then poured a couple of glasses of Germany's best red wine and served it on an elaborate tray.

Rocky, a 32-year-old average-sized Chinese man from the China Fukien Province (or Formosa) was well mannered and deliberate. He wore a three-piece double-breasted blue suit. His hair was straight, thick, and black and his round, smooth face showed no signs of aging.

Leo smiled. "Tell me," he said. "Is it safe to phone you whenever I need to see you?"

"Sure," Rocky said, "but only to make an appointment."

"Your phone is tapped?" Leo asked.

"Let's say that someone likes to listen to my conversations; a recent development. " Rocky said.

"Because of you?" Leo asked.

"Perhaps, or perhaps someone is trying to get inside information on one of my operations. There have been so many rip-offs lately, I find it necessary to use messengers or couriers within my circle," Rocky replied. Leo's face relaxed as Rocky handed him his drink and then sat in a chair directly opposite, crossed his legs, and raised his glass in salute. "Don't worry; we're on top of it." But it's wiser at the moment to play along with them, give them no hints to arouse suspicion." He glanced at his watch. "How may I help? What are your plans?" Rocky asked. "Prentice has told me some interesting things about you. It seems you've done a magnificent job with your outlet."

Leo smiled. "Thanks for the compliment," he said. "But I'd like to get out of the hash business, and convert the operation into a heroin network." He paused.

"Problems?" Rocky asked, around the glass of wine.

"No, not really," Leo replied. "It's just that most of my dealers have begun to complain. They claim that ever since the Army started withdrawing our troops from 'Nam and sending them over here to Europe, there's been a much greater demand for heroin than hash. And they'd rather sell the heroin because they could make more money, and it's easier to conceal."

Rocky grinned. "An interesting point, wouldn't you agree?"

"Absolutely." Leo replied with a serious look on his face. "And that brings me to the other reason for wanting to see you. I've been studying the possibility of expanding my operation into the United States; Florida in particular. But there are still a few issues to be worked out." He smiled. "Not to mention my lack of experience, as a smuggler. But I'd sure love an opportunity to establish a wholesale network there." Leo paused. "You think it's a good idea?"

Rocky scratched his temple, thought a bit, and then spoke. "When you're smuggling heroin in Europe, there is no relief from anxiety, from the suspicion that your presence is known in advance, that you are doomed to spend the best years of your life at slave labor. That is the horror. Visitors are routinely watched.

You sweat fearing even the odor of perspiration will betray you, and sweat all the more. Your mouth is dry. Even your breath stinks from fear. Anyone or everyone may be the many-headed dragon. Cut one head off and it will be replaced by two more. The most innocent-looking person may be D.E.A.; a young woman or an old man. At any moment you may be arrested. The moment may come with a small gesture, a polite request. You wonder what you'd do, run, shrug, what? However it comes, the result is the same: there is no deportation save at the leisure of the German and French governments. Notions of justice are quaint in trials for heroin smugglers. Such trials are theater staged for the outside world. The outcome is determined in advance, if not the precise punishment like a labor camp deep in the highlands of the Russian Front at the latitude where it never thaws. 20-years are taken from your life. American officials may protest, but what can they do? You knew the dangers going in. And no one will know how much human agony you're going through, for they will have nothing to do with you. You must consider these things, before you begin such an expensive operation." Rocky said. "And if it's something you still want to do, then do it."

Leo pondered, and then sighed. "Yeah, Prentice gave me a stern warning as well. He suggested that my visit to the Netherlands would best be served if I took Bagetta, Elfi, and Hillery along. He said you've worked with them before, and I could trust their judgment."

Rocky smiled, his eyes held something of the old zest. "Yes, they've covered a lot of territory," he said, "and they always came through."

Leo pondered again. "I was just going over their backgrounds in my mind," he said. "Elfi is working toward her Master's in Chemistry. Bagetta is a travel agent, and Hillery, an airline stewardess." He laughed. "Hell, if I use my assets right, the ability to recruit hundreds of new couriers may be possible."

Rocky laughed. "I suppose that's stretching it a bit," he said, "but smuggling is a high risk business."

"I know you're a smart operator, despite the danger, but how do you manage to be so careful?" Leo asked.

Rocky remained unemotional. "I was in the business of being careful from the day I was born." He said. "My office is in a nice old house, narrow, four stories high... on a large congested street in Northwest Holland. The top floor... I made into a communication center. Below that, two rooms of maps, a reference library and a special temperature vault waiting to be emptied. Then there's a floor for our borrowed computers, code ciphering and deciphering machines, and other devices. I have a full staff and some foreign contacts already established. The floor above the main hall is for legitimate business, with Import/Export dealers handling any actual request for our services. The entrance hall is for reception... and security."

"Import/Exporter's?" Leo wondered. "I'm amazed!"

"Just part of our many services," Rocky continued smoothly. He glanced at his watch again, pulled himself out of his chair, opened his attaché case, and then handed Leo a Kilo of 98% pure heroin. "This my friend...is PINK ELEPHANT," he said enthused.

Leo stood and looked at the heroin. When he saw the color, he frowned. During the entire time he'd been involved with drugs, he had never heard of PINK ELEPHANT, nor seen pink-colored heroin before. He was highly disturbed. "I'm sorry, Rocky," he said, "But I can't sell this shit looking like this. Man, the moment my people see this stuff... they'll laugh me out of business! I thought you sold that quality stuff, like Persian-brown or China-white?"

Rocky looked at Leo like he was nuts. He reached for, and picked up his hash pipe, lit it and took a hit, watching Leo's eyes. "Please, have a smell," he suggested, around the pipe. "It's apparent… Jerry didn't tell you everything." He was suddenly smiling.

Leo tore open the cellophane, leaned and smelled it, then without warning, he suddenly became extremely lightheaded and dizzy, then he bent over as if he were going to puke! He covered his mouth and nose with both hands and jerked away quickly. His eyes were watery and burning. His breath quickened. "Goddamn!" He said anxiously. "That shit is dangerous!" He became frightened. He wiped the sweat from his forehead with both hands. "I damn near puked from that shit, and almost fainted! Even the odor, will kill you!"

"It was necessary to get your attention," Rocky said. "You didn't exactly give me much of a choice." He gestured down at the heroin. "You're looking at the highest quality of heroin… ever sold on the market." He paused. He noticed Leo's boyish excitement.

Leo interrupted. "How potent is this shit?"

Rocky laughed. He poured them both another glass of German wine. "It comes from Thailand. It's only 98% pure," he said in a conceited tone of voice.

Leo blinked. "Say what!" He shook his head and sighed heavily. "Damn! Boy don't I feel stupid. You must forgive me, Rocky. I'm really sorry I doubted your intentions."

Rocky waved his right hand, and then said, "Consider it forgotten. Your good intentions are noted." He sipped some more wine, and then passed Leo the hash pipe. Leo lit the pipe with his cigarette lighter and took a long, slow draw, then felt a nervous feeling wash through his stomach. He suddenly felt good about himself again and wanted to know more. He approached the heroin cautiously this time. He was interested in examining that peculiar but interesting looking 2 x 3 inch paper seal affixed to the outer portion of the transparent cellophane.

"Hey, this is one of those prehistoric elephant's," Leo said enthused. "What's with the seal, Rocky... and what does this Chinese writing say?"

Rocky smiled. "It's called a mammoth. And a trademark frequently used by the China Mafia. The writing, translated into English says: 'Pink Elephant'."

"Oh, I see. I was wondering how it got its name. Are you one of them?" Stegner asked candidly.

"Of course, my family was born into their organization. They even sent me to school to become a chemist. After I graduated, they had a position waiting for me."

Leo looked surprised and rested his chin on the palm of his hand, then crossed his arms. "How clever," Leo said. "So, they avoid the unnecessary risk of hiring outsiders who may pose a threat to them at some later date, huh?"

"Exactly," Rocky acknowledged. He always maintained in discussions of this type that the best tactics were whatever was simple and direct. Too much tact can get you into trouble.

"Rocky, are many people aware of this trademark?" Leo asked.

Rocky sat on the corner of the table beside him, thought a moment, and then spoke. "Well, the C.I.A. and D.E.A. may have some knowledge... through prior drug busts, you know. But other than that, only members within our organization."

Leo nodded. "Ah, so the public isn't aware. Damn! It would make a helluva story. You should write a book someday."

Rocky laughed. "If I did... you, nor I would be around to read it. The Mafia is pretty high on keeping secrets," he said. Leo swallowed. Rocky continued. "Tell me, Leo, you've made lots of money from your military hash outlet. So why do you want to get involved in heroin smuggling into Germany and the United States of all places? Don't you realize a contract may be placed on your head if you're busted and decide to talk?"

Leo released the cellophane and peered at Rocky. He felt a sudden need to pee, but fought it back. He thought about his father, Joe Stegner, the humiliation, and promises he made to Joe while in jail, to devote the rest of his adult life seeking revenge for his murder. "For revenge," Leo replied angrily.

Rocky snapped to. "For revenge?!"

Leo nodded. "Yeah, a son-of-a-bitch murdered my father, and I'll get him... if it takes the rest of my life!"

Rocky interrupted. "Wait a minute," he said. "Who killed your father?"

Leo paused a brief moment to calm down, then he continued smoothly. "Listen. I'm sorry I got carried away. But... a few years ago, some mobster back in Florida killed my dad over a lousy gambling debt. He was never brought to trial. The prosecutor said they knew who was responsible but didn't have enough evidence to get a conviction since the murder was made to look like a robbery. So I'm going to take care of it myself! It will take money to complete the job, a lot of it. I'll have to plan, and then make the hit, and leave the United States forever. That's one of the reasons I joined the Army—to learn how to become a professional killer." Leo paused a moment to catch his breath. "Don't get me wrong, Rocky. I like being involved with drugs.

Number one, I like the adventure it brings into my life, and the beautiful girls here. Number two, I love Europe, and all it has to offer as well." Leo laughed. "So you see; I'm already a dead man. I'm not worried about getting busted, or the consequences!" Now he felt totally relieved from all his anxiety, pain, and burdens he'd carried for years.

Rocky sighed heavily. "Wow!" he said with a bit of a grin. "I'm not so sure I agree with what you intending to do back home, but I do sympathize with your cause."

Leo sighed heavily, and then said. "Thanks. You're the only person I've ever told, you know."

Rocky nodded. Suddenly he clapped his hands. "Enough of this, for now," he said. "I suggest you work the borders between here and the Netherlands, for six-months or so, and then once you get the hang of things, we'll study the feasibility of your U.S. distribution project. Agreed?"

Leo nodded, and then smiled. "Okay, agreed."

Rocky rubbed his hands together. "Now! When will I see you again and how much heroin do you think you'll need?"

Leo pondered a moment in silence. "Hell, I'm not really sure. I have over 180 pushers to supply."

Rocky interrupted. "Then let me make a suggestion."

"Okay." Leo said. "Go for it."

"Why don't you start with 3 Kilos? That's a little over 6-pounds. Then you'll know exactly what you need the next time," Rocky said.

"Fair enough," Leo said. "Then I'll see you in about 2 weeks. That will give me enough time to get with the girls, study the maps Prentice gave me, and bring everything together.

Danger to one is danger to all, you know?" They shook hands. "But what about the cost?" Leo asked.

"Just bring me as much as you can, and we'll work out the details later," Rocky suggested. "You'll end up a successful businessman yet," he added.

Leo laughed. "I certainly hope so," he said. "And I hope I didn't hold up your schedule." He noted the heroin in Rocky's hand, ignoring it politely. He left with a salute and a word of thanks to Rocky... an imposing figure standing beside the sofa, not one crease in his suit, not one hair escaping from his slick head, and not one furrow on that smooth benign face.

**

A few days later, Bagetta, Elfi, and Hillery had to smile. Leo's summer home was super deluxe. It was a two bedroom cottage with a giant living room and a sunken floor. It had a fireplace in the center with wall to wall carpet and stereo intercom installed throughout. He had the best antique furniture money could buy. Upstairs there was one master bedroom, a bath, and a patio. Leo's sacred den had everything from female centerfold pictures to a gun rack, and bookshelves.

"Ladies," he said. "I've asked you all over so we can have an orgy!" They all looked at each other startled, and then Leo laughed. "I'm kidding. I've made a major decision, so I thought I'd have a celebration with my friends."

"So can we assume the meeting the other night with Rocky went well?" Bagetta asked.

"Yes!" Leo said, excitedly. "Matter of fact, it was fantastic!"

"Did you find out a lot?" Elfi interrupted.

"I'll say," Leo said thoughtfully. "Much more than I expected; Rocky covered a lot of information about how to set everything up."

"Good," Hillery said spiritedly. "Does that mean you've negotiated a deal?"

"Yes," Leo said. "The four of us will leave for the Netherlands within two weeks. We'll be there a week."

"A week?" Hillery asked. She knew that part of the world. "Why a whole week?"

Leo looked at her intently. "Well, I figured we needed time to devise a plan," he said. "A way to get us back into Germany with the heroin."

"Just how much do you figure on bringing in, a ton?" Elfi asked, sarcastically. Leo frowned, the others burst out laughing. He tried to play it off.

"Don't answer that," Hillery said with a grin.

"No," Leo said. He was serious. "3 'kilos,' now. What's the safest way to smuggle it into Germany?"

"We are!" Hillery said. She sat back in her loveseat deliberately, her legs agape, rubbing her crotch. "You buy it, we'll haul it." She patted her pussy. "I can put seven ounces right here."

"Good move Hillery," Elfi said. "But we can't use it this trip. Unfortunately it's a little too small," Elfi gestured with her hand, "don't you think?" Everyone laughed but Hillery. She quickly closed her legs and pulled the front of her dress down.

Leo wanted answers. "Seriously ladies; I need to know another way to get 6 pounds of heroin into the country. And what about me; won't I have to provide some sort of smokescreen or distraction or something?"

Bagetta cut in. "To answer your first question: We'll have to make some long plastic tubes for the 3 of us... to pour the heroin into. And, since it's 3 of us, we each carry 2 pounds. Then, before we leave the Netherlands, we'll wrap the plastic tubes around the upper portion of our body and tape it in place, and make sure there are no leaks. Then we'll put a body corset on top of that so they won't be able to tell if it's the heroin or us, since they're not allowed to pat us down. To answer your second question, all you have to do is just drive, keep cool, and cover the expenses. We'll have ample cover, if no one starts questioning us too closely. But then, that's part of our job, avoiding the questions," she said.

Leo looked amazed. "That's great!" he said with enthusiasm. He felt a surge of energy. "I had no idea a woman could insert 7 oz. of heroin up her vagina," he said with genuine concern.

"Certainly!" Hillery said. She couldn't wait to get into the conversation. "After all, it was big enough to pack you in, wasn't it?"

"Yeah, but this is different," he said. "Besides, what kind of container, that's shaped like a penis, can possibly be used to put heroin in?"

"Condoms!" Hillery said, grinning. Leo looked amazed all over again.

"You mean rubbers?" He asked.

"That's right!" Elfi said. "Do you think we would kid you about something as important as this? She strolled toward him. Her light golden hair was shoulder-length and falling free. She was medium height and had an excellent figure. Elfi passed in front of him, turned her head to look at him, observed his glance.

Their eyes met, and held. Her dazzling blue eyes edged by curves of dark lashes were brilliant against the honey tan of her skin.

Leo touched her body, rubbing his hands up and down her thighs. "No," he said. "I don't think you'd kid me about a thing like that, but isn't it a bit dangerous? What if it bursts? It could happen, couldn't it?" He was asking, as Bagetta, his brown-eyed, black-haired, slender friend joined them. She sat next to him, each sensing the nearness of the other, enjoying it. He was actually becoming more relaxed, now that they were revealing the secrets of smuggling.

"Sure it could," Bagetta told him. "But I'll live." Her brown eyes looked contrite as she gave a reassuring smile. "You see, we don't have to worry about that. If one rubber breaks, the pussy is protected by five more."

Leo laughed.

Elfi cut in. "Yeah, it's really no problem at all," she said. "We like the French-Ticklers better, because they're thicker and hold more heroin."

Leo was impressed. He grinned and shook his head in astonishment. "How about the borders coming out of Amsterdam? Any suggestions?"

"Kleve is an excellent one," Hillery added.

"Where is that?" he asked her.

Hillery considered for a fraction of a second, "You're really new at this aren't you?" she said, as she remembered her first week when she had been overwhelmed by the strangeness of everything. "Don't you know Amsterdam at all?" Leo threw both hands up in the air, palms up. He was naïve as they had been.

He grinned again and shook his head. "No, but I have a good map that Prentice gave me, outlining everything. I can't wait to check out their drug scene."

"That's right!" Elfi said. "You just recently got back from America, didn't you?" She pushed aside a heavy strand of hair from her brow.

"Yep, but I missed you guys every minute I was gone." Leo said.

"Yeah, we knew Striker wasn't coming back, but we didn't exactly know what your plans were until Prentice told us; America!" Elfi was impressed. "I'm envious," she exclaimed.

"It isn't too far off, nowadays," he reminded her.

"I know, I know, but…," she sighed. "It's maddening. Here I am about to end six years at London University and just across that little bit of water there's the rest of Europe, Rome, and America. Maddening because I don't know when I'll ever get to see them."

Leo's smile was broad. "Hey, you stick with me! You'll see them much sooner than you think," he said. "In fact," he gestured with his hands, "I'll increase what Jerry Prentice was paying you guys by one thousand dollars. Now what do you guys think of that?" He smiled and the threesome fell all over him rejoicing, kidding him, and touching him as though he was the Emperor Caesar himself.

"Now I can save up," Elfi said, "and fly over for a few months in America." She was happy.

"It's well worth it. Expensive though, as I found out," Leo said. "But it was a relief, in a way, to go home and stop figuring what the dollar had sunk to. Holland… what's in Holland except canals and windmills?"

"More than you think," Hillery said. "I had a pretty good time there." She was a few years younger than Elfi and somehow she always had to do the protecting. "But you're almost as unsettled as we are. I don't think you'll be here six months from now. I think you're deciding right now to take off like a bird."

"And why not?" Elfi ended gloomily. "He's free. Free to do what he likes."

Leo cut in. He said, "I like it here. And I'm here to stay." He kissed each of them on the hand. "Even if I decided to leave, I'll take whoever wants to go with me."

"Isn't that something," Bagetta said. Her thoughts were filled with dreams.

"Yes," Hillery said, "it's wild." They studied the map patiently for nearly 30-minutes, choosing from experience the borders they would smuggle the heroin across.

"Now, before I forget," Leo said, "When is the best time to travel? Morning, noon, or night?"

"It really doesn't matter," Hillery said. She was the expert on foreign travel. "We know the routes and the arrangement for the pick-up; now we need to rent a camper as a tourist front. Just pray to God we get some kind of bad weather; rain, snow, or fog, will do."

Leo frowned. "Why do you want to travel under those conditions?" he asked. "That takes the fun out of traveling."

"Well, don't get angry," Elfi said, "but you just don't step on a flying carpet and away you go. You have to capitalize on the vulnerabilities of the border officials. They get lazy you know. They don't like getting wet and they don't like working when it's snowing and freezing cold."

Leo relaxed. "Oh, I see," he said cheerfully. "Humans will be human, won't they?" The girls grinned in agreement. Leo sighed. "Okay, then we'll prey upon their weaknesses until they catch on." He sighed again. "You girls are so very clever."

Elfi cut in. "We're only doing what we get paid for," she replied.

"Well, let me be the first to say you all are well worth it."

That night at the cottage, Leo sat drinking a beer and thought about the day's encounter. It had gone well. Tomorrow night, the D.J. gig at the 'Playboy Discotheque,' and after that, a stepped-up schedule concentrating on his new military heroin outlet. The exchange of life stories, future hopes, and past disappointments with the girls, laid a foundation for friendship and trust. That's what he wanted now, he was sure of it.

Bagetta, Elfi, and Hillery liked him. He was sure of that. There was an attraction between them that was hard to explain, but it was there. Even so, he warned himself, don't let your guard down.

Leo pondered a moment. Was Rocky having me watched right now? Probably. Leo felt a chill. It soon passed. Leo had informed Rocky he had merged nicely into the European scene with no suspicions aroused.

One week later: Amsterdam, Holland, the Netherlands.

Hundreds of tons of raw opium and equal amounts of semi-processed morphine-base (the raw materials from which heroin was made), were being shipped from the Golden Triangle. And from that Southeast Asian continent, the illicit cargos were slowly moving closer to the United States. But Amsterdam, the eternal city, one of the world's greatest crossroads, a center of commerce and culture had become a center of heroin abuse as well. Hundreds of thousands of addicts were living proof that Deutschland had become a big part of the Southeast Asian heroin connection.

Leo could see the addicts in the historic places and along the bank of the canals, nodding their way through life. 90,000 junkies, twice as many as there were just two years ago. Finding heroin on the streets of Amsterdam was about as difficult as finding cigarettes or a newspaper. To prove it, Hillery Krefeld did it. She posed as a tourist searching for a vacation fix. The first buy was for a gram of heroin. The transaction involved a guy who'd just gotten back from Thailand. In the old days, visitors to that country brought home fine garments, but this guy came back with Thailand's latest cash crop, heroin.

Hillery negotiated a $150 deal on the bank of the Amstel Canal. The dealer was strictly small time. As she did business, many other junkies made their deals. When she walked further along the canal's span every other step uncovered discarded syringes. Given the time, she could have collected hundreds of them. She spotted junkie after junkie under a bridge stretched-out.

Amsterdam's heroin problem, while severe, was certainly not unique. Almost all of Europe was currently in the grips of an extraordinary epidemic of heroin abuse. West Germany was suffering an addiction rate... 3 times that of the United States. Heroin overdoses had become one of the leading causes of death among G.I.'s and German young people.

Meanwhile... the French Connection was in France, processing opium into heroin for eventual sales in the United States, and waging war against an international effort by American and European authorities, which nearly closed them down. Law enforcement agents in France had busted major heroin labs in Sicily, which tied-in to New York and other national organized crime smuggling organizations. The arrest of Reco Record and his co-conspirators, who figured prominently in the French Connection, as well as the intensified effort against street level pushers, demonstrated that the French and United States governments had taken the problem seriously, and the war against heroin wasn't going uncontested.

Dope peddlers, especially those with Mafia connections, were fighting back. Authorities who got in the way, were murdered, and the traditional organized crime links between Europe, the Mid-East, and the United States, had money moving back and forth, with the couriers carrying heroin. They bought into corporations and businesses in the United States, and then took the illicit funds back to the Mid-East; building and investing as legitimate businesses. 90% of the heroin hidden inside cargo ships, airline luggage, and on persons, was getting through. Tons of heroin infiltrated the streets of New Jersey; New York City; Miami; Los Angeles; Washington, D.C.; Boston; Atlanta; Philadelphia; Detroit; Houston; Chicago; and Baltimore. Customers came from all levels of society. They looked like ants, in and out, back and forth.

Leo discovered people could purchase almost anything off the street; just as much as they could pay for. At one point, Hillery had four different peddlers competing for her business. Leo noted the way most dealers protected themselves from undercover cops, posing as junkies, was to demand to see the tracks on their arms; the scars and marks left by the frequent injections of heroin.

Leo was acutely aware when the supply was low in Europe; the heroin was moderately cut and sold from 80% to 90% pure, whereas in the United States, the average purity of street heroin was as low as 20% pure. And when the supply was low, it was heavily diluted to 3% pure.

***

Leo's burning passion to re-establish himself during his very first month back in Germany had been realized. He wasn't afraid of being on the real-life front-line war against heroin, with very little fan-fair and recognition. Instead, he felt highly motivated and in control of his immediate destiny, of course, as long as he continued to sell drugs to the military. He had reasoned that: The U.S Army was a guaranteed source of income because he wouldn't have to compete with the dealer on the street, thus making his business much safer. Secondly, heroin was less bulky and easier to conceal than hashish. So converting his military hash outlet into a heroin network would be an easy transition. And, thirdly, he would take advantage of the fear that permeates every hour of every day, in the life of the American soldier; 'Going Cold Turkey!'

Elfi Drechsler had analyzed Amsterdam's street heroin to be approximately 65% pure, and if Leo was to have any possible chance of competing against the quality of heroin on the streets, it would be in his best interest to smuggle his own drugs, and that was where Rocky Congo Lee came in.

In March, there were thousands of tourists and hundreds of sight-seeing tour buses... as well as the usual commercial trucks to cope with. Today, there had been no complications at all. Elfi, the wisest of the four; had suggested they park the camper in a garage near Central Station and head for Rocky's place in a nice anonymous taxi. They wore nothing flamboyant, just old favorites that made them feel comfortable.

The man-made island, on which Central Station lay was well behind them. They headed North, then slightly to the East... to escape the main thoroughfares and their tedious traffic jams. Here, in the close huddle of the streets, medieval houses edging ancient canals, pointed gables, brick and sandstone decorated with elaborately trimmed cornices, made riding almost pleasant. Still there was too much traffic; torrents of Flying Hollander's on their moped bicycles. The taxi driver changed direction again, traveling a little to the West, to reach the long narrow stretch of Cuserstraat, where traffic was banned and pedestrians could walk without fear. Too many stops for Leo's taste, but he couldn't have everything. And most of Amsterdam, the tourists too; seemed to be window shopping.

Leo noticed that in true Dutch Fashion, Central Amsterdam seemed to be a complete geometric layout of side by side straight through canals and parallel streets with sudden twist and curves until the next sharp turn. On a map, the pattern would be logical and easy; but by way of car, especially for a stranger, it was mystifying. Leo mastered all of the short cuts in Amsterdam after his third visit.

Ahead of them were a bunch of tourists. Pausing in the stream of traffic, the taxi driver hesitated about their direction. Lots of backpackers on vacation swarmed the streets of downtown Amsterdam for a week or two of reclining on the grass, squashed together, unperturbed by the mixtures of music from a hundred radios or by the polite policeman on horseback trying to separate the heroin addicts from the dreamers on hashish. There were girls everywhere, slumped on top of backpacks. Most of them wore striped shirts that were tucked into tight Daisy-Duke blue jeans that didn't have a quarter inch to spare over their ass. Their blonde hair, shoulder length, was parted in the center to swing free.

Worldwide Export/Import read the legend above the doorway of one of the restored houses on Cuserstraat. The Worldwide Marketing Firm was not remarkable; tucked away as it was in the middle of a row of ancient gables. There were other commercial establishments on this old Amsterdam Street, including a main street market place, expensive restaurants, and a luxury hotel. Rocky's office was on the top floor, accessed by a very small private elevator installed years ago for someone's heart ailment: it could hold four people if they were thin enough and pressed in a tight embrace. Leo touched an ivory call button to signal Rocky. The elevator door was released, avoiding the staircase that would have taken them through the busy second and third floors, where imports of coffee, cheese and other dairy products were actually marketed.

Worldwide was authentic business, but it was also a false front for illicit activities. How Rocky Congo Lee managed to secure the whole building was something that aroused Leo's curiosity. Knowing Rocky's diplomacy; he wasn't surprised.

The corridor was short and narrow. Rocky's door, as old and heavy as all the other carved woodwork in this building had a new sign, large and easy to read: Worldwide Export/Import (by Appointment Only). The door swung open as Leo was about to knock and Rocky was there with his broad smile and firm handshake's to welcome them inside. "I trust you guys had a safe trip?" he asked.

"Yes," Bagetta replied, with a big beautiful smile. "No trouble at all."

"You had a peephole installed, Rocky?" Elfi asked, studying the carved upper panel of the door as it was closed and bolted behind them. The small cutout was centered in a wooden rosette, part of the door's decoration both inside and out, not noticeable except by close scrutiny.

"Ah-so...You notice," Rocky said. "It's necessary during these times." His round face tried to look both happy and serious. Now he was at his desk, arranging a chair in place for Leo, while the girls made themselves comfortable.

Rocky's office was noticeably different from when the girls had last visited it: dark paneled walls enclosed a large square room, with a large desk, a comfortable sofa and matching loveseat, nice cushioned chairs and an IBM microcomputer, some filing cabinets, and several telephones. There were two powerful lamps for evening work; by day, light beamed through the diamond-shaped panes of two windows, narrow and tall which stood close to the desk. Everything was well within reach. Leo waited while Rocky lifted the large food tray onto his desk wondering if the business that had brought them there necessitated all the security precautions.

"We'll lunch first and chat," Rocky said. He lifted the large cover off the serving tray and Leo smiled. Rocky wasn't about to let business interfere with regular mealtimes. Leo pitched in by sweeping blotting pads and letters aside and in the cleared space; spread out napkins which had covered the food. The large tray contained hot roast beef, various kinds of cheese and delicious treats, salad, bread, and several bottles of Dutch wine.

The ladies joined them, and in fascination, watched the deft way in which both men's hands arranged the items in logical order. Leo poured wine into five glasses; he smiled and gave a glass to Rocky. As usual, they saluted and bowed their heads in acknowledgement of their new beginning.

Rocky spoke, "Rumor has it that Prentice is resigning from the Playboy. Is this fact?"

"Negative. Only a rumor," Leo responded. "He's only thinking about it, he's getting up there in age you know."

"Glad it's only a rumor," Rocky said. "He still has 30 good years ahead of him."

Leo raised his glass. "To Survival," he said. They drank to that.

"So you really have decided to join us?" Rocky asked.

"Of course!" Leo replied. "Did you ever doubt it? Who else is crazy enough to step into Striker's shoes." They all laughed.

"I'll drink to that!" Hillery said.

"I wasn't sure," Rocky said. "I had to wait and see if you showed up." Rocky gave him a sheet of paper he took from his attaché case. "This diagram will give you a general idea of how we operate."

Leo took the diagram and began to read: Leo sighed, "Hmmm, this diagram is very informative."

"Well, you've made such an excellent start—I've decided to share a few trade secrets," Rocky said. "I must admit—converting the hash outlet to a heroin outlet was a good idea! Some more wine?"

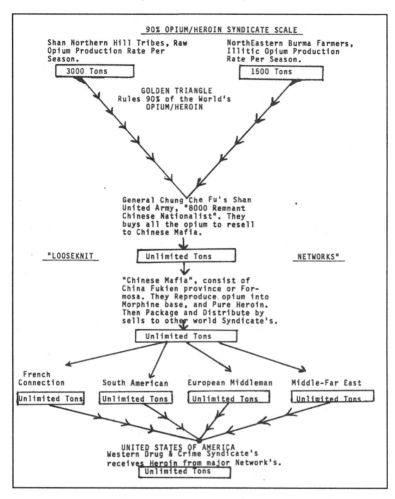

"No thanks," Leo said. "Dinner is a long time away. I think I'll make myself a sandwich." He selected a slice of roast beef, a slice of cheese, and cushioned them between two thick slices of bread. Bagetta, Elfi and Hillery were helping themselves to two of everything.

Rocky Congo Lee in all probability was marked to be the next leader of the 'Loose-knit Heroin Network'. He was immensely wealthy and legendary. He owned large fleets of cargo ships, several apartment houses, airplanes, loan companies, a huge fabric firm, and a few villas scattered around the globe. He was into everything. Rumor had it that he owned over five-hundred suits, ready at a moment's notice wherever he happened to be. He had a presence that was magnetic. When he walked into a room, people would turn to stare. His wife was an attractive, gracious lady and when he entertained on his yacht or in his private home she was by his side. If business required his absence, his wife was equally capable of stepping in and hosting an event.

Leo admired Rocky's stamina and idolized him. He began to pattern himself after Rocky and yet had only seen him twice. 30-minutes later they cleared Rocky's desk again and spread a small stack of newspapers.

"Shall we get down to business?" Rocky began.

"Yep, might as well," Leo nodded in agreement. He had finished his sandwich and was now onto dessert. He poured himself some more wine and lit a cigarette. The threesome (Elfi, Bagetta, and Hillery) kept on eating, kept on smiling, and waited patiently for them to finish. They, of course, had been through this routine dozens of times before.

"Next week, I'll be in Germany," Rocky said. "Why don't I meet with you at the Playboy?"

Leo smiled. "An excellent idea," he said. "I'll be there." He often wondered how the threesome must have felt when they were hired for their very first smuggling mission. Leo was more afraid than excited.

Rocky reached into his attaché case, found two surgeon's masks, handed one to Leo and tied the other around his lower face. Leo copied. He was excited, then terrified. There was absolutely no way they could work without it because the shit was lethal. The smell alone was toxic. They took the three kilos of 98% pure pink heroin packaged in cellophane, slit them open—with a letter opener, then poured all of it onto the newspaper. It was like watching a mini version of Mount Saint Helen erupting all over again. Large and hard, pink crusty-like rocks, fumed with the vapors of death, mushrooming toward their face. They got the hell out of the way in a hurry and allowed the heroin's toxic fumes to settle. The shit had their eyes burning and streaming tears like a faucet.

"I figured you guys would need this," Elfi said. She tilted their head back and dropped a few drops of Visine into their eyes. "There, that should stop the irritation." She rejoined the others, but not before Rocky and Leo thanked her for being so alert.

Leo shook his head. He had a solemn look about his face. "Wow, Rocky. This is the baddest shit I've ever seen in my life!" He whispered from behind the mask. "What did you pay for it?"

His boyish enthusiasm made Rocky laugh. "If I told you," he said, "you might want the same deal."

Leo shook his head again and grinned. "No, I'm not like that. I was just curious to know," he said. "Besides, what will I owe you for all this?" He paused briefly. "I only have $60,000 to spend," he added concerned.

"No problem," Rocky gestured with his hands. "Just give me what you have—and pay me the rest when you get it." He smiled and Leo frowned.

"But how much are you charging me per gram?" Leo asked frankly.

Rocky said nothing. He knew Leo was anxious, but he wanted him to sweat a little. "I guess I can let you have it for $75.00 a gram," he said.

Leo searched his memory quickly comparing Rocky's quote with U.S. and international street prices. His face brightened. "Only 75 bucks a gram? Okay, great!" he said enthused. He pulled the seal (Chinese Mafia's Trademark Seal) off the cellophane. "I'd sure like to know, who you know!" He held the seal up. "Can I keep this for luck?"

Rocky laughed. "Sure!

Leo smiled, then said "Well, you know how it is: it's my first mission and I don't want to miss out on anything."

"I understand completely," Rocky said. "I was the same way too, but whether you meet them, really depends on you." He folded the newspaper into one neat square, and then he took from his desk drawer, a plastic tablespoon, a large sifter, a small hammer, and a plastic bag, 2'x2' in size. "Okay! "he said, with a clap of his hands, "Let's put the heroin in this plastic bag and tie a knot at the end of it." Leo did just that. Then Leo handed Rocky the hammer. "Now pick out a nice clear spot," Rocky gestured toward the wooden floor, "and start crushing her up... Don't forget, the finer you crush it, the more you'll be able to pour into your strips." Leo knelt down quickly and got busy.

"Do you know...?" Leo was cut short by the ringing of one of the telephones. Unerringly, Rocky picked up the right one, possibly identified by the bell tone.

"Excuse me," Rocky said hurriedly. "This may be a report on some cargo I ordered." He was listening now, speaking in Chinese... listening, speaking, and listening. With his hand over the receiver he made a quick comment in English for Leo's enlightenment. "From my office to the Sauna place, okay Wong, I'll see you there."

Wong Lee was Rocky's assistant, reliable and competent, though a little long-winded at times. Leo waited patiently, his thoughts were on the heroin he was about to smuggle.

"What?" yelled Rocky into the telephone, "What?" Rocky repeated in a low-toned voice. "Are you sure? I'll be back this evening. Call me if you hear more." He clamped down the receiver, swung around to face Leo and the trio and then broke into English again. "Now where were we?"

"The mysteries behind this seal," Leo responded. There was a brief silence.

"Perhaps you'll meet them after I've gotten to know you better." Rocky wanted to evade the subject altogether. "Personal interest could distort judgment. No need for that, you know."

Leo nodded in agreement. He didn't want to appear too pushy. "You've got me curious," he said. "I understood most of the diagram you showed me, but I'm still not quite sure—what makes your heroin better than the rest?"

Rocky laughed openly and took the diagram (90% OPIUM/HEROIN SYNDICATE SCALE) from his desk. Rocky was glad Jerry Prentice hadn't sent him an asshole who thought he was so damned independent, thinking he can take on the world and come out winning. Then Rocky said, "First of all," pointing to the top left-hand corner of the diagram, "the Shan; Northern Hill-Tribesmen have an opium production rate twice that of the Northeast Burma farmers. But it's not so much quantity but the quality that counts. You see, Burma has some of the richest farmland in the world. Their crops produce the most powerful, natural alkaloids ever grown."

Leo was mystified. "Ah, so that's why the DEA is becoming more concerned." He pondered over the diagram a moment, and then continued to hammer away at the heroin. "So General Fu is just a middleman, eh?"

"Not really," Rocky replied. "He has labs scattered about the Golden Triangle too. But it's becoming more difficult for him to operate them with consistency now that Thai and Laotian drug enforcement agents are trying to shut them down." Rocky smiled. "Unsuccessfully, I might add."

Leo grinned. "But how do they convert opium into heroin?"

"I think perhaps, we should stick to those matters that will aid you in your operation and finish up here. You'll have plenty of opportunities to find out all you want to know." He took another chart from his attaché case and handed it to Leo. "Here," he said. "This should clear up a few questions you may have."

Leo took the chart, gave Rocky the hammer, and began to read: Leo was astonished. "So my profits are determined by how many times I can cut this stuff?"

Kinds of Heroin	Name Brands	Percentage of Purity	Color & Characteristic	Times it can be Cut or Diluted
Pink	Pink Elephant	98%	Pink, Grainy	12-15
Brown	Persian Brown	93-97%	Brown, Grainy	8-12
White	China White	83-92%	White, Fluffy	8-10
	Purple Smoke	83-89%	White, Fluffy	8
	Two Dragons	83%	White, Fluffy	8
	Number Four White	86%	White, Fluffy	8
	Golden Spider	94%	Brown, Grainy	8-12
	Lucky Strike	87%	White, Fluffy	8
	Salt and Pepper	87-93%	White & Brown, Fluffy & Grainy	8-12

HEROIN CHARACTERISTIC'S CHART

Name Brands	Prices Per Kilo or 2.2 pounds Asian, European, Mid & Far East	Prices Per Kilo or 2.2 pounds United States of America
Pink Elephant	$100,000 - 150,000	$250,000 - 280,000
Persian Brown	80,000 - 140,000	250,000 - 280,000
China White	75,000 - 130,000	225,000 - 250,000
Purple Smoke	75,000 - 125,000	225,000 - 250,000
Two Dragons	75,000 - 125,000	225,000 - 250,000
Number Four White	75,000 - 125,000	225,000 - 250,000
Golden Spider	80,000 - 140,000	225,000 - 250,000
Lucky Strike	75,000 - 125,000	225,000 - 250,000
Salt and Pepper	80,000 - 140,000	250,000 - 280,000

Pink Elephant

Rocky nodded. "You guessed it pal." Then he gestured in Elfi's direction. "You have one of the best chemists on hand." He smiled at her and she smiled back. "Just do as she suggests and you can't go wrong," he advised.

"Will do," Leo agreed. "But who came up with these names? Your people?"

Rocky grinned. "Not all of them," he said. "Most of them are used by other Provinces we do business with."

"God damn!" Leo said, highly amused. "There are enough drug organizations over here to control the world's economy!" They both had a sudden fit of laughter. But Bagetta, Elfi, and Hillery were laughing the loudest. *Damn! He's a very potent teacher. There is much more to Rocky than I originally surmised,* Leo told himself. *An Importer/Exporter, a businessman and heroin controller; without him I'd have accomplished little to nothing.* He studied Rocky's techniques just in case he had to repeat this process himself. Rocky rose and placed the heroin carefully on his desk.

"Drugs are an absorbing topic," Hillery said as she brushed by Leo to get closer. "There's so much to learn—with so little time to learn it."

Leo sighed and nodded his head in agreement. "You can say that again." He glanced over his shoulder. Bagetta was talking with Elfi and laughing, but everything was under control. "I'm just glad we're not on a long stretch of road going nowhere cause prisons in this part of the world aren't no health resorts."

Rocky laughed. "I thought you looked worried. Just look at it this way; if there wasn't a safe way of getting the heroin back to Germany, we wouldn't be taking a chance. Now...doesn't that reassure you?!"

Embarrassed, Leo said. "Yeah, you're right, I've learned a lot, quite a useful exchange of information."

"We better hurry and finish-up here," Rocky urged. "I have some pressing business.

"Say no more," Leo replied, "I understand completely." They quickly sifted the jagged fragments of crushed heroin into fine grains, while Elfi and Bagetta poured the heroin into soft plastic strips; 1 ½ inches wide by 65-inches long.

Hillery took care of the tedious part; checking the strips for leaks, reinforcing them with an additional plastic cover, then assisting Bagetta and Elfi in strapping the 2.2 pounds each, around their stomachs and waists.

Leo reached into the inside pocket of his jacket and pulled out a white envelope that contained $60,000 in large bills. He handed it to Rocky. "From Uncle Sam—with love," Leo said smiling.

Rocky bowed. "No need to count it," he said. "I'm sure it's all there. Next time, I'll show you how to deposit your profits in a numbered bank account in Copenhagen, using three banks in different cities, but not all in Germany."

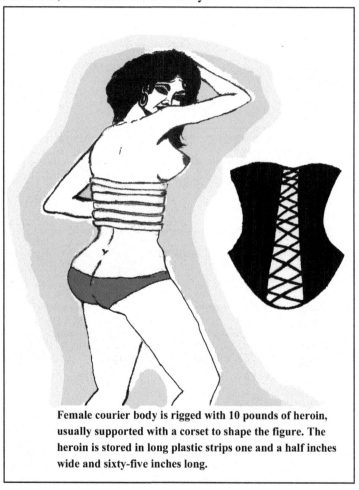

Female courier body is rigged with 10 pounds of heroin, usually supported with a corset to shape the figure. The heroin is stored in long plastic strips one and a half inches wide and sixty-five inches long.

"That's beautiful," Leo said. "I've always wanted to know how it was done." Rocky laughed. "A piece of cake, don't let it baffle you. I'll see you at the Playboy," he said as they shook hands.

"The sooner the better," Leo said as the women joined them at the door. There was another handshake and the door closed behind them.

"Almost two o'clock," Leo said with surprise as they reached the street and walked along the marketplace. "It was a useful exchange of information with more to come about the 'Golden Triangle'. Wonder where Rocky is headed?"

Rocky had left a lasting impression on him and Leo decided he was going to be the best 'International Heroin Smuggler,' in all of Europe.

"Who knows," Bagetta replied. "He's a very busy man."

Leo was startled by a sudden clap of thunder directly overhead. The tops of trees twisted and whipped in the distance. They watched the lightning dance and bounce across the canals. Beyond the river was the capital city. Thunder rumbled from the direction of the lightning. Wind ripped sheets of water across the brick street. A bolt of lightning struck the tops of trees not a hundred yards away. Leo was waiting for it but was still surprised by the crack of thunder that followed. There was an awesome 'crrraaccckkk' trailed by a hollow boom that shook the shit out of the trio (Elfi, Bagetta, Hillery), and the store windows too. Leo practically inhaled his cigarette.

Hillery lit a Virginia Slims Menthol Light, and turned to Elfi and Bagetta. "So is that it? Is that all Mother Nature has to offer."

"Yes," said Elfi. She liked smuggling during storms. "Remember when we were driving through Amsterdam once, or maybe it was Germany in an electrical storm that had been genuinely frightening? The clouds had come first, black clouds that rolled and billowed from the west. Then it turned dark when the lightning came and there was no place to stop, nowhere to go, nothing to do but drive on toward the border through the rain."

She did it because she knew the border police didn't like to check passports when it was storming. "Yes," Elfi said again.

"These storms are something else," said Bagetta. "Let's hope they continue and don't go away so we don't have any trouble at the border." They listened to the thunder roaring in the distance and watched the trees bend under the wind as they walked quickly to the camper.

Leo and his crew chose the Kleve border for their return to Germany. Traffic was heavily congested in the late afternoon. There were lots of trucks, but more sightseeing buses and small cars loaded to the top of their roofs with soaked holiday baggage. Outrageous gas prices were having little effect on vacationers northward bound. At the border, the rain had stopped and there was a general slow-up, unusual in the European countries where goods and people flowed easily across the frontiers. However, the terrorist bombings in Munich, Frankfurt, and Amsterdam were having their effect: closer scrutiny than usual of all vehicles leaving Holland.

Leo slowed his camper and joined the line of cars that edged their way forward; stopped, and moved forward again. A 'Europa' bus was released and sent on. One more car behind it, then a mini-bus, three more cars, and Leo's turn would come. That wouldn't take too long. He would make good speed on the road bypassing Eindhover, make some telephone calls to arrange heroin drops.

They noticed there was a small group of people gathered close to a white van. It had a tarpaulin strapped securely over the baggage on its roof. Would they have to open that up? Leo wondered in dismay, glancing at his watch. Kids, he thought, as he heard the small group break into laughter. Saw some light-hearted horseplay between three young men accompanied by three medium-height girls with oversized shoulder bags.

Leo looked at Bagetta, Elfi, and friend Hillery, in amazement. He couldn't believe how calm they remained; knowing they each carried 2.2 pounds of pure heroin strapped around their bodies.

All was in order; the group was called together and they climbed into the white van and drove off quickly gathering speed.

Then, as Leo looked along the road, he noticed a half-dozen Dutch officials approaching their vehicle. They instructed Leo and the girls to get out, giving them the third degree, while three officials went inside the camper searching it. They found nothing. Leo and the three girls departed the checkpoint. No terrorist stowaway and no evidence of drugs being smuggled or used. Leo smiled and shook his head at surviving that brief touch of suspicion.

They were days ahead of schedule. Leo would have to make up some time though, because he promised the girls a week of fun and excitement, unfortunately the weather was too bad to do anything. There would be no 'Dear Mama' letter written to Stella Stegner tonight: she'd be lucky if she got a postcard from Germany.

***

Rocky had allowed 30-minutes from the time Leo and the trio departed from his office before he left. The remnants of heroin from their luncheon gathered on the desk, plus the six kilos he retrieved from the special temperature regulated vault had been neatly placed into his attaché case. He had locked the $60,000 in his wall safe and the letters on his desk addressed to investment firms was locked away in his cabinet to be attended to later. The attaché case was tucked securely under his arm as he double-locked the door behind him.

He had already summoned the elevator, so it was waiting for him. Its' slow descent always reminded him of his maternal grandfather, the last Congo Lee to visit that top floor room when he stayed overnight in the city. Apart from a telephone operator at her switchboard, kept neatly out of sight under the curved flight of staircase; the hall was empty. From the floor overhead came the sound of a typewriter clacking away, making good time before closing hours.

The hall wasn't empty. A man was standing in one corner near the front door, leaning on his rolled umbrella, his neat brown suit blending into the mahogany wood paneling of the walls. His hair, cut medium length, was blond, and his thin face was unlined. He smiled shyly. "No receptionist here?" he asked. "How do I get in touch with the Personnel Manager?"

So he had just entered, wasn't waiting as I first thought, Rocky decided. His suspicion leveled off, but he still kept a distance from the stranger. "Try the telephone girl—you'll find her just around that curve of staircase."

"Thank you." The stranger came forward, but he was giving Rocky ample room to pass him.

"Not at all," said Rocky as he averted his face and made for the front door.

Suddenly, the stranger raised his umbrella, its ferrule pointed at Rocky's thigh; he felt a sting, hot and sharp. Rocky stared at the man, then at the umbrella. He raised his voice to shout and gave a strangled croak. He had no strength in his body at all. His legs were beginning to buckle. The man hit him sharply over the hand that held the attaché case. Rocky's grip loosened; the attaché case was pulled away. He saw only a blur as the dark suit turned and hurried to the front entrance. He heard only a faint noise as the heavy door closed. Rocky fell backward to the wooden floor, the traveling bag beside him. He tried to shout again, but knew it was useless. Only his brain seemed to be working. He made an effort to reach into his suit pocket, take hold of the card he always kept there in case of emergency. He could feel it, even gripped it, but he couldn't pull it out.

"What's wrong...? What's wrong?" It was the telephone girl kneeling beside him, looking in horror at the man who lay staring up at her. She screamed and kept screaming until the sound of feet came running down the staircase.

"He's alive," a man's voice said. "Get an ambulance."

"I thought I heard the door close. Then I heard a crash. He's trying to speak." The telephone operator said lowering her ear to his lips.

"He ripped me off. He stole my attaché case...," Rocky mumbled.

The stranger was a professional rip-off artist who prayed on the vulnerabilities of big business heroin distributors. He had injected Rocky with a powerful tranquilizer, which paralyzes the system for several hours. Rocky had lost about 13 pounds of pure pink heroin. Unfortunately, rip offs was a common occurrence among heroin dealers in Europe.

"Get an ambulance!" The telephone operator was yanked to her feet. "Call now!" The man's voice insisted, alarmed.

"What's in his hand?" The operator asked.

Rocky's hand was pulled open gently.

"A card; 'Emergency,' it says. A telephone number, a name: Wong Lee. Here," the man's voice said, "Call this number too, first the ambulance, and then the one on the card. Quick, quick!"

The skinny, ugly lady in high heels retreated.

"She's always so damn slow," said the man's voice. "Hurry!" he yelled after her. "What did he say? Could he speak?"

"Didn't make any sense," the telephone operator called back. "Sounded like umbrella."

"Stupid, as well as slow," the man told the rest of the small crowd. "Umbrella; but he wasn't carrying any umbrella. Heart attack, don't move him. Keep back and give him air."

Somberly, helplessly, Rocky could sense the small crowd watching him as his eyes stared up at the vaulted ceiling. Moments later Rocky's lips could no longer move, and then he passed out.

***

By the time Leo had crossed the Dutch frontier into Germany it was dark and had stopped raining. He kept his speed steady like other travelers on the road, which made for pleasant driving: with no one weaving in and out of traffic like a demented hornet, nor tailgating and forcing the pace. The girls were laughing and telling jokes about the old days. Leo could relax now thinking only of Germany and Amsterdam; of Elfi, Hillery and Bagetta and the monies paid out to Rocky; but mostly of the girls and how valuable they had become to him. In the beginning, Leo felt like a pawn with one or two exceptional moves because Striker had been calling the shots, but as time went on he found himself in a position of strength now that he was in control of his own fate. He began to feel a lot more confident about smuggling. Nearly once-a-week for 6 months he, Bagetta, Hillery, Elfi, and sometimes Eva, traveled through every border on their listed itinerary. They smuggled heroin through several European cities. Then when their faces became too recognizable, they switched from automobile to train.

Meanwhile, on the International Scene; in France, Reco Record; head of the French Connection and one of the biggest financial contributors to the Argentine government had just been kidnapped. The surprising news was... Record had been kidnapped by American Drug Enforcement Agents, then smuggled into the United States for prosecution.

The Argentine Republic had more than its share of heroin distributors who sought refuge abroad when the heat became too great. However, it was the news of how the American D.E.A. kidnapped Reco Record that caused the temporary disruption throughout the 'Looseknit Heroin/Opium Networks' standard flow of operation. This outrageous move on the D.E.A.'s part caused the drug networks to become more powerful, secluded, and work more closely together. No one was safe and everybody was a target.

CHAPTER 5

"Nothing to Declare"

Winter 1973

Several months had passed, followed by a severe cold front that changed weather conditions from bad to worse. The temperature was below zero. It was a cold dampness with white sparkling snow covering the roads and railway lanes.

Leo's sudden departure from The Russian Front though discreet, had become necessary. Hillery, Elfi and Bagetta couldn't blame him for that. If the German Border Patrol had even one piece of real evidence against him, they would have arrested him three months ago when they, for no reason, suspected them of smuggling and tore his Mercedes Benz apart at the Kleve border, but found nothing. That was one of the major reasons Leo and the clique switched to smuggling by train because the authorities had suspected them of smuggling and put them on the 'Blacklist' and had them under close scrutiny at all the borders. Once out of Germany, he was free… no extradition possible unless there was evidence of a crime. However, this was no sudden exit… it was planned and carefully arranged by Rocky and him.

Leo had become a seasoned and successful negotiator. Leo would set up financial arrangements and oversee the selection of qualified wholesale heroin purchasers to begin operations later that year. Such things took time, but Elfi, Hillery, Bagetta, now Eva and Silki (two new members of his smuggling team), were more interested in the promised increase in pay, once East-West travel was established. As for Leo's itinerary, when he would visit these countries, how long he would stay, depended on the difficulties he might encounter.

***

He would meet Rocky in London on a journey to Hong Kong, Singapore, Burma, Laos and Thailand, and then finally to Florida.

***

Across the Atlantic Ocean, a cheerful morning, bright and sparkling was spreading its smile over the New York harbor. The huge TWA 747 Jumbo Jet glided past the Statue of Liberty before touching down on the long runway at J.F.K. International Jetport.

Arrival in New York was the usual holiday confusion when several major flights descended all at one time on Kennedy International. Perhaps, it was natural, that the attractive young woman who was traveling alone should look so helpless and harried as she waited for her luggage to appear on the roundabout. She stuck close to Leo on most of the long walk from the landing area, which caused him to be completely paranoid. She was American—or at least traveling on an American passport. It was odd she hadn't given him one small glance. Most of the transatlantic passengers had noticed each other, exchanging the usual cursory look as they angled for the best position to grab their suitcases or compete for the attention of a porter. For someone who was now standing at his elbow it was strange that she seemed totally unaware of his existence. Their luggage should be arriving any moment. Would she ask for his help, delay him enough to let them go through immigration together? Delay him enough to let them leave together? Or would she take a taxi to follow his?

Leo lit a cigarette as she faced his direction briefly. His lighter missed twice, flaming on the third try. He had just enough time for a couple of pulls before he saw his luggage next to two dark-brown suitcases, a matched set varying only in size, circling slowly toward them.

"Oh!" she said, pointing to the larger of the dark brown cases which lay far up on the conveyor and needed a long arm to be reached.

Leo pulled his luggage and helped with her larger case, a nice excuse to let the smaller piece of luggage continue around the conveyor belt. He placed the luggage at her feet. "Don't worry," he told her. "The other piece will come around again… in 3 or 4 minutes." And with an encouraging smile that was met by her look of complete frustration, he left for the customs checkpoint line. *No porters available either*, he thought with some satisfaction and reveled in her misfortune.

There were eight lines, one customs official per line. There weren't any weapons in plain view, any dogs, or special devices. So Leo hustled to the shortest line realizing that in the world of smuggling it was always a game of matching wits against U.S. customs officials. He opened both suitcases with enthusiasm and allowed the official to pick his way through the clothing. The customs official appeared to be getting frustrated, then lifted his head and asked in an authoritative tone of voice, "How about these candles? They look awfully expensive!"

Leo smiled. "No, not at all. They were unique, so I decided to get them for my mother. I paid $69.00 bucks for them. They better look worth something." He smiled again, but the official didn't appear amused.

The customs official pondered a moment, and then asked another question. "You have anything to declare?"

Leo shook his head from side to side, and then replied. "No, nothing to declare!"

All of a sudden Leo noticed two plain clothes Drug Enforcement Agents heading in his direction, reaching inside their coats. Leo's eyes stretched wide and chills rushed throughout his body. *Damn! I've been busted,* he thought with fear and anxiety. One agent reached and grabbed his arm, then pushed him aside while the other agent rushed past him. Some idiot had allowed a seven-foot long Asian Cobra to slip out of its' weaved basket and slither its way onto the baggage counter. The commotion startled the hell out of Leo. Caught between a rock and a hard spot, Leo contemplated weather he should bash the snake's head in with his attaché case or run.

The customs inspector allowed Leo to close his baggage and move on, but Leo was still anxious and upset, and a bit stunned as he exited. During Leo's last rendezvous in the Netherlands, Rocky sold him a pound of pure pink heroin to take to Florida. Before he left Germany, he 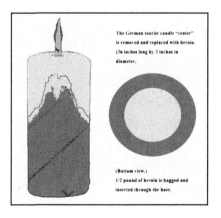 divided the heroin into equal halves and concealed them in the core of two huge souvenir candles nearly 36-inches long by 3-

inches in diameter, with medieval impressions carved onto the outer surface.

Leo, no fool, but with plenty to worry about, reasoned, he would smuggle the heroin in this way, just this time, until he was sure customs didn't do body frisking on the male transatlantic travelers.

Customs had caused him to be separated from the beautiful but strange woman at the luggage carousel; but here she was beside him again in the main hall with the midday sun, streaming in from the street outside.

Taxis, buses, and a row of limousines with drivers at their wheels lined up at the curb, where people on the sidewalk and people darting into the roadway tried to grab a cab. It took Leo several minutes to secure one. He threw his luggage inside to stake his claim but noticed one limousine in particular. Its driver, seemingly impatient, stood by its opened door, scanning the crowded sidewalk. As the limousine driver caught sight of Leo about to enter a taxi, he slipped back into his seat. His way out into the swelling stream of traffic was blocked by a tourist bus that had halted; to unload a group of foreign businessmen.

Leo briefly glanced at the sidewalk to catch one last view of the young woman from the baggage claim area. He smiled for a moment thinking how impatient she appeared; even abandoning her large suitcase in her desperate haste. He tried to stay focused and not leave any telltale signs of smuggling behind with his money safe in his pocket. Leo pondered, then asked himself if he overlooked the limo driver, with thick wavy hair and rugged face, or the seemingly innocent woman who could be a sky marshal, he used as a diversion. He didn't want to take any chances getting busted.

"LaGuardia Airport," he told the taxi driver, relaxing back in his seat and not worrying about the meter. He gazed out into the bumper to bumper traffic, daydreaming about New York, the pulsating center of power, with 90,000 junkies in the streets and how much heroin it would take to supply them. He had always thought of California as the heartland, but New York was one of the most exciting places he had ever seen with billions of illegal drug dollars floating around.

Leo and Rocky's plans had gone smoothly so far. For JFK International appeared to be a pushover without any major complications. Leo also knew that once he saw the right people, the merchandise would speak for itself, and the heroin pipeline into the Gulf Coast of Florida would become more of a probability than just a possibility.

Leo arrived at LaGuardia Airport 30-minutes before the Eastern flight was scheduled to depart. Several hours later, just as the sun was heading west, they landed at McCoy International Jetport, in Orlando, Florida. The weather was hot and humid. Security at LaGuardia and McCoy were a breeze.

Leo found a cab and headed to the Sheraton Twin Towers, a busy hotel located across the street from Universal Studios on Orlando's Southwest side. The deeper he went into the city, the more Leo felt like a stranger in the city where he had spent much of his life. Police patrolled every major street corner, watching everything that moved. It made Orlando appear as though it was being run like a police state; with Walt Disney World, Sea World and Universal Studios as its draw card.

Everything seemed different. The little city that Leo once knew had grown tremendously. Every booming town has a distinctive image, a personality that gives it its own special personality. Orlando had become a restless, dynamic giant— crude and without manner. It was a kingdom that belonged to

Mayor Langford, the Albertson's, the Langston's, and the Phillips, and the domain of cool professional gangsters like Holland Blackburn, Joe Gambino, the Linetti's, and a host of others

Leo arrived at the hotel. He felt comfortable but alert in his surroundings as he hurried to get his thoughts in order before Thomas Scalli (better known as Mr. "T") arrived. With so many distractions at hand, Leo found himself thinking about his brief encounters with former girlfriend Guyda and wondered how she was doing. Guyda had a beautiful smile, but in a girly naïve way she appeared to be pure and innocent in Leo's eyes, but in reality she was a sexual vixen waiting to pounce.

Leo thought Guyda would be either married or divorced and have had a child out of wedlock, or fell into the submission of the "Family Business" drugs and corruption. All of a sudden he snapped out of his daydream and quickly telephoned Scalli. "Raring to go," Leo told Scalli over the phone. "I'll be leaving by the end of the week. Let's get together for lunch or a drink? I know you're a busy tax consultant, but…" He left the suggestion hanging. If anyone were listening to this conversation, its context might seem negligible.

"Just let me have a look at my calendar. Let me see…" Scalli's deep, rumbling voice hesitated, as if he were really consulting his engagement book. "The Fourth of July today, New York tomorrow… Dammit. Finding a prospective investor; that could take until Thursday. Then Friday is the start of the weekend. Why not join us at Bay Hill? The kids and their friends will be there, a full house. But we'll always find room for you, and did I mention Guyda, too!" Leo had to smile. Scalli's spacious condo had three bedrooms, a giant living room where the stereo played well into the night and Scalli's lavish den with everything from trophies to gun racks, struggling for space among the bookshelves.

Leo took the concealed hint. "I'd like that, but my new job in Amsterdam doesn't allow for holidays."

"What about tonight? There's a cocktail party at my place. We are celebrating Guyda's 25th birthday and we've just landed a big contract, so I thought I'd have a 4th of July celebration for my staff and our happy clients," Scalli said.

"Tonight is pretty well-planned; drinks, music, and good times," Leo replied.

"Drop in, if you can manage it. It will be a madhouse; you know how these things multiply. Too bad you didn't let me know when you were planning to pass through Orlando," Scalli said. "Guyda's asked about you since you returned."

"I really wasn't sure myself. Next time, I'll...," Leo was saying, before Scalli cut in.

"The party begins at 10:00pm, but no one will be there before 10:30pm, I hope. I've got an emergency meeting downtown at 4:45... an important client," Scalli said, "And I need to pick up her gift before the party."

"Gift?" Leo asks.

"You'll see later." Scalli replied.

"Then you better hang up," Leo said, "It's almost 4:30 now."

"Damn it! So it is," Scalli said. "So I'll see you at my place, it's just a few miles south of you. Remember...? Good to hear from you."

Leo replaced the telephone on the side table and stretched out on the bed. Scalli would be there at 4:45; Leo's room was booked by him.

149

At 4:45 p.m. exactly, the door to Leo's suite was opened for Thomas Scalli's arrival. "You look well," Leo told him, studying the 6-feet 9-inch tall and solidly trim, dark complexion man who weighed about 269 pounds, as he closed the door and locked it. Scalli had lost weight in recent years and his face—large and craggy showed permanent grooves. His fine, dark eyes were more serious, almost sad in expression. His style of clothes hadn't changed, though they hung more loosely on his big frame: thin light-gray suit worn neatly, was slightly wrinkled. Leo gave Scalli a warm handshake and then a quick embrace with several hefty pats on his shoulders. "Good to see you, Thomas. Pick a chair."

Leo knew Scalli well. No problem there. He was a former wide receiver for the Miami Dolphins. He had been placed on waivers and never went back. Leo had met him unexpectedly at a house party, before joining the Army. Scalli had introduced Leo to his sexy cousin Guyda Henderson while working the party, and propositioned him to work selling bags of marijuana. Leo knowing so little about drugs declined Thomas Scalli's offer.

Thomas Scalli never went anywhere without protection; he had put the .38 special in the console of his car, then he mounted a small derringer on a special-made clip that he had designed on the back of his large, sterling silver belt buckle. Big game hunting was one of his specialties.

"You still make a good telephone call," Scalli told him as he chose one corner of the sofa, glanced around the green-and-white room, and took his turn observing Leo.

Leo poured a moderate sample of heroin on an elaborate serving tray.

"Well," Scalli was saying, "You know what they say about the typical Floridian. He has the best intentions—but he's always impatient and eager to get down to business." Leo laughed. Scalli pulled himself to the edge of his seat, and then went on. "So, what do you have for me?" he asked.

Leo laughed again, this time louder. He knew Scalli couldn't wait to see the package. "Just a little something I brought from across the water," he said. "Here, check it out."

Scalli frowned as he took the tray of heroin and lowered himself into his chair. He couldn't believe what he was seeing. He stretched out his long legs, raised the tray near his nose, sniffed the heroin and used his finger to taste it. Then Scalli snorted a tiny one-and-one in each nostril. "Damn!" he said. "I didn't expect this shit to be so pure." He was blinking his eyes, trying to keep them from tearing. He scratched his bald head, then down to his crotch. He could feel the pink heroin's devastating effects immediately.

"Damn it," Leo said. "I forgot to tell you that it's never been cut." He raised his glass of Pepsi in salute.

"Say what?" Scalli reacted. "That wasn't cool. Not cool at all! Leo."

"I'm sorry, Thomas," Leo said. "You might vomit and feel a little sick, but you'll be all right. Besides, it only demonstrates my purpose for coming home," he grinned.

"Yeah… I can dig where you're coming from," Scalli said, nodding his head repeatedly. His words dragged he struggled to express himself. "But you didn't have to let me—be the human guinea pig. Anyhow, why didn't you mention this shit at our last meeting? Why, I haven't seen anything like this—in over 10 years. What can it stand? A 8?" Scalli asked, thoughtfully. Then he jumped up and ran to the bathroom and vomited.

"No," Leo fired back abruptly. "More like a 15," he said with a grin.

Scalli braced himself, frightened. "A 15!" he shouted, struggling to bring himself under control. "Are you fuckin crazy? And you let me snort this shit?" He paused briefly, examined himself... then the heroin and said. "This goddamn shit could have killed me!"

Leo laughed out loud. "Sure it could've. But now you know what it's like before they cut it," Leo said. "Just think about the tremendous amount of money and power we'd gain if we established a major heroin distribution network---in every major city throughout Florida or perhaps the United States."

Scalli tightened his lip and shook his head in disbelief. "I'm thinking! I'm thinking!" he repeated and gestured with his hands. He was so fucked up from the heroin; he could hardly keep his composure. "I can handle all of that," he continued. "My football career enabled me to travel, and I've got connections all over the United States." Scalli paused momentarily. "But what concerns me is—who's gonna foot the bill? And who is bold enough to bring this shit into the country? It must cost a fortune!" he added with emphasis.

Leo laughed again, this time even louder. "You need not concern yourself with all of that. That's taken care of. Let's get down to business. We have a lot of traveling to do in the next few months, and I'll have plenty of time to explain it all to you," Leo said.

Scalli and Leo drove out to the condo and spent the weekend celebrating their newly developed plan to become the largest heroin distribution organization in the Northwest Atlantic region. Leo and Guyda had also spent the weekend reigniting their passionate affections for one another and reminiscing on their brief affair before Leo was shipped off for duty.

Tomorrow, he and Scalli were heading for Miami to visit a man called Nassau, then eight weeks later head to Amsterdam for an undetermined tour to make arrangements for a shipment of heroin to be smuggled into the United States.

The end of September... it couldn't come too soon. Suddenly, Leo's mind was jolted out of all those neatly planned prospects as he remembered his promise to Elfi and the other girls for the beginning of October: a MoneyGram, ready and waiting at the American Express office in Frankfurt.

Leo had become one sly operator. He slipped into Orlando, made the necessary appearances with his family, his real estate agent, and of course, his new lieutenant, Thomas Scalli; in charge of his U.S. heroin distribution network. Leo and Scalli had made a list to see financially distinguished people in Florida, Georgia, Texas, Detroit, New York and New Jersey; to schedule major heroin purchases, as well as, give each contact a sample to be analyzed, diluted, tested, and retested before any deals were made. They would stay clear of the U.S. Mafia and only sell heroin to wealthy merchants, bankers, doctors, lawyers, stock brokers and professional athletes.

Due to the increased pressure from Drug Enforcement Agencies and the FBI many Mafia "Dons" up north were moving down south.

Hell and damnation, Leo thought intensely. After conferring with Scalli he found out that it was going to cost him a little over a half million dollars to order a hit on an entire family of mobsters, but he remained determined in his cause. *What a price I have to pay to get revenge, having to smuggle heroin all the way from Amsterdam; of all goddamned places. But somebody took my father's life. He loved living. And someone is going to pay for it.*

***

The following morning, days after he and Scalli's meeting at the Sheraton, Scalli drove so Leo could catch up on his sleep and get his mealtimes back to normal.

Leo dropped his bag into the back seat with a "Hi, Thomas!" before he slid into the front passenger seat beside Scalli. Scalli locked the doors and raised the windows of the black 1973 Lincoln Continental Mark III and they headed for Miami. Leo informed Scalli that Rocky had sworn him to secrecy and that's why he couldn't tell him everything. As far as Leo was concerned, the less Scalli knew, the safer he—and the information would—stay.

Scalli's large frame and long legs occupied most of the front seat. His bald head was almost hidden by his battered hat. He had the look of excitement and welcomed Leo with a broad grin.

Thomas Scalli was studying Leo. "Long journeys, huh?"

"Yeah delays at London and at LaGuardia. Sorry if I'm not so talkative," Leo replied.

"Not at all, you're on time," Scalli said. "How was Germany?"

"It was fine. I miss it," Leo replied.

"You heard from Rocky yet?" Scalli asked.

"At eight this morning," Leo said, "I told him everything was going well and that I would get back to him later. He and a client were about to board his Lear Jet for Hong Kong."

Scalli wanted to know so much more about Rocky. Leo continued to pause… and pause… and pause… the long flights and time changes had left his mind foggy. "No details, of course… I'll hear more when I meet Rocky in London, in a few months," Leo added.

Scalli was freaking out. "Damn!" he said. "Rocky must know some pretty heavy people."

"Yeah… heavy enough to blow our fucking heads off—if we're not careful," Leo replied.

Thomas Scalli looked at him… then they both laughed. "Don't worry," he told Leo. "Everything will be okay."

"That's good," Leo replied. "Now… where are we headed first?"

"Miami!" Scalli said. "Cecil Beckman's place, it will take us about three hours to get there."

***

Cecil Beckman stood about 5 feet 11 inches tall and nearly 200 pounds. He was carefully groomed, dark-haired, dark-eyed, dark mustache, and middle-aged, with an authoritative look on his face. He was well-dressed for his size and lived in a secluded area populated by Cubans—on Miami's south side. From the street, Leo and Scalli entered Beckman's house briskly. His home was unobtrusive, soft, and warm. His home was a five-bedroom split-level with a typical modern look. People called him Nassau. He was a stock broker with a chain of restaurants, loan companies, and houses.

In the mid-1930's the United States government placed an embargo on the importation of tomatoes from the Bahamas. Cecil Beckman and his fellow farmers on the island searched desperately for another market for their goods, but found none. One by one they succumbed to the economic disaster that had ravaged America and was now spilling over beyond her borders. Reluctantly, Beckman made the hard decision to leave the

Bahamas and try to find work in America. Beckman stayed with friends and after many frustrating months found a job as the manager of a bicycle repair shop. After 2-years for reasons unknown to him, he lost his job and was unable to find another. With ends never quite meeting in the face of his best efforts, he turned to drugs and started selling heroin and cocaine.

***

Cecil put on an impressive introduction, showing them $50,000.00 in cash. But when Leo poured the pink powder-like substance onto the large mirror Beckman had placed on the table, Beckman's face quickly switched from that of excitement to a face full of skepticism. Leo pretended to ignore it by continuing to inform Beckman what he could expect in terms of immediate and steady shipments, providing the money was right.

Beckman's assistant examined the heroin closely, using a heroin tester. Beckman and his partners couldn't believe their eyes when the drug proved to be 98% pure heroin. It had been years since heroin of such quality had passed through their hands, but never that color.

"Is this shit synthetic heroin?" Beckman said. Suddenly in his native tongue, Beckman had a violent exchange of words with his assistant, and told him to get one of his runners to pick up a couple of junkies off the street and bring them to him.

Half an hour later the runner returned with two human guinea pigs; they were very beautiful women. In Miami, the female junkie was often used to test the drugs. The majority of dealers and distributors believed that women have a much stronger body metabolism than male drug addicts.

Beckman's assistant scooped several grains of the pink substance, mixed it in a tablespoon of water until it dissolved, drew it into the syringe, and handed it to the blonde. She injected it quickly, while the rest of them looked on. "Hey! This mother-fucking-shit won't kill me—will it man?" she asked.

Scalli couldn't believe what he was hearing. He broke and laughed out loud, then said, "Can you believe this bitch!... She picked a helluva time to ask!" He paused, and then laughed out loud again. "She'll be lucky if she can stand!" he blurted.

The addict became frightened. "It won't kill me will it?" she said repeatedly, paranoid and scared to death.

"No," Leo said reassuringly. "He only gave you a few tiny grains. But if I was you," looking at her with a real serious look on his face... "I'd take that syringe out NOW!"

First she relaxed, and then she refused to allow anyone to remove the syringe from her arm, disregarding Leo's warning. She was feeling pretty warm inside—that warm feeling that addicts get after a fix. She wanted to get a faster rush, so she boosts it (Pumping the handle of the syringe back and forth several times) before she came to an immediate halt. She felt drowsy and woozy, with deep breaths, followed by fear that overwhelmed her. She fought frantically to regain control, but it

was too late, her body began to sway.

Leo became alarmed, then frightened and somewhat sympathetic. He grabbed her by her arm and removed the loaded syringe. Beckman became angry; he was not so sympathetic and insisted the experiment continue. Leo released her reluctantly so she could stand on her own, but the blonde girl's body was too rubbery. Her skinny legs could no longer support her. It was as if her feet were nailed to the floor, while her body swayed back and forth, then crumbled slowly. She passed out.

Remembering one of the counters against heroin, Leo ordered a glass of milk and gave her immediate first aid. He felt responsible and guilty. He hadn't quite lost respect for life yet like the others. The milk caused her stomach to sour and enabled her to vomit most of the excess heroin that had settled in her digestive system. This prevented a possible overdose. Salt and water were also commonly used which was just as effective.

Beckman, still not convinced, questioned the pink substance' ability to withstand being cut (diluted). He ordered his assistant to put a "10" on a gram of the substance, after Scalli had informed him it could be cut 15 times.

The other female addict was fearful, but she was game, out of desperation for a fix. The tall, red haired, black girl, (both girls were escorts and models), injected the syringe in a vein on top of her left hand. She boosted the syringe several times, using her right hand. She got her rush, then moments later went into a nod. Beckman's fat face lit up with a broad smile. He was very pleased.

Beckman had used Baneda, a light weight substance to cut the heroin instead of Lactose. Baneda was white in color, shaped like a bar of soap, easier to sift and didn't take much strength away from the heroin. Like snowflakes, it was hard to find on the black market. It was sold mainly in northern states: New York, Washington, D.C., Chicago and sometimes found in Florida and Texas at $30.00 a bar. In contrast, Lactose is much heavier, off-white in color, prescribed as a baby formula and used by many dealers when Baneda wasn't readily available. Lactose was easily obtained and sold commonly in many major drugstores.

***

Back on the road, Scalli took the usual evasive tactics, driving around, and then ducked into a side street here and there before he headed for their next journey. They made sure no one followed.

Leo met all Scalli's connections during the two weeks, without incident and landed solid commitments from each of them. It was clearly established that each connection could handle $50,000 worth of heroin or better. It was Leo's first real tour of the United States and he enjoyed it. They took time out to scout various states airports, only to find customs to be moderately efficient at each of them.

Most of all, Leo's plans had been well-implemented with all the pieces coming together. The heroin couriers were on standby and his new U.S. drug network was now established. Leo's life with Guyda had entered a new phase, steady but constantly accelerating. Guyda had become an important part in Leo's life and his future.

CHAPTER 6

"Fire Aboard Flight 502"

By the first week October of 1977, Leo was on his way to London, England. He contacted Rocky and told him of his expected arrival. Leaving Florida at daybreak Leo arrived in London early that night. It was the usual confusion when several major flights descended on London/Heathrow Airport at the same time. Flights delay upon flight delay.

Leo had been in a thoroughly bad mood partly due to U.S. Customs officials scrutinizing passports with heavy frowns and no contraband found, and partly due to the long delay at JFK International waiting for connecting flights. Finally he was free to leave.

At London/Heathrow Airport, Rocky was in the car that met Leo. His slick black hair was almost hidden by his fashionable "gangster" hat and his well-tailored suit. Leo dropped his luggage into the trunk before he slid into the back seat with a "Hi Rocky. What's happening?"

At the wheel, Wong Lee smiled, all the brighter by contrast of his Chinese complexion. His thick straight hair was dark too and he was about the same age as Rocky. He and Rocky grew up together in Singapore and trained as a team in Heromoto's Temple, a Martial Arts Institute, both receiving black belts some 15-years ago. Leo could hear the Mercedes tires squeal against the hard brick road as they peeled away quickly from the airport.

Rocky was studying him. "Welcome back," he said "A bad journey?"

"Delays; at Miami and at JFK." Leo said.

"Glad you made it. How was Florida?" Rocky asked.

"Just fine, the weather was beautiful, and the people..." he laughed, and then said, "Would kill to do business with me."

"So, you've never had it so good, huh?" Rocky asked.

Leo smiled. "Matter of fact," he said, "I haven't!"

They laughed and rode through London taking in the sights, engaged in heavy discussions of strategy. Rocky had issued Leo stern warnings—regarding the importance of secrecy in the operation and praised him for being efficient, knowledgeable, and unafraid to take risks. He also praised Leo for establishing the connections—that inspired expansion and growth, and a stronger foothold for the China Mafia into the United States of America.

Leo was enjoying his new adventures... being where he wanted to be, doing what he wanted to do, the people he met, and Rocky, whom he respected and felt closer to every passing moment. While in London they hit the Victoria and the Woolpack strip clubs, pulled some girls, and enjoyed a satisfying number of orgies.

***

Leo heard a screech of tires and was jostled violently in his seat awakening him from a short nap on the London to Netherlands leg of his trip. After breezing through customs at the

Amsterdam Airport Schiphol in the Netherlands, Leo flagged down a cab which dodged in and out of traffic and with a screech of tires similar to the plane landing deposited him at the Sheraton Amsterdam Airport Hotel on Schiphol Boulevard. Leo decided against checking in immediately and walked to the strip club La Vie en Proost in the Red Light District, for a much needed drink and settled in to wait for Eva, Bagetta, Silki, and Hillery to arrive. There was a calendar on the wall with the dates superimposed over a photograph of a woman's breasts. Three women dressed in G-strings and nipple cups were dancing. They wore garter belts for tips; for thirty Euros they would show some pussy or bend over. The men stared without blinking, their blood pressure increasing.

Leo watched as one of the other men took a bill, folded it neatly lengthwise, and held it at his crotch for the dancer to retrieve. She did so without using her hands. She worked herself rhythmically against him for a long minute. She turned around and spread her ass for him as she removed the bill. She winked at Leo and slipped the folded bill under her garter.

One of the other young women walked over to Leo. "Would you like a drink?" she asked

"Vodka, please, "Leo replied.

"Straight vodka?" The girl, a medium blonde, looked surprised.

"Yes, please," Leo said.

The girl went to the bar, poured the drink, returned with a shot glass of vodka. "When you're ready for another, let me know. You can stay here as long as you like and drink as much as you want." She paused, and then added, "Within reason, of course.

"Certainly," said Leo.

The dancer set Leo's hormones racing. He was on his second shot when he looked at the clock over the bar and saw that it was seven o'clock. Suddenly, he was filled with panic. He slapped some bills on the bar and headed toward the door.

When Leo arrived at the hotel, his room was dimly lit: not much sun came through the flower-patterned curtains that covered the windows. The room had a suitable front view of the Amstel River, City Square and portions of downtown. Leo tipped the bellboy and sent him on his way.

Leo telephoned Elfi. "Hey, I just arrived in Amsterdam. Alert the others. Tell them to bring their own body corset." The new, long, soft, plastic strips had been uniquely designed to carry up to 40 pounds of heroin around their body.

Leo had tested and retested six of the plastic strips for leaks, including his own. He didn't want to even think about one of them walking through some foreign airport with a trail of heroin spilling behind them. Miami and other international airports had gradually converted their customs and immigration departments into more technological operations with metal detectors and x-ray scanning devices, thus throwing their occasional body frisking and luggage rummaging techniques out the window.

***

The young women had already checked into their room on the same floor and settled in. Leo and the five girls who were now alternating between euphoria, excited talk, wild plans, high laughter and sex play were overwhelming him.

Silki, who had been recruited by Elfi and one of the newest female courier's /smugglers in Leo's organization didn't know which portion of the plan scared her more as she picked out the Brazilian dress she hadn't wore since she left Venezuela. But, when Leo began emptying money out of his attaché case onto the bed, then gave them $5,000 each… and an additional thousand when the job was complete, Silki became brave. "Nothing will spoil this," she said intently, "nothing!"

The next day after spending an exciting night out on the town, Leo and his crew were wasting no more time. The girls put on their fancy dresses, combed their hair, fastened their earrings in place, picked up their scarfs and shoulder bags and left.

Leo stuffed their luggage into the trunk of the taxi; a four-door Mercedes, loaded the five young ladies in, then headed for Rocky's place: another of his secluded safe houses he used on an alternate basis—as a result of the rip-off nine months ago at his import/export business. They had just enough time to meet Rocky, fasten the heroin around their body, and catch the KLM Flight 502, to New York.

The taxi driver drove slowly through the City's Square, then crossed the Eider Bridge over the Amstel River. His pace increased as they got out of the city and the houses on the harbor road came into sight. Joined together to form a continuous line, they seemed so similar that the taxi driver might have passed Rocky's place had Leo not spotted Wong Lee in front of its entrance.

Wong greeted them and took them inside. There was a short wait. To Leo, it seemed an eternity. No one around him had much to say: they were all a little dazed.

Rocky and Wong aided them in strapping the heroin around their bodies. The ladies carried 10 pounds each. Leo had 20 pounds of heroin wrapped around him. There was the usual lecture from Rocky… about the precautions they should take. "Okay guys I know you've smuggled many times before, but this is the big one. Everything is on the line," Rocky said.

"You can kiss us for luck," Hillery told him. "Just don't talk about precautions anymore." Rocky's smile was broad. He kissed the young ladies for luck.

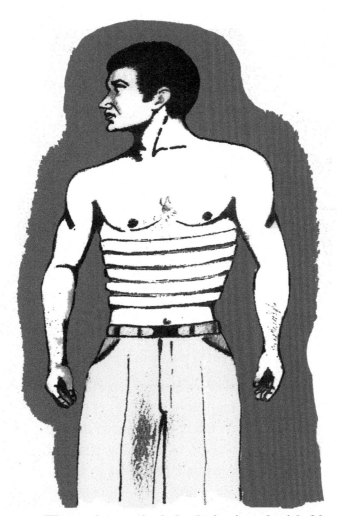

The male courier's body is rigged with 20 pounds of heroin, usually supported with a corset similar to a woman courier's device.

Elfi led the way to the street where the taxi had drawn up at the curb. She noticed Rocky wasn't following. She and Silki turned and waved, "See you when we get back," she said.

Rocky nodded. In haste, he checked the rooms to make sure they hadn't left any form of identification behind. He and Wong were going to Thailand where they'd need to exercise caution more than ever.

Leo and the girls settled into the taxi with squeals and laughs at meeting Rocky again, everything forgotten except the excitement of the journey ahead. The car moved off. Leo looked at his watch. It was twenty minutes to eight o'clock.

"Time to get to the airport," he said aloud.

They were nearly twenty minutes early, which was probably a record in punctuality for Leo. The taxi driver parked in the space reserved for taxis. Leo checked each girl's papers to make sure they were in order, and then sent them into the Amsterdam/Schiphol Airport in three minute intervals. They all cleared immigration, checked in at the KLM departure gate, and boarded the KLM aircraft, Flight 502. They were all assigned different seats so no one could put them together.

Amsterdam Tower had received a report on the weather in London. A blanket of fog would roll in by 9:00 p.m. with zero visibility expected. It was too late to abandon the operation; they were too far into the process to abort the plan. The pilot was under the assumption there might be a break in the weather by the time they arrived, but the report was the same. The London airport was fogged in. The jet was equipped with automatic landing gear and the pilot was unafraid and showed no willingness to turn back. The first half of the flight was boring and by the time they were over the Atlantic, it was partially dark. Greenland lay below in a mantle of snow when the pilot announced over the intercom that fog was blowing in from the North Sea and getting thicker. The pilot, Captain Copeland expressed regret for the bad luck in the weather and now Copeland and Air Traffic Control had to decide whether to risk an instrument landing at London or fly to an alternate airport.

In a radio news report later that evening, Leo heard a cockpit recording of what he experienced firsthand on the flight.

"Flight 502, this is Air Traffic Control, please be advised to alter your flight plan please." It was the tower at Greenland. The pilot had to make a decision swiftly. He could still land at Greenland. The voice cracked over the loudspeaker again, *"KLM, Flight 502, will you alter your flight plan please?"*

"I hope so," Copeland replied. The captain told the radio reporter that at the time he was wholly absorbed in flying the KLM aircraft, listening to the frequent weather reports from Air Traffic Control every so often then responding to them. He was still hoping for a wind change, but 15 minutes out of London, the report was still the same.

"Copeland, this is Air Traffic Control. We're still experiencing HEAVY FOG and the air field is still closed to all air traffic except for emergencies."

At the same time the captain radioed Air Traffic Control, Leo had just returned from the restroom at the rear of the plane and had just completed his check on his female couriers, when all of a sudden there was a loud, thunderous explosion... "Vooooommm Wooooommmmmm!" Then the right engine caught on fire. The passengers that spotted the fire immediately began to moan in fear.

"God dammit!" Leo shouted aloud. "The fucking engine is on fire!!!" He spotted several stewardesses rush towards the cockpit doorway, and then heard a fire alarm go off in the cockpit.

According to the plane's black box recorder, the pilot switched on the fire extinguishers and the aircraft began to toss from side to side causing more passengers to panic.

"KLM Flight 502 to London Tower. Approaching airport from 20 miles Southeast of Cambridge, ETA 2200 hours," Copeland said.

Almost instantly a voice on the radio crackled back, "London Tower to KLM Flight 502. Our field is closed down. We suggest you go on to Greenland."

Captain Copeland spoke into the hand mike. "KLM Flight 502 to London Tower. Negative! Repeat: Negative!! We have an emergency!"

A new voice came over the speaker, "KLM Flight 502, this is Chief of Operations at London Airport. We are completely fogged in here. Visibility zero! Repeat: Visibility zero! What is the nature of your emergency?"

"We're on fire!" Copeland shouted. "My right engine will not extinguish, prepare for forced landing! Repeat: Prepare for forced landing!"

The radio went silent for a few seconds. Suddenly it exploded into life again. "London Tower to KLM Flight 502. You have an emergency clearance. We'll bring you in."

"Roger!" Captain Copeland flicked off the switch and continued to try and extinguish the flames by pressing the automatic extinguisher, than he turned to his co-pilot. "Landing gear down!" he ordered.

The co-pilot swallowed and said in a choked voice, "Landing gear down, sir?"

"You heard me, Sam. Landing gear down!" Copeland repeated.

Again, according to the black box, the co-pilot nodded glumly and reached for the landing gear handle and snatched it back, allowing the landing gear to come down and lock into place. Five minutes later, the plane was in the fog, wrapped in a soft white mist that wiped out everything but the dimly lit cockpit the pilot and his crew sat in.

It was an eerie sensation for Leo, cut off from time and space and the rest of the world. The stakes were life or death. One passenger had already suffered a heart attack. Not to mention Silki Kessler, who'd panicked and attempted to take off her corset and the ten pound heroin strip until Elfi slapped the shit out of her, which quickly brought her back to reality.

The news station report continued the cockpit broadcast, *"London control tower to KLM Flight 502. I am going to bring you in on ALS. You will please follow my instructions exactly. We have you on our radar. Turn 2 degrees south and maintain present altitude until further instructions. At your present airspeed, you should be landing in 10 minutes."*

At the time, Leo could only visualize the aircraft smashing into the runway scattering the pink powdered heroin all over the plane. Leo grabbed the arm rest to his seat with both hands and held on tight. He glanced over his shoulder at the girls to make sure they were all right as Captain Copeland made the connection and shut out everything from his mind but the disembodied voice from Air Traffic Control that was their sole link to survival. In Leo's mind, Copeland flew that plane as though it were a part of himself, flying it with his heart, his mind and his soul.

Leo was dimly aware of everyone on the plane sweating behind him. He could just hear the co-pilot calling out instrument checks in a low, strained voice from the open cockpit door.

Leo knew that if they came out of it alive it would be Captain Copeland who did it. Leo had never seen fog like this. It was a ghostly enemy, blinding them, trying to lure the captain into making one fatal mistake. The aircraft was hurtling through the sky at 800 miles an hour and the captain was unable to see beyond the windshield of the cockpit.

The first rule of flying through fog was climb over it, or fly under it, but get out of it. However there was no way out. Leo and everybody aboard were helpless as Copeland flew the plane at the mercy of the instruments.

The air traffic controller's voice came over the speaker again, and it seemed to Leo, hearing it via the news report, that it had a new, nervous, quality. *"London Tower to KLM Flight 502. You are coming into the first leg of the landing pattern. Check the landing flaps and begin descent...Descend to 1000 feet... 700 feet... 500 feet..."* Still no sign of the airport below.

Leo seemed to remember the ground rushing up to meet the plane at that point.

"Decrease your airspeed to five hundred mph... you're at 400 feet... airspeed three hundred mph... you're at 375 feet..." Leo could hear the Controller through the cockpit door but there was still no sign of the airport.

The blanket of smothering fog seemed thicker now. Leo's forehead gleamed with perspiration. "Where in the hell is it?" he whispered tensed—and in fear of the captain overshooting the runway. Leo leaned way out into the aisle to check on the pilots.

In the cockpit, the co-pilot stole a swift glance at the altimeter. The needle was edging down toward 300 feet. Then it was below 300 feet. The ground was rushing to meet the plane at three hundred miles an hour. The altimeter showed only 175 feet. Leo thought the pilot should be able to see the airport lights by now. Copeland strained to see ahead of the plane, but there was only the treacherous, blinding fog whipping across the windshield.

The black box would later reveal the level of tension in the cockpit. Copeland heard the co-pilot voice, tense and hoarse, *"We're down to 60 feet!" And still nothing. "40 feet!"* And the ground racing up to meet the plane in the darkness while the right wing continued to burn and melt. Pieces broke off causing the plane to shift and sway violently. *"20 feet!"*

"In another 3 seconds, the margin of safety will be gone and we will crash," Leo said to himself.

Captain Copeland had to make and instant decision. *"I'm going to take it back up!" he said, with a sense of urgency.* His hand tightened on the wheel and started to pull back, and at that instant, as he reported to a rapt audience listening to the broadcast of the near-fatal crash, a row of electric arrows blazed out on the ground ahead of them, lighting up the runway below. Eight seconds later they were on the ground taxiing toward the airport emergency area.

Leo silently thanked the Lord and Captain Copeland when they came to a stop.

Leo quickly got out of his seat and prepared to deplane. As he stood near the exit door, he looked into the cockpit again to see Captain Copeland switch off the engines with numb fingers and sit motionless for a second or two. The Captain quickly pushed himself to his feet trembling all over. The rest of the crew acted quickly in getting the passengers off the plane while rescue units tended to the blazing fire.

***

Leo looked around for the 4 couriers first, annoyed with the situation at hand and shook his head from side to side, grateful to be alive.

"Ladies and gentlemen… welcome to London/Heathrow Airport," a stewardess announced over the PA system. "We'll have a two-hour layover until the fog clears."

Leo and the couriers felt exhilarated from the challenge ahead of them as they boarded another KLM flight, without bother from customs and immigration, and headed for New York.

The mission was all that mattered. *We'll continue carefully*, Leo thought, *taking things slowly, coolly. Yes, that was the angle needed for this encounter at New York customs.*

Leo and his crew were temporarily separated. They passed through JFK customs and immigrations checkpoints without trouble and walked briskly to the exit.

"Let's flag a limo and get away from here," Leo sighed. "We still have to get through LaGuardia."

"Okay, "Elfi nodded in agreement. People were darting into the roadway to get hold of a cab. She raised an arm and waved over one of the limousines with a driver at the wheel. They loaded their luggage into the trunk, entered the limousine from both sides and sped to LaGuardia Airport.

The corsets used to support the heroin held up firm and snug. But, Leo and his sexy crew felt a tightening in their stomach's that cried for relief from the pink heroin's weight. They had smuggled a total of 70 pounds between the six of them. *It's not a boat load, but it's a decent shipment*, Leo told himself.

A couple of hours later at McCoy Jetport in Orlando, Thomas Scalli, Leo's devoted lieutenant, was waiting for them.

He wore a navy blue and white pinstriped suit, as planned, so Leo could pick him out even before he saw the familiar face. He gave no hint of recognition, either. As they drew near, Scalli headed for the main exit. At a leisurely pace, they followed the blue and white pinstriped suited man until he had stepped into his car... then, with one fast motion Leo heaved the entire luggage into the trunk, slipped in beside the couriers and they were on their way. For the next six weeks, Scalli would be responsible for Leo's safety.

Elfi, Eva, Bagetta, Hillery, and Silki would unload their heroin at Leo's place (a large spacious house he leased) stay there for the rest of the week, take-in some sights at Disney World, then return to Europe until the next assignment.

Scalli showed an intimate knowledge of the states, streets, businesses, and coastlines they visited, that one didn't find in a guidebook. He had been well educated and a Commercial Arts major. He had entered the University of Miami almost six years ago after he became a senior, then gave it all up for the NFL.

Leo Stegner's first heroin transaction in the United States took place on University Boulevard, in Miami's southwest side, near the University of Miami Medical Center.

***

Cecil "Nassau" Beckman, a major dealer on the streets of Miami knew approximately when Leo and Scalli were to arrive, so he waited. The transaction went smooth and quickly. Scalli pulled the car alongside of Beckman's car, and let the window down. Beckman shoved the briefcase full of money through the car window. Scalli shoved the briefcase with the 2.2 pounds of heroin in it, in the same manner.

"It's in $1,000.00 bundles," Beckman's driver/bodyguard said.

Leo counted the bundles quickly. "Yes, it's all here. All $250 thousand," he grunted.

Beckman tested the heroin. He was pleased. Neither of them wanted to hang around for small talk. Leo had many more miles to go. People who knew Beckman were attracted by his money. Nearly every person he met wanted something from him: financing for a business project, or simply the power that his friendship could bestow.

Leo and Scalli were back on the road again. While Scalli slept, Leo drove and vice versa. They took Interstate 95 past Palm Beach Gardens. The second transaction occurred in the small town of Jupiter, just off U.S. Highway A1A. It was an 82-mile drive from Miami.

Scalli was sure of himself and what to expect next, but Leo wasn't. He was suspicious; he didn't want to trust anyone. He insisted on Scalli finding a neutral place for this next rendezvous as well. Robert Stone and Thomas Scalli had agreed that the swamp near the Jupiter Inlet was a nice secluded place to make the exchange.

Stone was accompanied by his driver and bodyguard too. He was a fairly young man in his early thirties, 5'7", handsome and neatly dressed. He came into wealth after his parents died. Real estate, the stock market, and small aircrafts were his main interests. The exchange went down with the greatest of ease; the heroin was tested and the money was swiftly counted. Stone enjoyed the challenge of figuring out exactly what it was that people were really after, for it was seldom what it appeared to be. His analytical mind was skeptical of everyone he met, and as a consequence, he believed nothing he heard and trusted no one.

All the money was there. Leo's boldness and self-assurance had begun to soar. Now he was more determined than ever to complete each transaction. The businessman in Fort Lauderdale was out of town for the weekend, so they rode on.

Tampa was nearly 300 miles away. They took State Road 441 North to Lake Wales to Tampa. Tourism there had increased from several hundred thousand to millions of people annually. The Dark Continent was Tampa's largest tax revenue from tourist attractions. Championship wrestling and fishing on Tampa's west coast were other forms of sports and relaxation in this fairly populous city. Tampa was the home of the Budweiser Beer brewers industry, and the Tampa Bay Buccaneers, who were an expansion team halfway through their first winning season.

Sam Capelli was a 60-year old Cuban, short and thick, with a large, bridged nose. He was unusually different. Capelli had to be treated gently, with caution. He insisted they meet on his turf or no deal. He owned a chain of restaurants with a Mafia family out of Detroit.

They met Sam Capelli at the Oak Hill Golf Course and Country Club Resort. Capelli's setup was awesome. Bodyguards were stationed throughout his private clubhouse, while Capelli strolled about the premises as though he was the "Godfather of Crime." The people who chronicled his life, reporters, were permitted to see only his geniality and charm, the sophisticated urbane man of the world. They never suspected that beneath the surface, Capelli was a cold-blooded killer, a gutter rat whose instinct was to go for the jugular; just as he had done when he ordered the hit on Leo's father, nearly 10-years ago over his delinquent gambling debt. There was enough information on the assassination of Joe Stegner to crash an ordinary computer. Leo had read the police reports of the Orlando Police Department and various publications by Organized Crime Task Forces, which took up yards of shelf space. It was all there. Sam Capelli's name mentioned from start to finish, except who actually drew the 'blade' that gutted Joe.

Scalli had kept Leo well informed about each connection they'd met, so Leo knew what to say and when to say it. But Scalli had no idea that Capelli was responsible for Joe Stegner's death. In fact, Thomas Scalli never knew Joe or Capelli during that time. Scalli was too busy playing football for the NFL. He didn't cut into Capelli until his career turned sour. Scalli then worked off and on with Capelli as a dope connection.

Leo wasn't about to call Capelli a murderer, not to his face at least. He wasn't in a position to argue the point; he was frightened by the unnecessary bodyguards: they could have killed them, took the heroin and the money and went on their merry way.

Leo couldn't believe it. He had spent the last 10-years of his life plotting to kill a man he'd never met, until now. How had this happened? It was like standing in the middle of a dream. Revenge, sweet revenge, Leo thought with pleasure. *It's unthinkable to let this motherfucker live.* The walls of security would have to fall immediately or the hit would have to be made on him in a way to eliminate Leo as a prime suspect during any manner of investigation.

Capelli didn't know who Leo Stegner was. Not yet, at any extent. Capelli had been so mesmerized by the heroin's strength and unusual-looking color, the name Stegner hadn't even rung a bell.

On the road again, Leo thought intently, always conscious of being ripped off. As far as Leo was concerned, the odds of being caught by the police seemed better. They were merciful and most gangsters weren't.

Leo and Scalli headed north. Damon Novack, a big time cocaine distributor who migrated from the Virgin Islands and made his home in Atlanta, was so satisfied with the heroin, he turned generous and supplied them with enough cocaine to keep them awake all the way to Detroit and back. New York was nearly 865 miles away.

Scalli looked at his watch. "It's six o'clock. If we drive straight through, we should get to Maryland sometime tomorrow morning."

Leo laughed, then shifted in his seat and said, "What are you going to do? Make this bitch fly?" Scalli joined in his laughter and Leo continued. "I think we better have a hit of that coke. We've got some serious talking to do."

Scalli reached into his shirt pocket and handed Leo the plastic baggy filled with the cocaine. "No lecture," he said.

"No notes either," Leo replied. He looked hesitantly at it. "It'll help me stay awake."

Scalli grinned. "Amen to that," he said. Leo held the wheel while Scalli inhaled a few toots of coke too. "We have a long night ahead. I won't be worth a pinch of shit the way I am."

Seconds later, they were staring out at the blackness of Interstate 95 North, their minds speeding under the niceness of the cocaine. Leo sighed and—looking at Scalli over the top of a cigarette, told the story about Joe's death and Sam Capelli's involvement.

Scalli blinked. "Is this some kind of psychotic joke, Leo?"

"Hell no!" Leo replied. He reached into his wallet and pulled out the 10-year-old Orlando Sentinel newspaper article implicating Capelli in the murder of his father and began to read it to Scalli in an arrogant manner. He looked at Scalli who shrugged and dug at his ear.

"Capelli?" Thomas Scalli said surprised. He helped himself to some more coke. "So what will you do? You were thinking of a hit?"

"Yes," Leo replied. "But if anyone says anything about this conversation, ever, they are dead." He shifted in his seat and looked at Scalli over the cigarette again. "Listen, that's the only way it can be. We have to accept it, live with it, and keep our fucking mouths shut until I work this thing out. That bastard must pay for what he did to my father and nothing on this earth will interfere."

"Say no more," Scalli replied. "I understand completely, I'm out of it. I know nothing." He gestured with his hand.

***

Due to Leo's increased responsibilities, his military heroin outlet in West Germany, his on and off DJ commitment to the Playboy Discotheque—and his commitment to his U.S. heroin network, Leo ended his role as a courier/smuggler and continued to pay the five sexy female foreigners a steady commission to replace him.

Leo worked his couriers hard that following year and a half. He had them smuggling heroin internationally—once every three months. The couriers took direct as well as indirect routes, penetrating customs at: Sudbury in Ontario; JFK in New York; St. Paul in Minnesota; O'Hare in Chicago; Dulles in D.C.; Greenville in South Carolina; Hartsfield in Atlanta; and El Paso in Texas.

Leo knew that time and distance between he and Sam Capelli would serve as his ally. So he would take care of him later, in his own special way. What he had in mind would cost money, lots of it. Or it could cost him nothing, he reasoned, if he played his cards right. Leo didn't only want to hit Sam Capelli, he wanted Sam and all his boys. That way Joe would be pleased. A bit psychotic Leo thought to himself, but he didn't give a fuck. He just wanted Sam's ass dead.

CHAPTER 7

"The Golden Triangle"

Frankfurt, West Germany - June 1980

Richard Milhous Nixon had resigned and the United States military manpower in all of Asia had eroded. Not only had President Nixon sent 50,000 soldiers to their death in Vietnam, but Leo who worked as a Battalion S-1 clerk and a Company clerk was privy to viewing sensitive documents regarding troop strength and morale had surmised in a twisted sort of way that the president had indirectly aided the communist plot in turning 5 million veterans into drug addicts by sending them there.

***

Leo had returned to his spacious flat at the Playboy Discotheque. A three-month stay working as a disc-jockey would be a vacation, even if it was coupled with a little business (resupplying his military heroin outlet). Most of the American soldiers during this time were injecting heroin and morphine, smoking hashish, taking all kinds of acid, mescaline, and smoking opium.

Rocky advised Leo to play it safe and trust no one. No open phone calls to Amsterdam or to him. He believed he had a rat (an informant) within his organization picking up crumbs of information.

Leo had suggested they meet, but Rocky being the extra careful type told Leo he would keep him informed about his search for the rat and about the people responsible for ripping him off—which caused Rocky's temporarily paralysis, and about meeting his connections in Thailand.

In the three months that followed, Leo's business declined and he was at the point of deciding whether or not to postpone his trip to the United States. He had only a marginal supply of heroin left and in another few days he would be out.

Leo rose and went into the bathroom that September evening, pulled open the neck of his shirt and splashed some cold water over his face and began to comb his hair, while taking a real good look at himself in the mirror. *I look normal* Leo thought. Not like a man under the worst attack of anxiety Leo had ever experienced in a long time.

As Leo brainstormed, he realized that he hadn't heard any news at all from Rocky about the thief with the lethal umbrella, nor their proposed trip to Thailand, or about the informant in Rocky's operation.

Rocky knows I'm out of heroin, and that my length of stay here in Frankfurt will soon end before I need to continue the rest of my travels. So what's delaying him? Do I just hang around here hoping for a call from Amsterdam, Leo thought to himself. Leo packed his camera and tennis gear (part of his vacation myth disguise). His telephone rang; a call from the lobby downstairs. A special messenger had arrived with a sealed envelope to be delivered to Leo Stegner.

"I've checked it," the blonde front desk assistant on duty explained. "It's from Amsterdam, Holland. The messenger's credentials are in order, too."

"Then have it sent up, will you?" Leo said.

"That's the trouble, Mr. Stegner. The messenger has instructions not to hand over the envelope to anyone except you.

Shall I have him escorted up to Mr. Stegner's room?" the bar waitress asked the front desk assistant; overhearing the conversation as she handed the messenger a glass of water. The front desk assistant repeated the question to Leo.

"No...Tell him the house rules," Leo pleaded.

Rocky is really taking no chances, Leo thought.

"I've tried that, Leo. He insists he must see you. He says it's confidential and can only be given to you," she replied.

"I'll come down," Leo said. He reached for his keys, pulled his shirt sleeves into place and left.

The lobby of the Playboy Discotheque was crowded and bustling at this time of the afternoon. Between 40 and 50 people, some in military uniform, some in civilian clothes, were in constant movement in and out of the Playboy. A Staff Sergeant and several PFC's were at the bar near the entrance. No sign of any messenger. "Where is he?" Leo asked.

"Over there Leo, standing by the photo display. Gray hair with a brown uniform," the waitress replied.

"I see him," Leo responded. The man was holding the large, white, letter-sized envelope tightly against his chest, "Doesn't trust anyone, does he?" Leo asked as he started toward the expressionless messenger. A man who takes his duties seriously,

Leo thought as the stranger caught sight of him and, after a moment's hesitation, came to meet him.

The envelope contained only one sheet of typed paper giving this weeks' destination—in Burmese alphabet code-that read:

Come………..to……….Amsterdam……….Immediately…

Stop……….Destination……….Thailand

Rocky

Various Alphabets--Burmese Signs
Often Used As Special Messages
By .Foreign Heroin Syndicates

Sign	Equivalent	Sign	Equivalent
	HPA		GHA
	PA		SA
	HA		HSA
	LA		FE
	GA		KI (OR) KL
	WA		QU
	DA		QA –
	BA		QI
	ZA		QI –
	TAI		QU –
	HTA		QEI –
	NA		QE!
	NYA		QAN –
	THA		JAN
	MA		
	YA		DRU
	KA		
	HKA		

Leo returned to his room, poured himself a glass of Liebfraumilch (mild German white wine) and settled down to the coded alphabets. Then he telephoned the Flughafen (Frankfurt

Rhein Main Airport) to postpone his trip to the United States and rescheduled it for the Netherlands.

***

The following afternoon was Rocky's turn to wait near the telephone in Wong Lee's most private, secluded office, nestled behind the accounting department of the Dutch Gift Shop with a second door into the adjoining bookstore and a third door into a roofed passageway.

Rocky was alone except for one of Wong's men, a silent calm type, in charge of Wong's heroin sales to reputable clients. Wong Lee had already left for the private airfield to make preparations for their departure aboard his small Lear Jet 35.

Leo and the couriers had smuggled over 70 million dollars' worth of heroin to foreign buyers without a single arrest and Rocky was thoroughly impressed.

Rocky Congo Lee's second set of instructions, sent in code to the Amsterdam/Schiphol Airport before Leo entered Amsterdam were precise. Leo was to phone Rocky upon his arrival and then meet Rocky at 12:00 noon in the Molokai Building. Leo was to be well dressed. He was to avoid the 3 large (attended) elevators and make sure one of the smaller (self-service) elevators was empty before he used it. Leo was to get out at the 4th floor. He would be met by a red-haired man who would greet him in French: "It's colder in Germany in December."

Leo would reply in German: "And as hot as Florida." Leo would then be escorted to Wong Lee's office, pausing...if anyone should appear in the corridor to chat with his guide until they judged it was safe to enter.

Despite a sense of urgency, Leo felt real amusement as he stepped into Suite 414. Back in Florida, he wouldn't have seen anything comic in comparison between a secretive approach and an open rendezvous.

His escort entered an office on the right where Leo glimpsed a blonde, thick-shouldered man at a desk with an elaborate set of maps stretched across it. The door closed. Leo waited, looking at the elegance around him. The last comfortable office he had seen, the only one in fact, had been at Rocky's import/export company in Amsterdam. His critical study of Wong's working quarters ended as the door to his left opened and Rocky appeared. The few minutes' delay had been calculated, thought Leo. He overcame his surprise at Rocky's appearance. Apart from his height and weight, he was difficult to recognize. He was now a brown-haired man with glasses; a brown mustache on his short upper lip; slow in movement; and dressed in a blue silk suit.

But Rocky's voice was as crisp as ever as he greeted Leo in Dutch. His brown eyes had the same strange alteration of bland innocence and calm scrutiny. He was glad Leo had made the trip. "Over 4 months since we met," he said, shaking hands briefly. "You look well, Leo. Not too unpleasant a journey? Sit down. We have much to discuss. We must leave here no later than 1:00 o'clock; we have an important meeting at 6:00." He pointed to a chair on one side of a large desk and selected the one opposite that was firmer, higher and more commanding.

"I had a successful trip in all." Leo responded. "I wondered what had happened to you...," Leo began; slightly on the defensive.

Rocky's eyebrows lifted. "We had 3 objectives," he said. "First: Wong and I were to drop out of sight completely, leave the Dutch authorities and the D.E.A. baffled. Secondly, we were to recruit and encourage while we traveled, selecting only the most promising couriers/smugglers. Third, I was trying to smoke out the rat who leaked the location of 2 safe houses."

There was a brief silence. Rocky was smart, thought Leo. "Have you caught him yet?" Leo asked.

"Not exactly, but we're close to it," Rocky replied.

"I hope you get them," Leo said. "The rat could expose our entire network. Now, what about Thailand? Are we...? "

"Yes," Rocky said smoothly, "Your progress was very well received at the highest level." He smiled. "Let's review these maps quickly and get out of here," he suggested.

"Alright," Leo said, enthused. "Onward and upward!"

"Yes, I know," Rocky said, shaking his head. "That is what counts, Leo. Not today's quick victories, but tomorrow's permanent success." Leo smiled. He noticed that the maps on Wong Lee's desk had been color-coded to reveal the China Mafia's "Loose-knit Heroin Networks" primary location: The Golden Triangle, the opium heartland of Southeast Asia: 60,000 square miles of jungle and mountains, straddling the borders of Northeastern Burma, Northern Thailand, and Northwest Laos.

It was an uncontrolled wild place 'Beyond the Russian Front.' It was inhabited by various tribes organized to rebel against civil authority and considered to be Communist territory where Burma farmers grew over 1500 tons of opium each season.

The Golden Triangle was the turf of local warlords, large scale smugglers, underworld businessmen and syndicate figures, but more so the private domain of General Chung Che Fu who supplied nearly 90% of the worlds' opium, morphine, and heroin products, with 6,000 or more Chinese nationalists, entrenched in a strong defensive position, well-equipped and heavily armed.

Due to the pressure applied from civil authorities and special interest groups, General Fu had imported highly paid chemists from Singapore, Macao, Hong Kong, and Taiwan to set up secret laboratories in the Golden Triangle. The chemists stayed from 6 to 10 weeks to turn the opium crops into pure heroin. Rocky, a Chinese himself who haled from China Fukien Province, sent his two sons to college to major in Chemistry. Then his sons returned to the Province so they could learn more about heroin refining and go into production for themselves.

Then Rocky pointed to areas in the Middle East where 25 out of 50 different opium refineries were located in inconspicuous areas, protected by guards and local authorities, who were paid for their silence. On the same map, he pointed to another color 'code' pin-pointing the various clandestine plastic, cellophane, and paper-seal factories, which operated around the clock due to the increasing demand for heroin.

To Leo's surprise, Rocky had color-coded maps of the United States military presence in Europe and the Middle-East. Mostly areas where their heroin networks could use private planes, charter small flights, and use military aircraft to make illegal drops and pickups on military and out of the way airstrips.

"Our prime objective is not to destroy the effectiveness of the U.S. 'Military Might' abroad. Such as the intent of Communist aggression, but merely to meet the increasing demand for heroin by individuals," Rocky said and then continued. "Fewer people die from heroin overdoses than any other form of death in the world. You see… opium is a natural grown product like all other green vegetation and we have just as much right to free enterprise."

Leo grinned, and then said. "The U.S. authorities would take exception to that."

Rocky frowned, and then pointed to the color-coded areas that represented ocean drops, and then said. "We take the heroin wrap it in plastic and then seal it in 100-gallon metal drums. Then mark it with a buoy to be picked up within a specified time for the next destination."

The final color indicator and topic of their meeting before Rocky, Leo, and Wong departed for Thailand revealed several hundred direct and indirect smuggling routes. Mostly places where customs were considered moderate.

Wong Lee, a courier pilot, had been waiting at an out of the way airstrip in North Holland. Leo was still a little stunned, but secretly delighted with his sudden promotion within Rocky's hierarchy. The small automatic door ramp descended by its own power and they boarded the plane for the Golden Triangle. They made a refueling stop at Hong Kong's Kowloon Airport, and then hours later arrived over Northern Thailand. Wong circled the plane and pinpointed the private landing strip owned by Colonel Ngai Towng, a reputable member of the opium syndicate near the small town of Muang Khop. They landed and were greeted by Towng's armed guards and a drug trafficking guide who provided them with a Jeep. Lun Lutken, a soft-spoken Burmese gentleman would be their guide. The short, lean, skinny-legged man had been a guide since he was a youth and was now one of the most rugged guide masters in the Golden Triangle.

"It'll take about 8-hours to make the trip in and out. I know all the trails and compass bearings," Lun Lutken said. He was familiar with the contour lines which indicated treacherous country.

Certain areas they were not allowed to enter alone, and as far as Leo was concerned, he wouldn't have anyway. Lutken drove miles and miles and miles down Thailand and Laos steep hills and uneven roads toward Northeastern Burma to the town of Muang Sing; population of about 30,000.

Minutes before reaching town, they were forced to reduce their speed because of a large convoy of 30-horses, 15-trucks, 20-elephants and a band of armed guards. It was an opium caravan that traveled four times yearly that normally took anywhere from seven to ten days to reach the town of Muang Sing from the opium fields. The opium was taken to a factory and converted

into heroin, crude morphine, and rice whiskey. Leo had never seen so much raw opium at one time.

In Muang Sing, they were taken to the guarded palace of General Chung Che Fu, leader of over 8,000 Chinese Nationalists. The exterior of his Royal

Oriental Pavilion palace was an exotic fantasy of minarets and cupolas, pinnacles and pagodas, all constructed over cast iron frames. The dining hall had a domed ceiling painted like a spreading palm tree. Its Water Lilly chandeliers suspended from the cast iron claws of scaly dragons, lotus blossom lamps, Oriental lacquer ware, and Chinese Chippendale furniture that completed the décor.

In a revolt against the academic rationalism and scientific naturalism of his time, Chung Che Fu turned to Oriental mysticism. He thought that man should achieve peace with himself, harmony with his fellowman, and the ultimate release into infinity by renouncing personal ambitions and materialistic pursuits.

The Golden Triangle was inaccessible except by helicopter, small aircraft and yacht. Both the airfields and private harbors were patrolled 24-hours a day by armed guards with trained Doberman Pinschers and German Shepherds. No one was invited without an invitation. Over the years several kings, diplomats, ex-presidents and movie stars appeared on Fu's door step only to have the barrel of an AK47 shoved down their throat and interrogated before allowed entrance. Then the intruders/uninvited guests left in awe over the whole setup.

In the drug underworld, Chung Che Fu was the wealthiest and one of the most powerful men in the world. He had taste and style and knew how to spend the money necessary to create beauty. The town of Muang Sing was as busy as the New York Stock Exchange. It had one of the largest opium/heroin refinery/processing centers in the Golden Triangle. U.S. Federal Drug Enforcement Agents, the C.I.A., Interpol, and the press had been trying to get to him for years, but he had simply made himself unavailable.

Leo was anxious to meet Fu. Customarily, General Fu sat in his richly-paneled library; relaxed in a deep arm chair smoking a Thai-Stick (a commodity twice as potent as the common marijuana joint and known worldwide among pot smokers) and thinking about the illicit trades that would begin every morning.

Rocky introduced them. He had already informed General Fu of Leo's unblemished smuggling record, his amazing formula for recruiting more couriers, sparkling appearance, military heroin/hashish outlet in West Germany and his Florida distribution network that expanded to 10 Northeastern States.

Chung Che Fu was intrigued. He was a native of China's Fukien Province (Formosa), 40-years old, medium height, straight shoulders, with an oval-shaped face and a wide cheek line. Fu spoke to Leo in English even though he spoke Turkish, Greek, Russian, Burmese, Laotian, Thai, German and Dutch.

"It's an honor to meet you Leo. I've heard so many wonderful things about you," Fu said then continued. "My 'Loose-knit Opium/Heroin Network' remains powerful simply because I rule and I'm the only law in these parts. However, with the help of you and Rocky I'm on the precipice of expanding worldwide," he added optimistically.

Leo's smile became broad and then he grinned. "Sir, does that mean that Rocky and I are on the precipice as well? Or are you not receptive to spreading the wealth?"

Fu looked at Leo with a raised brow and then said, "Sure, I have a lot of contacts and I know how to get things done. In fact, I received a huge commission for leasing armed guarded facilities in Muang Sing and other towns throughout the 60,000 square miles of the Golden Triangle regions for the storage of opium, and the manufacture and storage of heroin and crude morphine."

The climate was blistering hot and humid. Eager to impress Leo, Fu jumped to his feet. "Let's go for a ride," Fu said. He took them to a distillery downtown, only a few blocks from the local police station where one of his main warehouses was located. He showed them large bundles of raw opium, tons of both pink and white heroin, and a brown morphine base.

"But General, why is the heroin pink?" Leo asked.

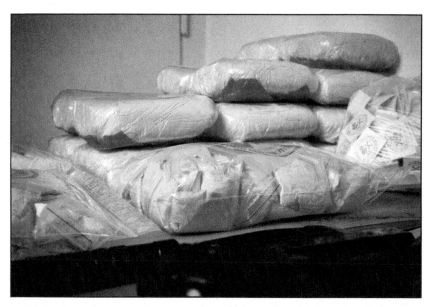

The General looked at Leo, and then frowned. "My friend that question requires a very very long answer. But in short, heroin is comprised of approximately thirty-two ingredients. However, the three most common ingredients are Opium, which is reproduced into Morphine combined with Acetic Anhydride. And the pure the ingredients are near the end of the production process, the pinker the heroin becomes. Rendering it approximately 98% pure."

"Wow," Leo said amazed. They left the distillery and rode a few more miles out of Muang Sing to a compound similar to that of a military outpost.

Along a busy section of town they saw young, adolescent boys on the street corners and squatting in alleyways cooking the uncut dope in bottle caps. Some were injecting opium, while others did heroin or

morphine. You name it, they had it, and they were just as unconcerned about their health as they could be. Such acts were considered a normal way of life there, but Leo was absolutely appalled. He had no idea it had come to this and that it would spread to the United States like wildfire in the years to come.

General Chung Che Fu had constructed several major complexes equipped with laboratories for extracting morphine from raw opium and capable of accommodating several thousand men. To discipline his men, their training course consisted of eight-weeks simulated aviation ground school, followed by an additional eight weeks of flight training. Since the trainees were not experienced pilots, the course was devised to serve many purposes: The first was to run through such subjects as navigation, radio communication, map reading, and instrument flying. Potential weaknesses were pinpointed and weeded out. And the second was to familiarize them with the new equipment they would be using. The instrument flying was done in a link trainer (a small mock-up of an airplane cockpit that rested on a movable base, enabling the pilot to put the plane through any maneuver including stalls, loops, spins, and rolls). A black hood was put over the top of the cockpit so that the pilot was flying blind, using only the instruments in front of them.

General Fu took Leo, Rocky and Wong to his private island. He had purchased the island near Lashio when it was just raw wasteland and then transformed it into a trillion-dollar enterprise-paradise.

"Is this one of your greatest accomplishments?" Leo asked.

"You may say that," General Fu replied.

"What a spectacular hilltop villa," Leo said.

"Thanks, I like the solitude of the island and enjoy it most when there's no other guest roaming about. I even have my own hunting reserve and a couple dozen guest cottages, with an artificial freshwater lake and a harbor where my 120-foot yacht, with four GM Diesel engines anchor.

Leo was moved and impressed by his intelligence and strength. General Fu trusted very few people in business, thus, he made his own decisions. "Are those your landing fields too?" Leo said pointing out into the distance.

"Yes I have several landing fields for my planes," General Fu said.

General Fu enlightened them on Burma's history. The rivers of Burma fell into groups: Naf, Kaladanlemro, and the An-Chaung, which flowed from the Arakan Yomo into the Bay of Bengal. All were rapid streams. The largest lake in Burma was a stretch of water in the Shan Plateau, known as Inle Lake. The hot season began in March and lasted until the end of October. The rainy season extended from June to October, the unpleasant months. The temperature and humidity were always high, and it rained almost constantly. More than a hundred indigenous languages were spoken in Burma, mostly among the hill tribes.

Only chosen tribes played an important role in the production of opium. The Shan Northern Hill tribesmen, who were animalistic in nature and sometimes called Head Hunters; and the Northeastern Burma farmers, mostly Buddhists, who believed in the existence of spirits that separate from the body after death.

They returned to the small town of Muang Sing and remained overnight as Chung Che Fu's guests at his local headquarters. General Fu extended an invite to Leo and Rocky upon their return visit to the Golden Triangle to meet him at his regional headquarters in the town of Lashio. He offered Leo permanent quarters and a responsible position in one of his nearby labs where personnel were being trained to extract morphine from raw opium and convert it into heroin, but Leo kindly declined the offer out of fear and paranoia.

The following morning what had been a fresh breeze turned into a cool wind when the sun came up. The light was strengthening. Almost 6:00 o'clock in the morning and wide awake, Leo turned over again on his queen sized bed. The mattress was very plush and comfortable. It was dead silent outside, making Wong Lee's snores seem even louder than they were from the room across the hall. Rocky lay still, gently breathing. They had fallen into a deep sleep by midnight, their heads buried deep into their pillows.

I'm tired, yet I can't sleep, Leo thought. *What's with this small room, and air-tight securely locked windows? What is Chung Che Fu so afraid of, prowlers or the night air? I'm suffocating.*

Leo rose, put on his green robe—sort of thick in weight, and pulled out a tiny flashlight from his pocket. He switched it on to search for his sandals, and then pointed its strong beam across the floor to lead him safely to the door. Quietly, he turned the key. "Keep this door locked," Rocky had said earlier that night as he told him goodnight. Leo drew the key out, closed the door and locked it, slipping the key into his pocket. He started along the corridor, which was dark and silent, and heard deep breathing from General Fu's room, with steady snores from Wong's room, and then slipped passed General Fu's private armed guards next door. Leo switched off his flashlight before he reached the entrance hall where one small candle had been left burning. The counter that served as a reception desk was empty. The manager must be in bed and asleep, lucky man. Voices were coming from the dining room. One meager light there—such extravagance, Leo thought with a smile; recognizing the manager's voice. It couldn't be the manager's son who had bustled around the dining tables, directing the waiters (four small Oriental boys, 12 and 13-years-old, anxious and willing, and overworked in order to feed their $600 a day heroin, morphine, and opium addiction).

Leo looked at the front door wondering if the manager or one of Fu's guards would hear the turning of its heavy key. It might be better if he told them that he only wanted ten-minutes of cool sweet air. But he knew what would happen; the guard would come with him then, make small talk and he would have to translate a language he really couldn't understand. No, he decided, not that. He'd be driven inside within five-minutes.

He reached the door. The key in its lock was massive. It wouldn't turn. Then Leo realized it wouldn't budge because it was already in the unlocked position. Some security, he thought: windows shut and covered with iron screens, and an entrance door left for anyone to enter. He stepped out into the yard, pulling the door closed behind him to cut off the murmur of voices from the dining room.

The sky was clear and beautiful. He drew long deep breaths, welcoming the cool air. Dawn was minutes away. No wind, only a breeze to stir the surrounding trees. The parked trucks, neatly placed, their color eaten up by the dust, were at one side of the yard. General Fu's Jeep, with its chrome shiny and polished and sparkling bright, stood aloof like some proud beauty. Its stripes were good, Leo admitted; custom-built, outside as well as in. It must have cost a fortune—no wonder he had it guarded constantly. Then as he studied it, he saw a faint, almost imperceptible glow spreading into the darkness from the mountains. Someone's out there watching us, Leo thought at first: Or it could be a hunter, he reasoned.

Leo hesitated, looked at the door behind him, and then thought twice about it, before alerting the guards. A false alarm and he would be apologizing all tomorrow for waking everyone up. Leo calmed down, he was more nervous than he previously realized.

Unbeknown to Leo, Rocky and General Fu, Thailand's Chief Drug Enforcement Officer, General Pao Sarasin and the United States Senior D.E.A. agent in Thailand, Robert DeFauw, had moved their field bases to the villages of Ban Namo and Louang Namtha to be closer to the local headquarters of the Laotian Drug Enforcement Authorities. They were closing in on General Fu's position.

General Sarasin provided leadership and people knowledgeable of the area, while Agent DeFauw provided contact with the Allies, arms, ammunition, and other forms of support. They had fanned out in units of 50 to 60 men to start their search-n-destroy operations against General Fu and his Shan Army.

General Pao Sarasin intelligence network had reached throughout the Namtha Valley and its approach to the South-East. He had given orders to build a thousand-foot long airstrip so that the troops could be taken in and out with greater ease and safety. In only a few weeks his agents had brought in such vast amounts of intelligence about the Shan Army daily activities and it was impossible for Sarasin to radio all of it to base.

Laotian Drug Enforcement Authorities sent more personnel in to join Agent DeFauw at Louang-Namtha. The newcomers infiltrated in through the trails as the original party had done. And, in case of an armed conflict with the Shan's army, Agent DeFauw reasoned that the most practical way to remove the wounded or sick was in helicopters or light planes. The Thai Air Force would control the air, while the light planes winging close to the treetops, could slip in unobserved.

General Fu and his Shan Army had hindered the D.E.A.'s efforts from infiltrating the areas sooner. For thatched huts had been erected on existing landing fields between Muang Khop and Muang Sing, so they looked like villages from the air. When a plane was expected, the huts could literally be picked up and carried to the side of the airstrips so that the planes could land.

Robert DeFauw's evening radio schedule with General Pao Sarasin contained intelligence information that led them to believe that within the next 17 days a large shipment of heroin would be smuggled out of Muang Khop. And that Agent DeFauw was to proceed immediately to Muang Khop, 60 miles away over the mountains. General Sarasin was to finish any necessary work on his landing strips. For, if there were Shan prisoners to be brought over land from Ban Namo to Louang-Namtha, his intentions was to fly in to bring them out.

***

At last everyone was awake. The world was waiting. The opium had been harvested, there was lots of work to be done, and General Chung Che Fu wanted to get back to Muang Sing to supervise it. General Fu, Rocky, Leo and Fu's men spent the next 2 days unloading the caravan and stockpiling the opium for future use. Leo and Rocky ate around 5:00 o'clock, still talking to General Fu about their future plans. By half past 6:00, well prepared, Leo and Rocky were on their way. The hillsides and its easiest routes to the airfield were becoming familiar to Rocky and Leo. The glow of the sunset spread warmly over the tall mountains that lay beyond the airfield's runway.

By 7:30, the moon was full and strong, the stars brilliant. Once their eyes became accustomed to the eerie shadows that played over the rough ground whenever a white cloud drifted across the sky, they found it a simple matter of putting one foot in front of the other. Leo had been prepared. Around his head, he had slipped a broad elastic band with its attached flashlight over his brow—ready to be switched on.

When Rocky, Wong, Leo, and Lutken reached the plane, they unloaded the Jeep, and then loaded the 200-gallon metal drums that contained approximately 175 kilos (or 385 pounds) of uncut heroin, aboard the Learjet 35.

The Learjet 35 was magnificent. It had thrust-enhancing winglets and high-performance Garrett turbofan engines. It was fuel-efficient and could fly up to 22 passenger miles for every gallon of fuel used. It had a coast-to-coast range, and a top-end speed of over 500 miles per hour.

"We're less than 800 miles from Hong Kong," Rocky said with his eyes glued on the runway ahead; for they were transporting a king's ransom in cargo and flying a powerful plane, but had a short runway, and that worried them. Rocky looked at his wristwatch, fastened his seatbelt, and then gave Wong Lee the "thumbs-up" sign for lift-off.

Leo sat aboard the Learjet in silence, a jacket around his hunched shoulders; staring out at the foliage and watching the wind-molded airfield on the left side of the runway… when all of a sudden Leo begin to shout "Hey Rocky!" craning his neck with a double take. "We better get this bitch in the air!!! There's freaking soldiers out there with guns!!!" Leo ducked low in his seat.

Rocky and Wong became tense, too. Then, just as Wong nodded in acknowledgement to take off, all-hell broke-loose as automatic gunfire rang-out across the left side of the Learjet's bow.

"I had a feeling this shit was going to happen!!" Leo said aloud. "It was just too easy to be true!"

"Just keep your head down!" Rocky shouted as Wong Lee jammed the Lear's throttle into full power. "They'll have to stop us to take us!" he added. The first round of fire had been fired with a mixture of tracer rounds. Warning shots, but the second hail of bullets was meant to kill. The bullets had been laced with white phosphorus tips as they poured in and around the plane like a hail storm. One bullet cut Rocky across the cheek and another grazed Wong on the arm, causing Leo to duck down in between the seats.

"Get this motherfucker off the ground!" Leo shouted. "Hurry, hurry, hurry, these motherfuckers trying to kiss us." Just as shots were fired again, the bullet riddled Learjet was up and away with alarm bells going off and all. They flew over the muddy Mekong River adjoined by Laos and Thailand. A few hours later, they dropped the heroin in the South China Sea where it was picked up by China Seamen.

***

Within 2 days Senior Drug Enforcement Agent Robert DeFauw had reached the Laotian authorities at Muang Khop, where he and his troops came over the hills crouched low, without clattering or stumbling, and moved within a couple hundred yards of the airfield. Agent DeFauw and his men had accelerated their approach to the evening's vantage point, but at the path to the airfield, they halted.

***

Earlier that week, General Fu had instructed his troops to dig deep, long and wide trenches between the hills and the airfield to give themselves the edge. The D.E.A. troops would have to get across the muddy trenches, filled with blood-sucking leeches, elephant manure, and God knows what else, in order to be in maximum effective range to halt the shipments of heroin.

Around 1:45 a.m. that night, they landed at Hong Kong Airport to service and refuel the Learjet for the next leg in their flight plan, Amsterdam, Holland. Wong Lee had flown the Learjet below radar, dropped the heroin into the China Sea, and then appeared on radar before they reached Hong Kong airspace. Whether or not Thai authorities had identified them and reported

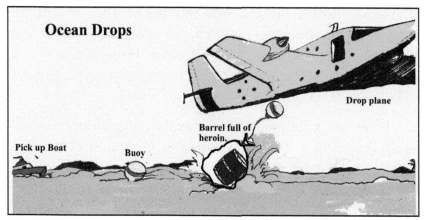

them to the authorities in Hong Kong, Bangkok, or Singapore, still remained a mystery to them, because Wong had headed the Learjet in the direction of Singapore, in an attempt to lead them to believe that was where they were headed.

Leo hesitated to pass the wide door at customs and immigration, afraid he, Rocky and Wong had been reported to Hong Kong authorities. The airport was a large, high-roofed modernized place, and beautiful. Several lines at the table; several serious-faced men in uniform gray jackets, an opposite set of doors firmly closed, and a host of notices around its walls. Nothing I can understand, thought Leo.

He heard Wong gasp, as he too stared at the notices. Leo held out his passport and waited for further directions... "Do you speak English?" Leo asked in his politest voice, adding a friendly smile to sweeten the atmosphere; two pairs of dark eyes staring at him, then at Rocky and Wong. Solemnly, the passports were studied. Solemnly, the expressionless eyes looked at them, and then looked back at the passports. Trouble? Leo wondered. Yet the officials must understand English, for they could decipher the passports. Or could they? They were talking together now, in a burst of indecipherable vowels and consonants that left Leo worried. How do a couple of idiots who can't understand a word of English manage to cope with this place? Then one of the customs agents with their passports still in his hand moved to a telephone. Definitely trouble, Leo decided. He looked at Rocky who had a bandage across his cheek, resting his weight against a table, white-faced and in pain, and saying nothing.

There was a long wait. Their small baggage was examined briefly, but closely. Leo and his friends spent most of the time watching the other travelers being questioned while parcels and baskets spilled out on the tables. Hotter by the minute, Leo thought, and wished that the opposite doors could be opened in case they had to make a break and run.

It did open. An authoritative middle-aged looking man entered briskly, well-dressed in blue. He was carefully groomed with dark-hair, dark-eyes and a dark mustache. He gave a sharp glance at the wilting men, a brief look at their passports, and then a massive exchange of words with the official who had telephoned. Then the stranger came forward, spoke in excellent English, his smile friendly. "Everything is solved now," he assured Leo. "Your friends are ill?"

"No," Leo replied. "Dog bites, but no communicable diseases being smuggled into Hong Kong; they're just exhausted from the trip. They'll be alright once we get to a hotel and get a few hours' rest."

"You have a specific hotel in mind?" the official asked.

"No, we thought we could get advice from a tourist bureau. Is there one near this airport?" Rocky interceded.

"Not here. Do you speak Chinese?" the official asked.

Rocky, Leo and Wong shook their heads. "No. Perhaps the tourist Police could direct us..." Wong responded.

The man brushed that aside. "You should have a guide and interpreter. Not expensive," he added quickly. "How long will you guys be here?"

"Until tomorrow," Wong replied again.

"One night?" Then you should consider one of the large hotels where English is spoken. For one night, not too expensive," the man suggested.

He knows who we are, Leo was thinking. What is he? Someone high up in the D.E.A., I bet that it's the Thai authorities doing. Somehow they have arranged all this. Leo drew from his jacket pocket the small hand guide of Hong Kong he had bought back in Amsterdam. A year out of date, but the streets stayed the same although hotels might change. He consulted the list he had marked. "I thought this hotel might be suitable." Leo said.

The official nodded his head, and then signaled toward the door from which he came. A much younger man approached. Chinese, Leo decided—those same dark brows and solemn eyes; but in dress and manner he could have passed for an American student. The young man stood still, smiling and pleasant, while his long name was rattled off in a quick introduction. Leo could only catch part of it: Matsuto, he thought... "Most reliable," the man in the blue suit told them, and turned away for a brief word with the immigration official who saluted. Actually saluted, Leo thought in amazement. Then, as quickly as he had appeared, he departed.

Matsuto said, "Everything is alright now. You guys can leave. I shall bring a taxi. Wait here!" He pointed to the doorway to the street, a street of high/low buildings and a maze of traffic movement, noise, and complete chaos.

They left Hong Kong's Kowloon airport. Matsuto was polite and efficient. He even directed the taxi to the hotel Leo had selected and stood on the walkway outside the airport until they rode out of sight.

***

Leo and his pals believed the Hong Kong authorities were trying to steer them into a set-up.

The hotel selected had been built of wood, one bathroom to a floor, lethargic ceiling fans, no dining room, and no English spoken in spite of its advertisement. Otherwise passible enough for a grade-"D" establishment, although the floors needed scrubbing and the lopsided curtains had a year's worth of dust ingrained in them.

"A change in plans," Rocky told Leo and Wong. The taxi pulled up to the Hotel Skylark. They got out of the taxi and walked into the lobby. Once the taxi was gone, they came back out and hailed another taxi.

"The Lucky Hotel please," Rocky said to the driver. When they arrived at the Lucky Hotel, Rocky went inside. Leo instructed the taxi driver to pull around the block. Rocky did a bogus check-in and slipped out the side door of the hotel. He briskly walked and jumped into the taxi with Leo and Wong and they sped off.

"The Red Light District," Rocky instructed the driver.

Hong Kong's Red Light District consisted of naughty massage parlors, prostitutes and sex dens.

"Stop here," Rocky said to the driver as he pointed at a prostitute standing on the side of the road.

Rocky, Leo and Wong got out of the taxi and looked around to see if anyone was following them. They approached the prostitute with an exchange of a few words and gave her the room key to the Lucky Hotel and then blended into the crowd. Moments later they hailed another cab.

"Take us to the Sheraton-Hong Kong Hotel… 20 Nathan Road," Rocky said. The threesome looked at each other and laughed.

Rocky made his phone calls from the Sheraton lobby. "All is settled, I directed the seamen who plucked the shipment from the ocean to the restaurant. Tomorrow afternoon, we sightsee! There will be lots of walking, many streets." He suggested, giving Leo a clue as to the place he had in mind for a meeting.

"Thank goodness," Leo gestured with his hands in a sigh of relief. "I have never been shot at before." Rocky and Wong looked at one another astounded. Then simultaneously looked at Leo and broke into laughter. They hit the sack early that night and the following morning treated themselves to the Sheraton's rooftop sauna, pool, health club, and shopping mall. Then Leo, Rocky and Wong partied a few hours with some ladies. After a short lunch, they felt crisp and confident as ever.

Rocky had begun his conversation in his usual way, by answering everything before it was asked. Rocky, Leo and Wong prepared to leave. They dropped all conversation as they reached the street and concentrated on finding a taxi.

The taxi driver took them to a small area of the walled and covered market place. There were more than 500 little shops jam-packed along narrow, twisting streets with the noise and confusion of bargaining everywhere. Chinese and foreigners all crowded together vying for the objects on display. It was easy to lose anyone overly interested in their movements. Rocky limited their choice of routes and Leo paid attention to the direction he followed rather than let his mind be sidetracked by antiques, furniture and gold bracelets.

Leo, Rocky and Wong left the Market Place and entered Yin Ching's Chinese Restaurant. Ching's restaurant hadn't changed. Red-and-white patterned still decorated the walls. An overhead fan rotated lazily wafting the smell of well-seasoned food throughout the dining area. Leo and Wong loitered among the crowd inside to make sure they weren't being followed and then rejoined Rocky, who was greeted by Yow Yin Ching and escorted to a vault-like room that was both discreet and comfortable in back of the restaurant.

"A good morning?" Rocky inquired politely.

"A very good morning," Ching said. He bowed and shook hands, then stood back to look at Leo, Rocky and Wong, not trying to conceal his pleasure. He was enthusiastic as ever and doing all the talking. Leo could only hope the afternoon could be as successful as the mission they just completed. "The drums of heroin came in this morning boss and we've already prepared your shipment," Ching continued to say.

"You're a good man, Ching," Rocky nodded, seeming pleased. "Now, let me introduce you to our new contact from the United States." He gestured in Leo's direction. "Ching, this is Leo Stegner. Leo, meet Yow Yin Ching, one of the best heroin controllers in the business.

Ching smiled. "Welcome to Hong Kong," he said. Leo and Ching shook hands. "I imagine you have an awesome responsibility, eh?"

Leo sighed, then smiled, and said, "Well, it wasn't exactly what I had in mind as a career move, but it's the best damn investment I've ever made." They all laughed briefly, and then suddenly became serious again.

"So," Wong said abruptly, "How is the canning business coming, Ching?"

Ching's smiled grew. "I couldn't be more pleased." Ching was urbane, witty, and fragile in manner, but very much in charge of Rocky's new $200,000-dollar Soybean Distribution Factory that also supplied Hong Kong's rapid growing economy with over 20,000 cases of caviar and pork-n-beans per day. The factory, now equipped with the latest canning machinery, was merely a camouflage to disguise Rocky's "Loose-knit Heroin Network," processing, packaging, labeling, and distribution facilities. His new facilities now enabled Rocky to create more innovative methods of smuggling heroin abroad, that would eventually revolutionize the entire narcotic smuggling industry. Concealing it in pressurized canned goods was one such technique commonly referred to in that part of the world as the "Shell Game."

Ching prepared them a large meal, then paid his courier pilot and sent him to Hong Kong Kowloon airport to fly the Learjet to a private out of the way airfield on the outskirts of Kowloon Hong Kong.

An hour later, they loaded the 20-cases of soybeans, at least that's what the labels said they were, but in actuality it was 200-pounds of uncut, now canned heroin, into the bed of Ching's delivery truck and escorted the driver to the airfield.

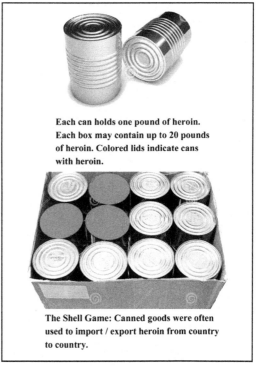

Each can holds one pound of heroin. Each box may contain up to 20 pounds of heroin. Colored lids indicate cans with heroin.

The Shell Game: Canned goods were often used to import / export heroin from country to country.

***

On the way back to the Netherlands, the trio smoked a few heroin joints (heroin mixed with non-mentholated tobacco) to relax their nerves. They streaked across Dutch Airspace, landed at Amsterdam Schiphol Airport without any fear of being arrested or suspected of any wrong doings. The trio cleared Dutch Customs, declared the Soybean cargo, then loaded the shipment into one of Rocky's Import/Export trucks, and later into a nearby lab for processing and distribution.

It was quite obvious that joining forces would work to the mutual benefit of both parties. Leo would provide the people to be trained as couriers/smugglers, the knowledge of areas within the United States, and the financial contacts, while Rocky would provide contact with the China Mafia via the Golden Triangle, heroin, leadership, and various forms of support. Their adventure to the Golden Triangle would be the makings of the most classic partnership between an American and an Oriental that would make the China Mafia's "Loose-knit Heroin Network" one of the most formidable narcotic trafficking organizations ever to operate.

Chapter 8

"The Snitch"

By the end of 1983, both the Shan Northern Hill Tribesmen and the Northeastern Burma farmers had harvested, sold, and transported a record 4,500 tons of opium to General Chung Che Fu and the China Mafia's clandestine processing labs.

Rumors of the huge shipments had reached the busy streets where heroin addicts were out and about looking for the next fix.

Leo, an avid reader of worldwide newspapers kept his eyes and ears to the ground when it came to current events involving the heroin dynasty throughout the world.

In Buenos Aires, Argentina, the heroin connections in the financially saturated San Martin territory waited nervously near the telephone, while the French Connection—who had the largest territories to supply, and others as far as the Middle East—lined the canals and seaports, in tugboats, speed boats, yachts, and seaplanes awaiting pickups from their individual connections.

The U.S. Mafia would be the last to get the word. Due to the dangers involved in smuggling heroin into the United States they would have to pay more, much more.

Leo was acutely aware that Mexico and other Latin American connections were independents.

Meanwhile, Military D.E.A., the C.I.A., Interpol, and U.S. D.E.A. abroad and in the United States were busy searching the

Senator
PAULA
HAWKINS
NEWSLETTER
U.S. SENATOR · FLORIDA

Autumn 1985
Volume 5 Number II

Senator Hawkins swears in a witness at a hearing on international drug smuggling. The witness' identity is concealed for his safety.

NARCOTICS CONTROL COMMISSION TO AID IN DRUG ABUSE WAR

In what promises to be a significant addition to the war against illegal narcotics, Senator Hawkins fought and won passage of her legislation creating the United States-International Narcotics Control Commission (USINCC).

The Commission, structured along the lines of the Helsinki Commission which monitors compliance with human rights treaties, will oversee and promote international compliance with narcotics control treaties. The USINCC will also monitor and encourage U.S. government and private programs to expand international cooperation in the war against drug abuse.

Over 90 percent of the illegal narcotics consumed in the U.S. is produced abroad. And although all major drug producing nations have treaty obligations to eradicate their illegal crops, world production of marijuana, cocaine, and heroin is at a record high. Several hearings she has held on international narcotics have revealed the extent of the problem.

"No problem is more threatening to the health and well-being of Floridians and all Americans than illegal narcotics," said Senator Hawkins. "If only the treaties we already have were followed, the flow of illegal narcotics into the United States would be drastically cut."

streets for clues and getting closer. Every major heroin connection throughout the world was trying to find a way to filter their supplies through the China Mafia's illicit "Loose-knit Heroin Network."

DRUG ENFORCEMENT SCORECARD: 97th CONGRESS

During the 97th Congress, Senator Hawkins targeted drug enforcement as a top priority. Here is a look at some of her activities in this area:

1. Created the Senate Drug Enforcement Caucus, which now has 26 members, to make drug enforcement a Senate priority and to focus national attention on the drug epidemic in the United States.

2. Held hearings, as Chairman of the Senate Subcommittee on Investigations and General Oversight, into the problem of drugs in the American school system and introduced legislation making it a federal offense to distribute illegal narcotics on or near elementary or secondary schools. The legislation, which also stiffens penalties for offenders, including the imposition of mandatory minimum sentences on repeat offenders, was passed by the Senate.

3. Introduced legislation that would effectively ban the manufacture and sale of methaqualone, or Quaaludes, a controversial and addictive drug which is the most abused narcotic among teenagers and young adults. Senator Hawkins also urged the government of the Peoples Republic of China to cease exporting methaqualone, pointing out that 90 percent of the methaqualone illegally sold in the U.S. comes from Red China. A positive response has been received from Chinese leaders and curtailment has begun.

4. Co-authored an amendment requiring countries receiving economic assistance under the Caribbean Basin Initiative to cooperate with U.S. efforts to control illegal drugs, an effort aimed at making drug eradication a foreign policy priority.

5. Formulated an eight-point program of Administrative initiatives to reduce crime, drug trafficking and illegal immigration in Florida. The majority of these proposals were incorporated into the President's South Florida Task Force.

6. Introduced a resolution urging the President to promote a United Nations Year Against Drug Abuse. This resolution also passed the Senate.

Senator Hawkins, Vice President Bush inspect drugs seized by Coast Guard.

***

That afternoon had been Leo's turn to wait near the telephone in his most private Bay Hill estate on Orlando's southwest side of town.

Rocky had dispatched Robert Plush, an international heroin smuggler who carried phony credentials that said he was a market researcher in the areas of foods and services. Plush's mission was to transport 30 pounds of 98% pure pink heroin, valued at 7.5 million dollars wholesale to Florida. Eva, Elfi, Hillery, Silki, and Bagetta had taken a badly needed vacation across the Swiss border. They had begun to draw suspicion because of their many trips through Customs and Immigration. Plush was to take a direct route from Amsterdam to Paris, to New York, to Miami, and finally to Orlando.

Thomas Scalli, Leo's right-hand man had already contacted prospective buyers, took their bids, and waited patiently for the soon-to-arrive heroin shipment. But Cecil Beckman, one of Leo's highest paying clients and Scalli's closest friend, just couldn't wait in Miami. The thought of having 98% pure pink heroin in his grips again seemed to have controlled his sense of direction and his will for patience. Beckman had claimed that he happened to be passing through Orlando on legitimate business and since he was there, he might as well save everybody some time and pickup his piece of the rock.

When Robert Plush telephoned Leo around midnight from McCoy International Jetport, Cecil Beckman and Thomas Scalli were with him. Beckman would go along for the ride, but Scalli and Beckman's driver would remain behind to monitor the phone calls. It was half past midnight when they pulled in McCoy's passenger arrival area in Leo's recently purchased Lincoln Continental Mark V. Beckman remained in the car while Leo went in to check everything out. Upon entering the airport's lobby, he spotted Robert Plush from the description given to him by Rocky. He was reading a Sentinel Star newspaper. He wore dark-tinted glasses, cowboy boots, a cowboy hat, and jeans with a red plaid shirt. Plush was clean shaven with a handle-bar mustache and sported a crew-cut, hair style. They talked a few moments, exchanged code phrases to make sure each was who they claimed to be. But when Leo asked Plush about the heroin shipment, Plush hesitated, and then replied, "I stashed it in locker 666 here in the airport."

Leo fumed… then grunted through his teeth in a demanding tone of voice. "A LOCKER! What in the hell is it doing there?"

Robert Plush, the shorter of the two, smoothed the front of his mustache with the back of his finger, then said, "Hey, I put it in the locker as a security precaution... How am I supposed to know what I'm up against?" He gestured with both hands.

Leo threw up both hands. "Okay! Then let's have the key to the locker."

"I don't have it," Plush replied. "I taped it on the back of the water fountain," he pointed.

Leo sucked in his breath and wondered momentarily if this guy was on the level. "Well let's go get it and get the hell out of here," he suggested seriously.

"But what about my fee?" Plush insisted. "My flight leaves in an hour. I was supposed to get...."

Leo, equally cautious, looked Plush directly in the eyes and fired back, "You'll get it when I see the goods."

At the water fountain, Plush drank some water, retrieved the key taped on the back of it and handed it to Leo. They strolled over to locker '666' and Leo opened it, removed the cases labeled 'Soybeans' and stacked them on the floor. Meanwhile Robert Plush flagged a skycap and paid him to haul the camouflaged heroin shipment to the car. There were 3 boxes with 36 cans in each. Each box contained 10 one pound cans of heroin and 24 actual cans of soybeans.

Stegner unbuttoned his suit coat, took a white envelope containing $4,000 from the inside pocket, and handed it to Plush. Plush grabbed the envelope, but Leo refused to turn it loose. "I think you have something for me" Leo said.

"Oh yeah, I almost forgot" Plush replied, seemingly agitated. He reached into his pocket and pulled out the 'Pink Elephant' seal. The back of it was laced with a thin hard layer of dry pink colored heroin. "Rocky told me to give this to you as a sign that everything is cool."

Leo took the seal and examined it closely both front and back, then he lifted up his left pants leg and stuck the seal inside the rim of his stock and sighed with relief. From the first time he saw the seal at Rocky's place in Amsterdam, Leo wanted it. To him, having it in his possession symbolized his membership in the China Mafia because the seal was a well-guarded secret unknown to the public at large.

Plush quickly stuffed the money in his pocket without counting it, and in a sudden urge said, "I've got to go to the restroom. I'll meet you at the car in a few to see you off... okay?"

Leo took a deep breath and said, "All right! But if you're not there when we're loaded, we're not waiting." *Delays and more delays; what is this guy up to?* Leo asked himself. Leo was anxious to get this problem, Plush, and Cecil Beckman off his hands.

Plush nodded, turned, and strode into the men's restroom.

***

It was empty except for D.E.A. Drug Enforcement Agent Miller whose feet were visible below the partition to the toilet.

"It's all set," said Plush.

Agent Miller unlatched the toilet and handed Plush an empty briefcase and a change of clothing.

Plush stripped off his trousers with his back to the door that opened to the interior of the airport. "Stuff these in there, will you?" He handed Miller his old trousers and motioned to the briefcase. "You and your people only have a few minutes to bust him, so you'd better hurry." He stepped into his new trousers and began tucking in his shirt tail. "I'll be seeing you in the Netherlands in eight hours or so." He stepped aside to let Agent Miller leave.

"Good luck, Robert," Miller said.

"No big deal," said Robert Plush. He finished mashing his cowboy hat and old clothes into the large briefcase Miller had left him. He waited five long minutes, and then casually walked out, briefcase in hand.

Leo and the skycap left the airport through the exit opposite the gift shops and reservation counters and headed toward the asphalt parking lot. Cecil "Nassau" Beckman, the dark-complexioned man sat in Leo's Lincoln Continental suppressing his urge to look back over his shoulder while staring intently down the Beeline Highway.

***

Agent Miller ran from the airport lobby. He signaled for his men to close in and follow his prearranged lead. Miller circled along the edge of the parking lot at the front of McCoy International Jetport, then through the Budget rental car lot. He radioed his agents and instructed them to seal off the entire perimeter. Leo and Beckman were totally surrounded. Miller always maintained in discussions of such kinds of duty that the best tactic is whatever is simple and direct. "Too much finesse can get you in trouble," he had warned Robert Plush.

Agent Miller and several of his agents snuck up behind Leo in the airport's parking lot. Miller tapped Leo lightly on his shoulder, and then said, "FREEZE!! Right where you are!" He reached around Leo's left shoulder and flashed his badge. "Put your hands up!" Miller demanded.

Leo froze, threw his arms up, and turned around, startled. "What in the hell...?" He started to speak but stopped. He was facing the muzzle of a cocked .45 caliber automatic pistol, and surrounded by a swarm of agents with Beretta's, pump shotguns and M-16's.

The agent said, "D.E.A. You're under arrest! If you twitch, I'll blow your balls off!" Miller lowered the muzzle of the pistol, and then began to search Leo. "You'll live, but it won't be fun!"

Leo's head jerked in the direction of the airport's main entrance. Plush was standing in the doorway smiling. "That son-ova bitch set me up!" Leo said. He looked in Beckman's direction. He was being placed under arrest as well.

"What are you talking about?" Miller asked.

"Robert Plush! That bastard over there!" Leo gestured with his head. There were some things Leo liked; the value of simply being clever. But he hated the prejudice, the deceit, and the way one always stabbed a friend in the back.

Miller grinned. "Rocky is next. Who's your friend? A bodyguard?"

"No! Just a friend here on vacation!! He asked if he could come along for the ride," Leo replied angrily.

Beckman quickly confirmed this and claimed he knew nothing about anything.

"Okay, you two have the right to remain silent and anything you say or do can and will be held against you in a court of law," Miller advised. He was accompanied by D.E.A. agents from Tampa, the Orlando Police Department, and the Orange County Sheriff's Department. "Why do you sell this stuff and take such chances?" And who else are you connected with?" Milder added authoritatively.

Leo laughed, and then said, "I have the right to remain silent, and anything I say can and will be used against me in a court of law. Isn't that what you told me? Now what about my car?"

Miller was unnerved as much by Leo's apparent indifference as by the enormity of his crime. "So, you want to be a smartass huh?" Miller said bitterly. He motioned toward the car with his pistol. "Well if I was you, I'd forget about that there car." He grinned. "Where you're going my man, you'll never see it again."

Leo backed off mostly out of fear Miller may try to take advantage of him on the way to the police station. Suddenly Leo had a flashback… a flashback to that moment when Detective Sergeant Hood struck him across the bridge of his nose with a weighted handkerchief. Leo had heard through the grapevine that OPD's Narco Squad had a reputation for making detours and fucking people up on the way to the police station. However Leo and Beckman were in luck. They were in the custody of the Orange County Sheriff Department.

"Stick those arms out. Hands close together," Miller ordered. His agents handcuffed both men's hands, running the handcuffs under their belts as they locked them shut. Then Miller ordered the bystanders to clear the area, while his agents stuffed Leo and Beckman in separate vehicles, then set off for the Orange County Sheriff's Department in downtown Orlando, calling ahead that they had apprehended suspects from the airport stake-out and were bringing them in for booking.

***

Unbeknown to Leo, Robert Plush had played his "snitcher's" role well, perhaps better than anyone had imagined. He had smuggled heroin for Rocky for several years, then got busted going through U.S. Customs in New York, with 30-pounds of heroin strapped around his body.

This happened around June of 1982, several months before Rocky was attacked by the stranger with the lethal umbrella who rendered him temporarily paralyzed. It was Plush who hired the stranger that day, after Leo, Bagetta, Elfi, and Hillery left for West Germany in the camper. It was Plush who hastily decided to cooperate with the D.E.A. and bust anyone connected with the China Mafia. And it was Plush who sensed that Rocky was getting too close then set Rocky and Leo up for the BUST. Through bits and pieces of information, Rocky suspected that Robert Plush was responsible, but wasn't 100% sure.

There was more; not only had Robert Plush, the Caucasian male in his early 30's from Tennessee arranged the neat heroin bust, but he had also double-crossed the D.E.A. as well. Plush, a creative scavenger had taken 33 of the 36-pound shipment of 98% pure heroin, except for 3 pounds of it before he left Amsterdam in route to the United States. He had replaced 33 of the 16-ounce cans labeled 'Soybeans', with some other soybean product. He then notified the D.E.A. of his expected arrival into the United States with 3 pounds of pure heroin—disguised in canned goods to set Leo up for a drug bust at the McCoy airport rendezvous.

Now Plush was on his way back to Amsterdam to meet Rocky and Wong for another prearranged rendezvous—to set them up.

***

The Orange County Sheriff's Department was located in downtown Orlando near Lake Eola on a road that led to several large bank buildings and resort hotels. It was built of discolored bricks and blue tile that resembled a successful business establishment.

On the way there, Leo remained silent. Leo thought there should have been something to say—some dramatic gesture he should have made. Instead, he stared out the window of the police car at the leafless, wintry landscape. His eyes stung, but he didn't cry. He couldn't. Leo was overwhelmed by fear brought on from thinking back two decades ago when he was arrested as a grand theft auto suspect.

It was nearly 1:30 a.m. by the time Agent Miller reached the Orange County Jail. He took his prisoners upstairs to the booking room and turned Leo, Beckman, and the case of soybeans concealing the three pounds of heroin over to Lieutenant Butch Reed who had just returned from the arrest scene. Officer Reed thanked everyone for their cooperation in modifying their appearance as airline ticket agents, porters, gift shop salesmen, and taxi drivers.

Leo watched Lieutenant Reed remove the heroin cargo and placed it in the evidence room, and then he fingerprinted both Leo and Beckman and put them in lockup.

An hour later, the door to the lockup swung open. A fat, sloppy dressed guard called out, "Leo Stegner, you have a visitor." The guard escorted Leo into an interrogation room. Agent Miller from the D.E.A. and Lieutenant Reed, who offered no deals and made no threats, was there to interrogate him. Agent Miller, after a few preliminary inquiries concerning name, age, address and characteristics advised Leo he could have an attorney anytime he wanted and had the right to make a telephone call. Leo chose to make the call.

Lieutenant Reed allowed Leo to make his call. The telephone booth was located on the 3rd floor, across the hall from the evidence room.

And when it was Beckman's turn he did the same. Cecil Beckman telephoned his people in Miami and told them to contact his attorney and bondsman. More important, Leo telephoned Thomas Scalli, who was waiting patiently at Leo's home to hear from them. He was astonished and devastated over what had happened. He was so upset he demolished furniture all over the room.

Leo calmed Scalli down, then told him in code to telephone Rocky in Amsterdam, inform him of his arrest and that Robert Plush was responsible— a D.E.A. informant, and that Plush was on his way back to Amsterdam that very moment with a posse of D.E.A. agents to arrest them. Leo also told Scalli to advise Rocky that he should relocate all the heroin safe houses immediately and get the hell out of the Netherlands altogether.

Leo heard later from Scalli that his warning was delivered to Rocky immediately. Within one hour Rocky, Wong and all their Mafia connections throughout the Netherlands, Europe, and the Mid-East who had any dealings with Robert Plush had relocated their labs and safe houses, then scattered to the four corners of the earth. They had an eight-hour head start over Plush and the United States D.E.A. agents.

Leo, who was now tucked away neatly in the holding cell, was being tormented by his own demons. He still had the China Mafia's seal in his sock and was soon scheduled to be strip searched. Leo didn't know what to do with the seal and now regretted having it. He knew that if he was caught with the seal in his possession, it would further prove his connection with the China Mafia when he stood before the judge. The court will surely give him life imprisonment. He pondered whether to destroy it, swallow it or hope the guards overlooked it. He heard the sound of shuffling feet. Two guards were coming in his direction. He quickly made the decision to destroy it for two reasons; Leo was afraid that for the first time in history of the China Mafia existence, he would be the one responsible for revealing the decade upon decade secret of the seal, thus making him a 'marked man' with no place to run, no place to hide, not even in prison. He was also afraid that this would ruin his chances for revenge on Joe's killer, Sam Capelli. Leo tore the seal into tiny pieces and dropped them into the floor drain of the holding cell.

He was taken to be fingerprinted and strip-searched, then placed back in the holding cell. Leo would've given a year's salary to see the expression on Plush and the D.E.A.'s faces when they arrived at Rocky's clandestine labs and safe houses to find nothing but trash and debris. Boy! How Leo laughed that night in his jail cell. The other inmates thought he was a little crazy! But the joke had been on the D.E.A. And Robert Plush would be a marked man for the rest of his life.

Leo often wondered who would be the first to put a bullet in Plush. The Chinese Mafia, or the DEA? Because in the streets, Plush would have been known as one of the worst kind of slime-buckets in the drug business... A SNITCH AND A JUNKY!

The following Monday morning, Leo and Beckman were arraigned at the U.S. Courthouse and Post Office Building before Judge Samuel Duncan, the United States Magistrate for a preliminary hearing. Persons present were U.S. Prosecuting Attorney Robert T. Briggs, Chief U.S. Probation Official, Rubin S. Lee, U.S. Marshal, Jerry Stonewall, and Stegner's lawyer, Dan Kirkland.

The Courthouse was overflowing with spectators and the Press. It was an enormous beige building that took up the entire square block of Hughey Avenue and Robinson Street. Of the many courtrooms in the building, only four rooms were reserved for criminal trials: 22, 23, 40, and 44. Room 40 had been chosen for this trail because it was the largest.

The corridors outside were jam-packed, and the U.S. Marshals in plainclothes were stationed at the two entrances to control the crowd. Newspapers from as far north as New York carried the accounts of Leo's heroin bust. There were long lines in front of the telephone booths and the sandwich stand near the corridor's entrance downstairs sold out of food in the first 10-minutes.

Jerry Stonewall, Chief U.S. Marshal in Orlando, personally supervised the security arrangements. Newspaper photographers were everywhere, and Stonewall managed to have his photograph taken with pleasing frequency. Passes to the courtroom were limited. The actual seating of the trial was commonplace. Courtroom 40 was on the 4th floor of the courthouse. Musty and old, it had been the arena for millions of legal battles which had taken place over the years. The room was about 50-feet wide and 80-feet long. The seats were divided into 3 rows, 6-feet apart, with 12 wooden benches to a row. A section of the room had been reserved for the press, with several representatives from: CBS, ABC, NBC, United Press International, and the Associated Press, among others. The circumstances of the heroin trial itself would have been sensational enough, but the persona-non-gratis (Leo and Beckman) were so famous that the excited spectators didn't know where to look first.

Leo smashed a camera on the way into the courtroom and adamantly refused to speak to the press. He wanted to preserve his anonymity in case he decided to get back into the business. He sat withdrawn and silent, an invisible wall around him. On the front row in the courtroom, Stella Stegner, Leo's mother, sat at the end of the bench, exquisitely beautiful, her honey skin a bit paler than usual, and dressed as though she had just stepped out of an Escada boutique. There was a regal quality about Stella that Leo wouldn't see again for a long time.

The excitement of the spectators began to heighten as their bloodlust for justice grew. The emotions that flowed toward Leo was so strong it became an almost physical presence in the courtroom. It was not a feeling of sympathy or empathy; it was simply a feeling of high expectation.

The case was listed as: United States of America vs. Leo Stegner, Cecil Blackman, Rocky Congo Lee, and Other persons unknown to the Grand Jury.

The Grand Jury Charges were listed:

Count One— From, on or about, October 29, 1986 to, on or about November 10th, 1986, in Orange County, Florida, in the Middle District of Florida, and elsewhere,

Leo Stegner

Rocky Congo Lee and Other persons unknown to the Grand Jury

Knowingly, intentionally, and unlawfully, did import or cause to be imported approximately 3 pounds of heroin, a controlled substance listed in Schedule 1, Title 21, U.S.C. & 812, into the United States from Amsterdam, Holland; in violation of Title 21, U.S.C. & 952(a) and 960(a)(1) and Title 18 U.S.C. & 2.

Count Two— From, on or about, October 29, 1986, up to and including November 10, 1986, in Orange County, Florida, in the Middle District of Florida and elsewhere,

Leo Stegner

Cecil Beckman

Willfully and knowingly did combine, conspire, confederate, and agree together, and with each other, and with Other persons unknown to the Grand Jury, to commit offenses against the United States of America, that is to knowingly, intentionally, and unlawfully possess, with the intent to distribute heroin, a controlled substance listed in Schedule 1, Title 21 U.S.C. & 812; in violation of Title 21 U.S.C. & 841(1); and in furtherance of said conspiracy and in order to effect the objects thereof, the Defendants did commit, among other acts, the following:

(1) That on or about November 10, 1986, at Orlando, Florida, Leo Stegner had a phone conversation with Robert Plush.

(2) That on or about November 10, 1986, Leo Stegner met Robert Plush at the Orlando International Jetport, Orlando, Florida.

(3) That on or about November 10, 1986, at Orlando International Jetport, Orlando, Florida, Leo Stegner, retrieved a key for locker number 666 located at the Orlando International Jetport.

(4) That on or about November 10, 1986, at the Orlando International Jetport, Orlando, Florida, Leo Stegner removed the contents of locker number 666.

All in violation of Title 21 U.S.C. & I 846, and Title 18 U.S.C. & 2.

Count Three— On or about November 10, 1986, in Orange County, Florida, in the Middle District of Florida,

Leo Stegner

Cecil Beckman

Did knowingly, intentionally, and unlawfully possess with the intent to distribute approximately 3-pounds of heroin, a controlled substance listed in Schedule 1, Title 21 U.S.C. & 812; in violation of Title 21 U.S.C. & 841(a)(1) and Title 18 U.S.C. & 2.

All morning Leo and Beckman sat listening to the testimony against them. The tidal-wave of words washed over them. Some of the words registered, some of them seemed untrue, but that didn't anger or excite them. It wasn't just that Leo Stegner, like many of the people in the courtroom and perhaps on the Grand Jury, had a hard time following the disjointed testimony. Leo didn't much care what was said. He didn't see that it would have any effect on him. He remembered clearly what happened the night of his arrest, and while some D.E.A. witnesses presented an accurate picture of events, he knew that when his turn came to testify, he would swear to an even more accurate version. The crowd in the courtroom reacted distastefully when Attorney Dan Kirkland entered a plea of not guilty on the Defendant's behalf. Kirkland who had been hired by Scalli was viewed as one of the most competent lawyers in the Central Florida area.

Leo knew no matter what he said now, he couldn't save himself. He knew the one thing he could do, was limit the damage. Tell his story in such a way that nobody else, including Beckman was hurt and nobody ever learned enough to ask him painful questions.

Attorney Kirkland scored poorly in round one. Judge Duncan found the evidence presented strong enough to deny Leo's bond, but granted Beckman's bond. Both cases were turned over to the Criminal Court.

Kirkland fought persistently despite oral argument and opposition from the Prosecutor, Briggs. "Your Honor I strongly object to your denial to set bond for my client" Kirkland challenged.

"Objection noted," Justice Duncan fired back. "However, the court doesn't know enough about the case, except for what I've read in the indictment and the court will not take the responsibility of setting your client free where he could leave the country." Duncan then adjourned court.

***

On November 30, 1986, Leo returned to the United States Middle District Court of Florida, Orlando Division, for round two which ended in defeat as well. "Your Honor," Attorney Kirkland said with a clear voice. "We're here for two reasons: to file another pre-trial motion petitioning the court for a Fast-and-Speedy Trial and another bond hearing." Attorney Kirkland attempted to present a clear picture of the events leading up to Leo arrest, but Justice Duncan, once again, didn't care to hear it.

"Good try counselor, but I'm denying your request on all counts." Judge Duncan fired back. "The way I see it, I'm doing your client a favor and might be saving his life in the event he decided to plea bargain. The court is well aware of your client's China Mafia ties, and I'm not about to let him slip through the courts fingers." Duncan refused to grant Leo a bond or the Fast-and-Speedy Trial, then rather abruptly adjourned court and insisted they not return until the trial.

Several weeks later, a certified letter addressed to Leo Stegner arrived at Orlando's Orange County Jail. The letter was from the Internal Revenue Service charging Leo one-million dollars in back taxes, for income tax evasion and tax on the confiscated heroin. It was a well-timed Christmas present. Now Leo began to realize that the Criminal Investigation Division of the United States government wasn't only out to put him away for good, but to break him financially as well.

Attorney Kirkland, well known throughout the state of Florida for his brilliance in handling murder cases had advised Leo to hire a good tax lawyer. But Leo, who was never one to blow money for someone else's advice, unless he felt he couldn't get the job done himself, decided to file his own appeal against the I.R.S.'s long list of allegations. However, down the road, he found that going up against the I.R.S. was like taking on a gang of street thugs single-handedly. The I.R.S. took his car, his house, froze all of his bank accounts and put a lien in his credit bureau file, and didn't leave him with shit!

On February 20, 1987 at 9:30 that Monday morning, two overweight U.S. Marshals arrived at Orlando's Orange County Jail to escort Leo to court. News photographers and reporters swarmed in front of the courthouse awaiting his arrival. Attorney Kirkland had already petitioned the court for a change of venue due to the overwhelming amount of pre-trial publicity, but the motion was denied.

When Dan Kirkland arrived, he advised Leo not to take the case before a jury and consider pleading to a lesser offense. He reasoned that U.S. Prosecutor Robert T. Briggs had sufficient evidence to get a conviction that could net him 45-years in prison. Kirkland informed Leo that Briggs would recommend no less than five years but no more than 15-years, providing he plead guilty to any one of the charges. There were 3 charges pending, each charge carrying a maximum of 15-years.

"Let's take that deal and run with it!" Leo said to Kirkland. He didn't want to serve 45-years in prison so he entered a guilty plea to Count Three: "knowingly, intentionally, and unlawfully possess with the intent to distribute approximately 3-pounds of heroin, a controlled substance listed in Schedule 1, Title 21 U.S.C. & 812: in violation of Title 21 U.S.C. & 841(a)(1) and Title 18 U.S.C. & 2."

Attorney Kirkland left the holding cell, his expression hopeful as he entered the U.S. Prosecutor's office with the word.

At 10:45 a.m., Court went into session under the Honorable Chief Justice, Alfred C. Turner. Turner had a cold passion against drug traffickers and it was well known among the inmates throughout the prison system. If it had been within Justice Turner's power to sentence them all to death, he probably would have.

Turner had been the first Federal Judge in the South to bring a gun (snub nose .38) into the courtroom and boldly set it in plain view, on the justice bench. Judge Turner was disliked and he knew it. He asked no quarter and gave none, for his life was constantly threatened. All the inmates dreaded to go before him and knew that Turner's motive for packing the rod was because several years back he had sentenced a drug peddler to life imprisonment and the guy freaked out and almost beat him to death.

"All rise," the bailiff said when Judge Turner entered the courtroom.

By this time, D.E.A. Agent Miller had met U.S. Prosecutor Briggs in secret to bargain for a deal of his own. Miller wanted the opportunity to offer Leo full immunity from prosecution, and identity change, relocation, protection, and money. All this providing Leo became a D.E.A. informant and aid in the downfall of: the Chinese Mafia; his military heroin outlet in West Germany; General Chung Che Fu and his Shan United Army; his wholesale heroin distributor connections in the United States; and the whereabouts of Mr. Rocky Congo Lee.

The offer seemed irresistible, but Leo had already lost his father over 10-years ago to one mob's gangland-style hit, and to him the world didn't seem big enough to hide in. Nor did Leo want to take the foolish chance of risking the future existence of the Stegner family. So, Leo decided to take his chances with the guilty plea—to the possession with intent to distribute charge.

Agent Miller was not only puzzled but pissed. He couldn't imagine why a man, Leo in particular, facing 45-years, would turndown freedom for the slammer. Miller knew that any prearranged deals made between the U.S. Attorney Briggs and Attorney Dan Kirkland weren't legally binding and couldn't represent the judge's final decision. As far as the court and the D.E.A. were concerned, he was still facing 45-years and only the D.E.A. could save him.

Out of a sense of duty, and not true concern of course, Justice Turner asked Leo to comment about his mental and physical well-being. Leo stood and addressed the bench, then said, "Your Honor, I've been incarcerated for 125-days without bond, and mentally I'm under a great deal of emotional stress." He paused, looked about the courtroom, and then went on. "Sir, it's bad enough just being there! But when you have the I.R.S. fucking with you and the D.E.A. sending you menacing messages, and the Prosecutor pressing for a deal, it's a wonder I haven't committed suicide!" Leo had paused again, this time in an attempt to draw a sympathetic reaction from the Judge, but there was none. So Leo continued. "Your Honor, Sir. Before I was arrested, physically—I was in excellent condition; but due to my inactivity in an over-crowded, cramped, incarcerated surrounding, my body is rapidly deteriorating. Sir! I protest being treated so inhumane. Why, I haven't been given the opportunity to exercise my rights, and my attorney has been denied every pre-trial motion he's petitioned before the court!" Leo sat down. Everyone was astounded by Leo's forwardness. Hushed whispers radiated throughout the courtroom, then all of a sudden, silence.

Leo stood up again. He decided to take advantage of the situation. He said, "Your Honor. No disrespect to you because I was not under your jurisdiction at the time, but I think this entire matter should be investigated by you or higher authorities." Then he sat down again.

Judge Turner pondered for a moment without comment. He noticed that Leo had become plenty upset. Turner said, "I'm going to accept your guilty plea to Count Three of the Grand Jury indictment, but before I impose sentencing, I'm going to place you on Pre-Sentence Investigation and order a Psychiatric examination, and a hearing to follow, to determine if you're competent enough to enter a plea of guilty. Court adjourned!" Judge Turner left the courtroom.

On March 6, 1987, at 10:00, Thursday morning, Leo was seen for approximately 45-minutes, in a private cell by Dr. John Sheppard, the court appointed psychiatrist. Sheppard's evaluation procedure consisted of a wide variety of tests: tolerance to change, attention span, concentration abilities, answering questions as to anatomical matters, I.Q., personality changes, and tolerance to frustration and irritability.

On March 29, 1987 when court reconvened, Dr. Sheppard testified under oath that in his professional opinion, Leo suffered from a moderate case of depression and should be moved to a more pleasant institutional environment as soon as possible. He added that Leo suffered from no known neurotic disorders and he was mentally competent to enter a plea of guilty to Count Three of said indictment.

Then, Chief Justice Albert N. Turner ordered that the guilty plea should stand as previously accepted by the Court on February 20th, and ordered sentencing to be imposed on April 12, 1987 at 2:00 p.m..

Meanwhile, Agent Miller visited Leo at Orlando's Orange County Jail on one particular occasion before he was sentenced and showed Leo several photos. "Do you know any of these guys?" he asked Leo Stegner.

"Yes I've seen this guy before, but I'm not telling you shit!" Leo fired back in a fit of rage.

"If you don't cooperate," Miller said raising his voice. "I'll have no other choice, but to recommend to the judge to give you the MAX!" Miller reassured him in an angry tone of voice.

"Then go ahead and do what you're going to do because I'm not telling you anything unless you drop all the charges against me and my entire network. Shit! I've had many restless nights, anxious and without sleep. Freedom at this point would taste real sweet, but if you don't back the fuck off I'll notify the media of the sordid story of Plush underhandedness and how you allowed Plush to rip both of us off for the 33-pounds of uncut heroin before he left Holland. And how the D.E.A. spent millions of dollars in manpower on the word of a heroin and barbiturate addict, who ended up leaving the country unescorted and causing an endless search for Rocky and the Chinese Mafia's that may take decades to find," Leo said.

Miller glared at Leo intently, and then in one swift motion he snapped the number two lead pencil in half with one hand. Leo stared without a glimmer of emotion as Miller stormed out of the interrogation room madder than hell saying, "You must be out of your fucking mind. Plush was just a tool to be used and discarded. We don't give a fuck about how much money we waste to get bastards like you. I'll see you in hell first and I'm going to do everything in my power to get you the maximum sentence allowed by law. And you can believe that!" Miller had been given the covert undercover assignment initially in an attempt to smash the Chinese Mafia's "Loose-knit Heroin Network" operations and bring persons involved to trial. Miller had engineered Leo's arrest and he was considered as the best U.S. Foreign Intelligence Agent among his colleagues.

Most heroin traffickers, who had heard of or knew of Miller, labeled him a 'heartless slime' who commanded an unlimited number of confidential informants in the United States, Europe, the Middle and Far East. Miller had become the type of slime who'd turn his own mother into an informant if she gave him half the chance. Agent Miller so wanted the court leave Leo under his jurisdiction where he could interrogate Leo in his own fashion, he knew he could have gotten results. Miller knew if he got Leo in his care, Leo would lose the contemptuous look on his face in a hurry, but nobody at the local drug enforcement level would allow him to resort to torture.

During the interrogations, Leo wanted to talk. He wanted to tell everything he knew, but was scared. Leo knew he would have to serve time, and was willing; otherwise the D.E.A. would have the liberty to use him for life and his hopes and dreams to be someone productive would have surely been lost.

By now, Cecil 'Nassau' Beckman had already been convicted and sentenced by Judge Turner to serve a maximum term of one year of imprisonment. He had been released into the custody of the U.S. Attorney General, and then transferred to the Federal Penitentiary in Atlanta, Fulton County, Georgia.

Beckman's lighter sentence had offered Leo a glimmer of hope until Leo's attorney, Dan Kirkland, advised Leo he wouldn't be as lucky. Leo's case had drawn so much public outcry, Judge Turner had no other choice but to make an example of him.

On Monday, April 12, 1987, at 2:00 p.m., the United States of America vs. Leo Stegner case continued. It was Leo's day for sentencing and he had begun to visualize himself behind Federal bars. Leo had already come to accept the fact that for him there would be no more: orgies, no D.J. gig at the Playboy Discotheque, no more foreign military hashish/heroin outlets, no plush cottage or elegant clothing, no more smuggling through small foreign borders in neither Germany nor the Netherlands, and no more flights abroad. He was really going to miss Jerry Prentice, Elfi, Hillery, Bagetta, and Silki. But most of all, he would miss Rocky, Wong, Scalli, and how to reproduce opium into heroin, and the mystery that lies within the Golden Triangle borders.

In court, oral arguments had begun. Stella Stegner was filled with rage and anger wondering if her son, Leo would be stupid enough to return to society with the intent to reorganize the million-dollar heroin network or if Chief Justice Turner would be inclined to put him away for life.

Leo had already been tried in the newspapers and in the minds of the populace, and had been found guilty. No one doubted his guilt for a moment.

Among the inmates, Attorney Kirkland was considered one of the greatest criminal lawyers in Florida. However, the experts at the Orlando Sentinel's legal department and the Florida Bar Association agreed while Kirkland might be competent enough to handle routine cases, he was hopelessly out of his depth in this one.

It was like playing mental chess except Leo was the pawn and the stakes were 45-years to life imprisonment. In the past, Leo had been careless with his future, recklessly squandering time as though it were eternal. Now he was having second thoughts and wondered if he would ever see daylight again, thus more have any kind of future.

Justice Turner read off the charges, reminding Leo of the seriousness of the crime, and the harm heroin had caused today's generation and to society. Leo had no previous juvenile or criminal record. He had always taken the idea of prison lightly and had no idea how much life meant to him until that moment. He had aged 10-years in the few months. He looked gaunt and haggard and his clothes hung loosely on his frame. Leo's eyes held his mother's attention when his sentence was imposed. They were the eyes of a soul that had been through hell. Judge Turner, without leniency, informed Leo that count three of his indictment carried a maximum sentence of forty-five years, and then imposed a sentence of nine years, with a three-year Special Parole term to follow, and counseling at a Drug Rehabilitation Center once he got out.

Leo's knees nearly buckled as the judge read his sentence. Adrenaline surged throughout his body as he listened to the Judge's last words in shock and disbelief. For the web of justice had been woven. Leo stared at Turner, his eyes filled with pain and hate. He wanted to kill him.

When Leo spoke, his voice was husky with outrage... "Oh Hell No! Wait a God-damn minute, here!" He yelled, pounding his fist on the Defendant's table, in defiance. "I was told I would get no less than three and no more than 6-years if I plead guilty to any one of the counts!" A bailiff stepped forward and took him by the arm.

"That was only a recommendation. It's not legally binding, Mister. And besides, I call all the shots in this courtroom!" Turner snapped back.

Leo looked at him intently, and then said. "Why you low down, dirty, son-of-a-bitch! I'll get you for this... I'll get your fat-ass for this! You... You bastard!" Another bailiff hurried forward, but he was too late. Leo had vaulted over the wooden table, and then quickly climbed his way up and over the top of the 6-foot raised dais and hit Judge Turner up-side the head with a barrage of elbows and fists, then strangled him with his bare hands. Somehow, Turner managed to fumble the gun into his right hand. As he pulled the trigger, Federal Marshals and the courtroom bailiffs rushed the Judge's bench from both sides and deflected his aim just in time. The bullet struck the rear wall of the courtroom. All hell broke loose! People were ducking and dodging; some were swearing and cursing. Order was finally restored. Leo was lucky that day; the bullet barely missed his forehead. The people in the courtroom didn't know whether to stay or leave. They didn't know what to expect next.

Turner, who didn't have a conscience, had sent many cons to the gallows in his days. He was a big, heavy man whose bloodhound-looking face stretched with unbelievable fright and terror. He ordered Leo out of his courtroom and vowed to give him life if he ever saw him again.

Leo tried to jerk away from the bailiffs, but the handcuffs were snapped tight on his wrists and he was yanked away. The Marshals transported him back to the county jail and to his 3rd floor cell. Leo stared at the traffic below on Magnolia Avenue. He saw men, women, and children hurrying home to be united with their families. For the second time in his life, Leo felt frightened. His illusions about any chance of freedom completely dwindled now that the conscience of an outraged society had been satisfied. The court hearing would be the last time he would ever be around anyone, other than criminals without a set of bars between them. The realization hit him hard.

***

Leo was committed into the custody of the U.S. Attorney General. A week later, he was transferred from Orlando's Orange County Jail to the Federal Penitentiary, in Tallahassee, Florida.

F.C.I., or the Federal Correctional Institution, was a grim, crowded and dangerous place. Leo had to be careful with whom he socialized with or constantly run the risk of being gang-raped, jumped or beaten. Leo was determined not to be indoctrinated by the institutionalized thugs. However, F.C.I. had changed. Inmates and the prison staff alike had reassured Leo that the institution was being run like a drug rehabilitation camp or vocational school, rather than a concentration camp or prison.

The small cellblocks, close supervision, and the single cells had been changed to reduce the threat of violence, especially sexual attacks, since F.C.I. adapted psychotherapy programs and a variety of educational and recreational facilities.

What Leo hated the most was he didn't have the opportunity for an early release. In his case, and in those of the adult or "hardcore" penitentiaries, he would have to serve three and a half years before being eligible for a parole hearing, whereas other inmates received an annual review of their case. Not only would he have to serve one-third of his sentence, he would have to score eight points or better on the Salient Factor Test:

The points were usually determined by prior convictions, prior incarcerations, age of first commitment, commitment offense, the number of paroles revoked, history of drug abuse, educational level, verified employment, and a parole release plan. The third major criteria for his release consisted of two simple questions: Is Leo dangerous to society now? And, has he been rehabilitated? Leo didn't believe he had ever been a danger to society, and with no previous convictions, he thought there was nothing wrong with him from the start. He was convinced he would be out after his first eligible parole hearing three and a half years away.

Although it was in many ways a progressive prison, unique in Florida and seldom matched anywhere in America, F.C.I. had a bad reputation in 1988. Among the inmates, F.C.I. was the most dreaded institution in the state. It got the dregs—the people with lousy rehabilitation potential. According to the current medical director of F.C.I., Morris Macy, the inmates sent there would've been rejected by most private practices. Under Florida's strict definition, the inmates were all sane; but they had severe psychiatric problems or low I.Q.'s, a history of sociopathic behavior such as convictions for rape, murder, organized crime, and repeated serious drug offenses.

F.C.I. however, had a strict parole policy. Leo learned that if he was found to be a defective delinquent, he would receive an indeterminate set-off (no possible chance for parole in the immediate future), while someone else convicted of a far less serious crime might remain at F.C.I. long beyond his eligibility for parole. In theory, if Leo did not respond to therapy or his rehabilitation goals or he could not convince the Parole Review Board he was reasonably safe for society to terminate his confinement and treatment, he could be imprisoned there for the rest of his sentence.

F.C.I. stood on acres of flat, neatly manicured lawn just off Route 19/27 in Tallahassee. The grass, the trees, and the flowerbeds gave the appearance of a college campus. The double chain-link fence bristling with barbed wire enclosed the grounds along with four strategically placed gun towers that offered the guards an open field of fire in every direction. And it left no doubt in Leo's mind that the heavyset red-brick buildings with iron gates and metal doors were a prison.

When Leo arrived that sweltering afternoon in April, the F.C.I. reminded him of the P.J. Phillips Convalescent Home in Orlando. The feel of the place and the look of the other inmates weren't like jail. He thought it was much worse.

Leo was locked in the quarantine wing where he remained until he underwent a thorough evaluation. He found himself among men who paced the cellblock, never saying a word, sitting rigidly still, but wouldn't stop babbling. The others that never left their cells appeared limp from the heat, possibly from drugs or depression and lay on their bunks night and day; until their ill-fitting brown uniforms gave them the appearance of rumpled sacks of dirty laundry.

One night a young man cut both of his wrists and was bleeding like a hog. The guards carried him away and Leo never saw him again. Nobody had any idea the inmate had just received a 'Dear John' letter until the hacks found it on his bunk after they hauled him out.

Frightened and depressed by this place, Leo felt wasted. He had not had a full night's sleep in 5 or 6 months now. He couldn't relax; he had to stay on guard. Everyone had warned him; sometimes in a friendly fashion, other times with scarcely veiled threats to never let your guard down and what would happen if he did.

While Leo knew nobody there; they all appeared to recognize him. His case had drawn so much public attention everybody in the institution had heard about his arrival to the joint and most of the homosexuals wanted to see what he looked like. They wanted to test him for weaknesses and throw themselves all over him if they could.

One day in the shower a homosexual stepped close to Leo and brushed up against his penis. "Hey, baby-cakes, how about slipping on back here? I got a friend who wants to be fucked by you."

That wasn't the first time somebody had come on to Leo in such an inappropriate way, so he knew he was just being tested.

Nobody would say anything if a homosexual meant to crack on you, but Leo was plenty pissed. Leo was tired and still tense from the trial and being transferred into that zoo like atmosphere full of freaks. He went over to the gang of homosexual friends. Everybody was watching. Leo was a muscular 45-year-old man, weighing approximately 170 pounds, naked and soaking wet, ready to take them all on.

He stuck out his penis then yelled, "Here it is! You like it? Nice, isn't it? Come and get it!" Then he started stomping around screaming, "Just try! Because the first fucker that touches me is dead. I'll kill you motherfuckers. I'll kill every one of you!"

At first a few of them thought it was funny, but when he went on screaming they stopped laughing and the looks on their faces changed. This one Hispanic dude said, "Hey, that bastard is crazy!" One by one, they got the hell out of the shower room.

When Leo was back in his cell, he realized what he had said. He was already convicted for 9-years and here he was threatening to ice somebody. It sounded sick and he wondered if he might ever get out.

The way Leo figured it, he didn't have a choice. He had to play crazy if he hoped to survive. He had to come on like a stone-cold killer to keep the homosexuals from propositioning him. He saw himself going on like that for the rest of his life, spending half the time trying to convince the case manager he was rehabilitated, and the other half working to show the homosexuals or cons that he was nobody to fuck with.

＊

Then at last, Leo saw a very un-liked, but familiar face. "Don't you remember me?" the inmate asked. "You and Scalli sold me a couple of kilos in Tampa." Leo had never forgotten him. He was the man who ordered the hit on his father, Joe. They would never be close friends, but Leo was glad to see him now. Capelli seemed glad too.

"When I read you were here, I was hoping I'd get the chance to say hello before I leave," Capelli said.

"You're getting out?" Leo asked.

"Yep," he said, grinning, "3 days and a wake-up."

"What are you in for; murder?" Leo asked sarcastically. At F.C.I. that question was taboo. If it slipped out in group therapy or in the course of a conversation, fine, but you never fished for information.

Capelli frowned. He had a guilty, suspicious look on his face. "No! Whatever gave you that impression?"

"You! You son-of-a-bitch!" Leo's inner rage was undiminished, his resolve unchanged. "You killed my father Joe! Remember Joe? Joe Stegner. Over a lousy debt you tried to extort." Leo's heart was thudding, his blood hammered at his temples, his brain was swarming with all sorts of thoughts. "I've been pursuing you for 15-years."

Capelli became frightened. He remembered the hit on Joe. As he gazed at Leo, his gray eyes wide and expectant, he appeared frozen, like a deer in the headlights. He didn't speak, or try to flee. He simply raised his right arm, perhaps appealing to him, perhaps in a futile attempt to protect himself.

Without thinking, Leo threw several punches. One ripped past Capelli's arm and into his face. The second punch slammed against his chest. Then Leo lost control and the next two blows landed wildly. Capelli staggered and fell on the ground with blood bubbling at his nose and mouth.

"You're a dead man, Capelli! A dead man!! You got that?" Leo looked around quickly to see who was watching. He kicked

Capelli repeatedly while reciting John 3:16 to let him know he meant business. "For God so loved the world," he kicked Capelli. "That he gave his only begotten son," kicked him again. "That whosoever believeth in him should not perish," then kicked him again. "But have eternal life," and kicked him real hard. After pulling himself together, he moved with a strange sort of weightlessness that reminded him of swimming. Buoyant, inhaling air in rhythmic gulps, he glided across the ground, not thinking, barely registering impressions. He no longer felt sick to his stomach; he no longer felt anything at all except the urge to kill Sam Capelli. He went to his cell chatting with a couple of inmates, keeping his encounter with Capelli private.

***

Leo heard from Capelli's cellmate that Capelli tossed and turned and couldn't sleep at all that night, and that he was talking about plans of escape. Leo imagined that he must have fantasized about his turbulent past relationship with Joe. Leo hoped Capelli had bad dreams over his present conflict with him, while contemplating how death may come, now that Leo was aware how 'short' his time there was. Leo knew Capelli wouldn't go running to the Warden demanding protection because he was a murderer and could get the "electric chair."

***

The next morning Leo notified the guards of Capelli's plans to escape. Leo went to breakfast that morning bursting with joy over the fact that if Capelli attempts to escape, he himself would be responsible for putting the final nail in Capelli's coffin.

Leo thinking like Capelli reasoned that the best possible opportunity to escape was during shift change at the guard towers. Later that morning, Leo tailed Capelli throughout the prison compound remaining out of sight. And sure enough just as shift change occurred Leo spotted Capelli acting skittish by constantly looking around heading for the fence. Leo reacted quickly.

He rushed over to a guard who was in close proximity then said, "Excuse me officer, I think we have a runner" pointing in Capelli's direction.

The guard radioed the guard towers with his walkie talkie, "We have a runner! We have a runner!"

***

Capelli was 'hauling ass.' He was running with his head held high and his arms whaling. Capelli had totally lost it; he hit the fence hard as he climbed up to the strands of barbed wire. A guard with a bullhorn ordered him down—just as he was about to clear the second fence, but Capelli slipped gingerly over the wire and dropped to the ground on the other side. When he ran for the woods, the guard's voice changed. It sounded as if he was begging him to stop. There was a flood of automatic weapons fired from two of the towers, and Capelli fell in a sprawl—several small holes in his back—several big ragged ones in his chest—where the shells had ripped through. Capelli died instantly before they could get him to the infirmary.

Leo clinched his fist to his face then shouted, "Good they got that FUCKER! ...FUCKKKK!!!... I wanted that motherfucker for myself! I wanted my own sweet revenge... That son-of-a-bitch! He's in less of a hell than I had in store for his ass. All those years of prepping and planning my revenge; enlisting in the Vietnam war to learn to kill, and all those meetings with higher-ups in the different Mafia's to hone my motherfucking skills just for this fucker to get away!"

***

Leo stayed in his cell fuming, lying there listening to the inmates in the hall. All he knew was he'd seen just 2 men get out of there. One slashed his wrists. The other was shot dead, so he stopped trying to convince himself that the F.C.I. didn't seem like a fucking jail, and he stopped jiving himself that he was going to talk his way out.

Leo no longer had any illusions he would be released. The way he was going, he'd be lucky to stay alive. And lucky for what reason, he wondered; to last another day, another month, another year? For what? To watch another inmate stand in the window stroking his meat? To spend every waking hour worried that he was about to be jumped? To lie awake every night thinking?

Just before dark, the 'dealer,' an older con, rapped on Leo's door, and asked if Leo needed anything: cigarettes, beat-off books, dope, whiskey, pills? But all Leo wanted was sleep.

"Gimme something that'll put me out," Leo said.

"Sure, my man. Feeling a little low? Try one of these red pills. It'll pick you up." The old con suggested.

"I don't want to be up. I want to sleep!" Leo replied.

"Well, I got five of these yellow birds. How many do you need?" the old con asked.

"All of them," Stegner responded.

For an instant, the man hesitated. "One or two will do you," he suggested.

"Are you selling or not?" Leo asked. He was pissed.

"Sure, my boy. Just space these bad-boys out. I'll get you some more next week," the old con said assuring.

When the man left, Leo dropped the five pills into his cup, filled it with water at the sink, and drank them all down. He then lay back down on his bunk. Although he had no idea what the pills were, he figured five of them should do it. He would sleep the night through, and if he got lucky, he'd never wake up. However, five yellow birds were not enough.

For two days Leo drifted in a semi-conscious state, dreamless and incoherent. Then he woke with a thundering headache and an enormous hunger.

He never attempted suicide again. He reasoned that under desperate circumstances the decision not to kill his self was as incomprehensible as the decision to do so.

Immediately after making up his mind not to commit suicide, he had to decide whether to get involved with the homosexuals. He'd had proposals. A few homosexuals had offered cigarettes, money, and companionship, and warned him he'd never survive alone. Regardless, Leo went his own way and started lifting weights and running, hoping that muscle, along with his reputation as being crazy, would keep him safe. Although he would never grow taller than 5'11", he gained 25 pounds, most of it in his shoulders, biceps, and chest, and eventually resembled a medium-sized "Incredible Hulk."

With the same numbing, metronomic rhythm as he pumped iron daily, he began 'doing time'—an expression that has little meaning to anyone who hasn't been in prison, serving a nine-year sentence.

***

Leo's initial goals established by his case worker while serving time consisted of: improving his academic grade level, voluntary college participation, improvement of clerical skills, learning to accept responsibility, and learning to function without resorting to the use of drugs.

Within eight months' time, Leo had completed the high school refresher course and received C.L.E.P. credits toward his first two years at Tallahassee Community College. He also participated in a drug abuse program at the institution and responded in an above average manner.

While he was enrolled in college, he worked as a clerk in the Classification and Parole section. Later, he was assigned as a clerk in the institution's hospital. The hospital administrator, Morris Macy rated him as being outstanding in response to supervision and instructions, and above average in his ability to learn.

As time went on, Leo continued to exhibit an above average interest in his job, and did extra work to improve his skills. He planned his work well and exhibited an ability to work independently. His quality and quantity of work was rated as excellent and he became very proficient in the many clerical skills needed in the hospital department.

The graphs and reports in his files appeared to indicate progress. To Leo they seemed random, pointless, and repetitious. Like the exercises, tens of thousands of curls, reverse curls, dead lifts, and bench presses that filled out his body—the tests, therapy sessions, and academic and vocational courses were at first only excuses to fill up his days. He didn't believe they these activities were leading anywhere because he had a seven-year regular adult sentence with a three-year special parole term to follow that required him to do a third of his time before seeing the parole board. So with his kind of sentence, where could it lead? He was just killing time before it killed him, as far as he was concerned.

At F.C.I., Leo was rated as one of the more cooperative men in the prison and constantly assumed the leadership roles in institution activities. He had actively participated as a chairman of the institution town meeting program and represented the needs of the prisoners to the warden in a positive manner. His relationships with his peers and the prison staff had been rated by Warden Adolph Payne as above average, and he was not seen as aggressive unless extremely provoked. Leo had done all of this because he was now desperate to get out of prison. He knew that without these accomplishments there was no way in hell the Parole Board would consider him for release after doing a third of his time.

A year later, Leo found the courage to write Judge Turner and apologize for his hideous behavior in court, and sent him copies of his outstanding progress, and assured Turner that he'd never resort back to selling drugs or violence as a means to an end. He asked Judge Turner if he would consider and approve his Rule 35 (a Motion requesting a sentence reduction) that he had sent along with his letter of apology, based on the facts that: he was a Vietnam era veteran, honorably discharged; with one prior arrest, no convictions nor any prior history of drug abuse; he had maintained an excellent prison record without a disciplinary report; and that he had only acted hostile in court out of his fear of incarceration and arrogance.

Some three months later, Judge Turner granted Leo's motion, but with some reservations, of course, and reduced his sentence from nine years to seven years, with a three-year Special Parole term to follow.

***

Stratified into four tiers, the F.C.I. prison was run according to the behaviorist theory principle, with reinforcements given for good conduct and the appropriate response to treatment. As an inmate advances from one tier to another, he enjoys more freedom and better facilities until finally, on the fourth-tier; the prisoners virtually govern their own lives. They spend less time in lock up and are allowed to decorate their cells with plants, pictures, and personal belongings which are forbidden on the lower levels. There was also a game room where inmates could entertain visitors and throw an annual Christmas party. During the summer months, inmates on the fourth-tier were permitted to picnic on the front lawn every Sunday with their families and friends. The F.C.I. even provided tables and brightly colored umbrellas. Each man's case was reviewed every three months and their privileges could be revoked for infractions of the rules or failure to make progress in therapy.

Leo graduated from Tallahassee Community College, receiving an Associate in Arts degree in Clinical Psychology. He was an active member of the institution's International Jaycee Organization and had participated in their local community programs. Leo had been assigned minimum custody and during the Christmas holidays visited his family in Orlando for five days. He initiated his parole plans by enrolling into the University of Central Florida in Orlando, but in group therapy he could not bring himself to speak out. It wasn't just that he didn't care to discuss his crime or the darker secrets of his childhood— he didn't want to reveal anything about himself. Already the other inmates knew too much about him and he felt they wanted to use him for his contacts.

Because of the way he spoke, and his criminal profile, many of the inmates accused him of being a snob. He remembered one guy in group therapy saying, "You asshole, you had it made. You had money and a nice house and a good family. And you blew it. You just fucking blew it!" How could he convince the guy, who probably came from a slum somewhere, those things don't matter and that their struggle was virtually the same?

There was only one way he could win. Whenever he talked in therapy, they accused him of sounding like a stuck-up bastard, and if he kept quiet, they asked, "What's the matter? You too good to talk to us?" Before long he got the message. They were going to keep jumping on his case until he dropped everything he had picked up at home, college, and in Europe. Well, one thing he learned, he was adaptable. He would turn into a Goddamn Chameleon if it was a question of surviving.

In addition to continuing his weight training, he took on protective coloration in the form of jailhouse tattoos; a symbol of physical toughness and imperviousness to pain. He talked like them, too. Good grammar deserted him, his slang was now that of the slammer, not the schoolyard, and he peppered every sentence with obscenities. The thing was, he didn't want to be different or stand out and become a target. However, on a brighter note, the warden and his staff was impressed by Leo's achievement in being the first of two people to receive a college degree at F.C.I.

On July 9, 1990, after serving 3 ½ years, including county jail time, Leo was released on parole to an approved parole plan, but with special drug aftercare conditions. He had to participate, as instructed, in a program approved by the Board of Parole, for treatment of drug dependency which included urine testing to determine if he had reverted to the use of drugs.

Chapter 9

"Pleading for Presidential Pardon"

Click. That was the sound of Leo Stegner's life going from crooked to straight. The clicks of guns cocking, the click of the lock on the jail-house door as it slammed shut. Click, the sound of the judge's bullet barely missing Leo's forehead, and now click... The noise inside Leo's head, then the horror clears and the realization hits; it's time to change.

Leo stepped up to the podium to shake the hand of the College Dean at the University of Central Florida, Summer Commencement Ceremony the 27th day of July 1992. Leo had finally graduated with his Bachelor of Arts degree in Clinical Psychology.

Guyda had even attended the big event. Stegner's rehabilitation from International Heroin Smuggler to a College Graduate was the way the penal system was supposed to work, but often doesn't. He and Guyda partied all night; just dancing and fucking the night away.

***

On August 10, 1992, Leo was released from early parole, receiving a Certificate of Early Termination, but he still had to remain under supervision for the three-year Special Parole Term to follow, which was subsequently granted. Meanwhile, Leo and Guyda got married then had a baby girl. Leo had become so successful as a Private Investigator he was able to finance Guyda's way through the same college he had attended. Her major was in Radio-Television Production, with a minor in music and voice.

***

On March 11, 1993, Leo received a Certificate of Restoration of Civil Rights from the Office of Executive Clemency, in Tallahassee.

***

On December 11, 1993, Leo Stegner went before Governor Fred Graham, and the entire Florida Cabinet, and was granted a full pardon and granted the specific authority to receive, possess, or transport in commerce a firearm. Leo had previously been denied this right by the Parole and Probation Commission.

***

On January 11, 1994, Leo was granted the specific authority to receive, possess, or transport in commerce a firearm, by the Department of Treasury of the United States government.

***

On March 1, 1994, Leo was granted a Class A license to operate his own Private Investigation Agency, by the State of Florida, Secretary of State Office.

***

Leo had become so successful as a private investigator and Special Process Server appointed by the Orange and Osceola County Sheriff's Departments, as well as, a certified process server appointed by the Chief Justice of Brevard County; he was able to finance Guyda's way through the same college he had attended.

***

The biggest task was yet to come, convincing the President of the United States of America, George W. Bush, to grant Leo a Presidential Pardon.

On February 23, 1998 Leo Stegner filed an *"Application Petition for a Presidential Pardon"* with the White House in Washington, D.C.. Months went by, and then finally the FBI called, and then came by Leo's house to interview him. The FBI requested Leo write a more complete explanation as to why he should be pardoned other than the information filed with his application.

Several months later word finally came. Stegner opened the letter with expectations of positive results until he read:

"Dear Mr. Stegner; your pardon application has been carefully considered in this Department and the White House, and the decision has been reached that favorable action is not warranted. Your application has therefore been denied. Under the Constitution, there is no appeal from this decision. As a matter of well-established policy, we do not disclose the reason for the decision in a pardon matter. In addition, deliberative communications pertaining to agency and presidential decision-making are confidential and not available under existing case law interpreting the Freedom of Information Act and Privacy Act. I would like to take this opportunity to emphasize that Presidents have granted very few pardons in recent times, and the decision in your case does not reflect adversely on the progress you have made toward rehabilitation since your conviction. Sincerely, Roger C. Adams, Pardon Attorney."

Leo was crushed. It seemed as if all his hard work didn't matter. *I'll apply again and again Leo thought.* Leo had already visualized himself being pardoned and was ready to be "the President's representative" on prison reform and rehabilitation; speaking at prisons, reformatory schools and high schools, and testifying at religious institutions how his faith in God had helped him turn his life around and become a role model for gangs and dysfunctional youths throughout America.

A light bulb went off in his head. He would write a book, telling his truth to everyone who would listen and title it "Sin and Redemption: The Pink Elephant Connection" in the hopes the people of America would be willing to dig deep within their hearts and forgive him by granting him a people's pardon just in case the next president does not.

***

On January 20, 2009, Barack Obama was sworn in as President of the United States. He officially assumed the presidency at 12:00 noon, EST, and completed the oath of office at 12:05 pm, EST. He delivered his inaugural address immediately following his oath.

Leo was excited as hell. He saw the Obama presidency as an opportunity for him to reapply for Presidential Pardon once again. On March 12, 2013, Leo submitted his application for Presidential Pardon which was received by the U.S. Department of Justice, Office of the Pardon Attorney which acknowledged that the application is being processed.

Leo's application is still pending to this date.

THE END

Appendix A
Corroborating Documents

Document 1: Notice of Action.

Document 2: Certificate of Parole.

Document 3: Certificate of Early Termination (from parole).

Document 4: Clemency / Restoration of Civil Rights.

Document 5: Permission to own and use a firearm.

Document 6: Department of Treasury Acknowledgment of Firearm Use.

Document 7: Private Investigator, Firearm, and Process Server certifications.

B-2 part 2
(Rev. 4/74)

NOTICE OF ACTION - PART II - SALIENT FACTORS

Case Name __James E. McCarthy__   Register Number __19682-101__

Item A --- [1]

    No prior convictions (adult or juvenile) = 2
    One or two prior convictions = 1
    Three or more prior convictions = 0

Item B --- [2]

    No prior incarcerations (adult or juvenile) = 2
    One or two prior incarcerations = 1
    Three or more prior incarcerations = 0

Item C --- [1]

    Age at first commitment (adult or juvenile) 18 years or
    older = 1
    Otherwise = 0

Item D --- [1]

    Commitment offense did not involve auto theft = 1
    Otherwise = 0

Item E --- [1]

    Never had parole revoked or been committed for a new
    offense while on parole = 1
    Otherwise = 0

Item F --- [0]

    No history of heroin, cocaine, or barbiturate dependence = 1
    Otherwise = 0

Item G --- [1]

    Has completed 12th grade or received GED = 1
    Otherwise = 0

Item H --- [1]

    Verified employment (or full-time school attendance) for a
    total of at least 6 months during the last 2 years in the
    community = 1
    Otherwise = 0

Item I --- [0]

    Release plan to live with spouse and/or children = 1
    Otherwise = 0

Total Score --- [8]

James E. McCarthy

The United States Board of Parole
Washington, D.C. 20537

RECEIVED

Certificate of Parole

JUL 0 7 1975

U. S. PROBATION OFFICE
TAMPA, FLORIDA

Know all Men by these Presents:

It having been made to appear to the United States Board of Parole that

JAMES E. McCARTHY, Register No. 19682-101, a prisoner in

the FEDERAL CORRECTIONAL INSTITUTION, TALLAHASSEE, FLORIDA,

is eligible to be PAROLED, and that there is a reasonable probability that he WILL REMAIN AT LIBERTY WITHOUT VIOLATING THE LAWS and it being the opinion of the said United States Board of Parole that the release of this person is not incompatible with the welfare of society, it is ORDERED by the said United

States Board of Parole that he be PAROLED on JULY 9, 1975,

and that he remain within the limits of MIDDLE DISTRICT OF FLORIDA until

FEBRUARY 13, 1980;

Given under the hands and the seal of the United States Board of Parole

this 7th day of JULY, nineteen hundred and SEVENTY-FIVE

UNITED STATES BOARD OF PAROLE,

By *Thomas R. Holsclaw*
THOMAS R. HOLSCLAW, REGIONAL DIRECTOR

[SEAL]

ADVISOR ....

PROBATION OFFICER ROBERT EVANS, CHIEF, USPO

This CERTIFICATE OF PAROLE will become effective on the date of release shown on the reverse side. If the parolee fails to comply with any of the conditions listed on the reverse side, he may be retaken on a warrant issued by a Member of the Board of Parole, and reimprisoned pending a hearing to determine if the parole should be revoked.

INMATE COPY

Parole Form H-15
(January, 1977)

UNITED STATES DEPARTMENT OF JUSTICE

United States Parole Commission

~~Washington, D.C. 20537~~

Atlanta, Georgia

CERTIFICATE OF EARLY TERMINATION

RECEIVED

JUN 5 1978

U. S. PROBATION OFFICE
ORLANDO, FLORIDA

Name __JAMES EDWARD MCCARTHY__ Register Number __19682-101__

Date sentence imposed __July 27, 1973__ Date supervision began __July 9, 1975__

District of supervision __MIDDLE DISTRICT OF FLORIDA__

Inasmuch as you have successfully completed a period of parole supervision, and the United States Parole Commission is of the opinion that you will not again engage in conduct which will violate any criminal law:

YOU ARE HEREBY DISCHARGED FROM PAROLE

By this action, you are no longer under the jurisdiction of the United States Parole Commission.

J. ROBERT COOPER
(Regional Commissioner)

JULY 5, 1978
(Date)

cc: USPO Little
Orlando, FL

FCI
Tallahassee, FL

Note: If you have a Special Parole term to follow you are to remain under supervision on that term only.

JPS/ks

PAROLEE COPY

FPI-MAR—2-11-77-45M.SETS-6996

James E. McCarthy

OFFICE OF EXECUTIVE CLEMENCY
Tallahassee, Florida

CERTIFICATE OF RESTORATION OF CIVIL RIGHTS

WHEREAS, the Governor with the concurrence of the requisite members of the Cabinet of the State of Florida have filed an Executive Order on _____October 23_____, 19__80__, with the Secretary of the State, in compliance with Article IV, Section 8, Constitution of the State of Florida, which grants

JAMES EDWARD McCARTHY

restoration of civil rights in the State of Florida for any and all felony convictions in any state other than Florida, or in any United States court or military court for which this person has been duly discharged from imprisonment and/or parole or probation, and for which this person has not been heretofore granted clemency; provided, however, that a person who has been convicted of a felony and has been released from prison by expiration of sentence shall not be exempt from the registration requirements of Section 775.13, Florida Statutes.

NOW, THEREFORE, I, the Coordinator of the Office of Executive Clemency, pursuant to said Order, and by virtue of the authority vested in me by the Governor with the concurrence of the requisite members of the Cabinet of the State of Florida, do hereby issue this certificate to

JAMES EDWARD McCARTHY, DOC 172274   DOB 11/4/50

and the same shall be evidence to all persons that this person is restored to all civil rights in this State, except the specific authority to possess or own a firearm, lost by reason of any and all felonies this person may have been convicted of in another state, federal, or military court; provided, however, that if this person has been convicted of a felony and has been released from prison by expiration of sentence, this person shall not be exempt from the registration requirements of Section 775.13, Florida Statutes.

Dated this _____23rd_____ day of _____October_____, A.D., 19__80__.

Alice S. Ragsdale
COORDINATOR

State of Florida

Whereas, At a meeting this day, at which were present

His Excellency, _____ BOB GRAHAM _____,

Governor of said State, _____ GEORGE FIRESTONE _____, Secretary

of State, _____ JIM SMITH _____, Attorney General,

_____ GERALD A. LEWIS _____, Comptroller,

__ BILL GUNTER __, Treasurer, __ RALPH D. TURLINGTON __, Commissioner

of Education, and _____ DOYLE CONNER _____, Commissioner of Agriculture,

of said State, who under the Constitution of said State, have full power to grant full or conditional pardons, restore civil rights, commute punishment, and remit fines and forfeitures for offenses, it was determined that JAMES EDWARD McCARTHY,

who was convicted in the United States District Court, Middle District of Florida, July 27, 1973, of the offense of Possession With Intent To Distribute Heroin, and sentenced therefor to serve nine years in a Federal Penitentiary, to be followed by three years special parole; sentence amended November 26, 1973, to seven years in a Federal Penitentiary, to be followed by three years special parole, and who was granted restoration of civil rights in the State of Florida on October 23, 1980, should now, upon showing made, be granted specific authority to receive, possess or transport in commerce a firearm.

Therefore, Be it Known, That the said JAMES EDWARD McCARTHY, be, and he is hereby granted specific authority to receive, possess or transport in commerce a firearm.

In Testimony Whereof, We have hereunto set our hands,

this ___ 10th ___ day of ___ December ___, A.D. 19 80.

_____
Governor.

_____
Secretary of State.

_____
Attorney General.

_____
Comptroller.

_____
Treasurer.

_____
Commissioner of Education.

_____
Commissioner of Agriculture.

I certify the foregoing to be
a true and correct copy of the
original order.

_____
Coordinator, Office of Executive Clemency.

James E. McCarthy

DEPARTMENT OF THE TREASURY
BUREAU OF ALCOHOL, TOBACCO AND FIREARMS
WASHINGTON, D.C. 20226

OFFICE OF
THE DIRECTOR

JAN

C:I:F:TVF
3270.10

Mr. James E. McCarthy
2925 S. Semoran Boulevard, Apt. 261
Orlando, FL 32807

Dear Mr. McCarthy:

Reference is made to your application for relief from
Federal firearms disabilities. We are pleased to advise
you that we have granted your application pursuant to
18 U.S.C. § 925(c).

You are cautioned that this action provides relief only
with respect to your Federal firearms disabilities
arising from prior criminal convictions. It does not
relieve you from any firearms disabilities to which you
may now or hereafter be subject by reason of any State
laws or local ordinances.

Appropriate officers of the Bureau responsible for the
enforcement of firearms laws are being advised concerning the favorable conclusion of this matter.

Sincerely yours,

Director

261

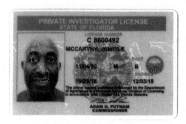

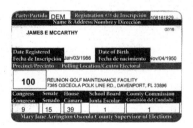

Appendix B
Description of Characters
Chapter 1

Leo Stegner: Son of Joe and Stella Stegner, a member of the Ring Eye Gang, a confidential mail courier for TWA at the Kennedy Space Center, a soldier/Company Clerk in the U.S. Army in West Germany, a DJ at the Playboy Discotheque, a hashish and heroin dealer then became an international hashish and heroin smuggler, a prison inmate, a college graduate and a Private Investigator.

Joe Stegner: Leo's father who was a gambler and a car porter

Stella Stegner: Leo's mother who had three children

Robert Stegner: Joe and Stella older son

Doris Stegner: Joe and Stella youngest daughter

Lester Stegner: Stella's father who was called over to console her after the death of her husband

Nick Machinso: The primary hit man from upstate New York who was paid $25k to do the hit

Ted Morgan: Leader of the Ring-Eye-Gang

Detective Sergeant Hood: Orlando Police Department's finest officer of 19 years who interrogated Leo at the police station

The Old Drunk: Old man who Joe gave money to deliver a torn page from the bible to the hitman

The Ring-Eye-Gang: A teenage gang of professional car thieves; one of the best in Florida at the time

Florida Mobsters: Professional gangsters who extorted money out of people to settle gambling debts

The Tail: Secondary hitman hired to fulfill the contract if the primary hitman didn't complete the job

The Guard: A guard at the Orange County jail who stopped Detective Hood from assaulting Leo

The Preacher & Church Members: A bald preacher and members of the Mount Sinai Seventh Day Adventist Church

Chapter 2

Werner Von Braun: Director of NASA space exploration

Alfred Nelson: Leo's supervisor at the TWA mailroom at Kennedy Space Center

Three Apollo Astronauts: The first three men chosen to go into orbit on the Apollo flight

NASA Security: Wackenhut security guards

Chapter 3

Guyda Henderson: Thomas Scalli cousin and Leo's girlfriend from the hood

Colonel Bob Bronson: Commander of the 3rd Armored $3/36^{th}$ Infantry Division and a combat intelligence officer who had served seven tours of duty in Vietnam during the 60's

Lieutenant Paul Underwagger: Senior DEA Officer transferred from the Pentagon

Private First Class Darwud Shaw: Leo's roommate who gave Leo lessons on how to make out with German girls and a saboteur

Private Ricky Dicks: Leo's roommate who controlled everything that moved in the supply room for the Headquarters Infantry Company

Lieutenant Karl Rukyser: Officer of the guards at the Russian Embassy

Sergeant Vladimir Krouse: Embassy guard carrying the AK47

Corporal Ivan Koloff: Embassy guard carrying the AK47

Four- Star General Alexander Haig: Commander of NATO forces in Europe

Sergeant Benjamin Striker: Leo's mentor and best friend. Disc jockey at the Playboy Discotheque, military drug distributor and Platoon Sergeant over Leo's Platoon

Andre Cooper: Rapist and escape convict from the Mannheim Stockade

Jerry Prentice: Owner/Manager of the Playboy Discotheque and he taught Striker everything he knew about drugs and drug smuggling

U.S. Army Military Police Sergeant: Officer who served the arrest warrant on Andre Cooper

U.S. Army Medics: Administered first aid to Andre Cooper

Playboy Discotheque Tenants: Residents that lived above the Playboy Discotheque

Elfi Drechsler: Leo's girlfriend and heroin courier

Eva Vermeil: Elfi's roommate and heroin courier

Bagetta Fritz: Darwud Shaw girlfriend and heroin courier

Hillery Krefeld: Ricky Dicks girlfriend and heroin courier

180 GI Drug Peddlers: Striker's military drug dealers who was stationed at different military Posts throughout West Germany

Chapter 4

Leo's Old Friends in Orlando, FL: Leo's friends from the hood

Rocky Congo Lee: Leo's Heroin mentor and China Mafia connection

Taxi Driver: German taxi driver

Amsterdam, Holland's Drug Authorities: Maintain a black list of suspected smugglers coming in and out of the country **Wong Lee:** Rocky's assistant and pilot

Border Officials: Border officials at the Kleve Border between Germany and Amsterdam

Richard Record: Head of the French Connection

American Drug Enforcement Agents: Kidnapped Richard Record

Telephone Operator: Attended to Rocky after he was ripped off

The Stranger with the Umbrella: Professional rip-off artist who prayed on the vulnerabilities of big business heroin distributors

Personnel Manager: Managed the building complex where Rocky fell victim

Crowd of People: People in the office building who responded to Rocky's aid

Chapter 5

Silki Kressler: Bagetta's best friend and heroin courier

Young Attractive Woman: Tourist that Leo became suspicious of while in the airport

Customs Official: U.S. Customs at JKF International

Asian Cobra: Cobra that escaped while going through customs

Taxi Driver at JFK International: Taxi driver that took Leo to LaGuardia Airport

Thomas Scalli: Guyda's cousin, former Miami Dolphins wide receiver, heroin distributor and Leo's right hand man in the U.S.

Orlando Police Department: Police officers that constantly patrol high profile drug areas

Cecil Beckman: Bahamian nationalist who migrated to the U.S. and was one of the biggest cocaine and heroin retailers in the South Florida area

Beckman's Assistant: Assisted Beckman with examining the heroin shipments being purchased

Beckman's Runner: Assisted Beckman in finding human guinea pigs to test the heroin

Two Female Models/Prostitute/and Junkies: Injected the heroin in their arm to show how potent it is

Chapter 6

Captain Copeland: Senior Pilot who navigated Flight 502

Sam: Co-Pilot who assisted in the navigation of Flight 502

London Tower: Assisted Flight 502 with an emergency landing

The KLM Airline Stewardess: Maintain order and calmness throughout the plane during the crisis

Chief of Operation: Cleared the air field for the emergency landing

The Passengers Aboard KLM 502: Spotted the fire on Flight 502 and began moaning in fear

Robert Stone: A big time drug dealer out of Jupiter, Florida

Sam Capelli: Ordered the contract on Joe Stegner

Capelli's Bodyguards: Stationed throughout Capelli's private clubhouse and over saw Capelli's safety

Damon Novack: A big time cocaine distributor who migrated from the Virgin Islands and now made his home in Atlanta

Chapter 7

Waitress at the Playboy: Assisted the special delivery courier

Special Delivery Courier: Delivered a sealed envelope from Rocky to Leo

Playboy Discotheque Customers: 40-50 party goers moving in and out of the club

Wong Lee's Assistant: In charge of heroin sales to reputable clients

Amsterdam Airport Red-Haired Man: A liaison and guide for Rocky

Blonde Men: A map reader and guide

Lun Lutken: A Burmese guide familiar with treacherous terrain

Opium Caravan: Consisted of 30 horses, 15 trucks, 20 elephants and a band of armed guards

General Chung Che Fu: Leader of 8,000 Chinese nationalist who purchased Opium from the hill tribesman and oversaw the Opium be converted into heroin for distribution

Young Laotian Street Boys: Adolescent opium/heroin/morphine addicts

General Fu's Guards: Shan soldiers who guarded heroin/opium shipments throughout the Golden Triangle

Thai Drug Enforcements Agents: Drug Enforcement Officers under General Pao Sarasin conmand

General Pao Sarasin: Chief DEA Officer in Thailand

Chinese Seaman: Made heroin pickups in the South China Sea

Hong Kong Customs Officials: Customs official at the Hong Kong Airport

Matsuto: Head of concierge

Taxi Driver: Picked up Leo, Rocky and Wong from the airport and drove them to the Hong Kong Red Light District

Yow Yin Ching: Owner of a Chinese restaurant that sold large quantities of heroin out of the back rooms

Robert DeFauw: Chief U.S. DEA Liaison Officer in Thailand

Chapter 8

Newspaper Reporters: ABC, NBC, CBS, United Press International and Associated Press

Courtroom Spectators: General public

Alfred C. Turner: U.S. Federal Judge

Dr. John Sheppard: Court appointed psychiatrist

The Courtroom Bailiff's: Orange County Sheriff Department officers

Federal Marshalls: Assigned to transporting Leo from jail to the courtroom

FCI Inmates: General prison population

Prison Guards: Prison employees

Adolph Payne: Warden of the Federal Correctional Institute prison in Tallahassee, Florida

Prison Caseworkers: In charge of Leo's prison progress reports

Parole Board: Reviewed Leo's chances for release from prison

Morris Macy: FCI's medical director in the prison hospital

Chapter 9

Jim Adams: Pardon Attorney for President Bush

Jeff Kunts: Newspaper Writer

Bill Ryder:

Howard Hunter: Newspaper Writer

Harold Dickerson: Director of U.S. Treasury for restoration of federal rights to possess a firearm

Kenny "G": Leo's Federal Probation and Parole Officer

Fred Graham: Governor of the State of Florida

Jim Firestone: Secretary of State for Florida

Tim Smith: Attorney General for the State of Flroida

James Lewis: State Comptroller

Robert Gunter: Treasurer of the State of Florida

Alan E. Turlington: Commissioner of Education

Boyle Conner: Commissioner of Agriculture of the State of Florida

Lieutenant Butch Reed: Orange County Sheriff Department DEA Agent

About the Author

James E McCarthy is a retired self-employed Private Investigator and Tax practitioner who was born and raised in Orland Florida. After High School he worked for TWA as a mail courier at the Kennedy Space center until he was laid off. He volunteered for the United States Army during the Vietnam era and was sent to Germany to serve his tour of duty. Upon returning home he attended Tallahassee Community College graduating with an AA degree in clinical psychology then further his education by attending Southern College obtaining an AA degree in computing programming then attended the University Of Central Florida, graduating with a BA degree in clinical psychology.

Upon completing college he worked for most of the major Law Firms in the central Florida area as a self-employed private investigator at Investigators Inc. and as a self-employed Special Process Server as well as a Certified Process Server for approximately fifteen years with the Department of Children's and Family attorneys for Seminole County. At the end of those careers he worked for less than a year as an Investigator I, with the Public Defender's Office then left there and became CDC Certified and worked at the Orange County Health Department as a Disease Intervention Specialist chasing down individuals whom had contracted Aids, Syphilis, Gonorrhea, etc. and getting them into the clinic for treatment. At the end of those two short careers he open his own Tax Practitioner Service as a tax preparer and consultant until he retired but to this day he still maintain a class "C" PI License.

Ordering Information

Sin and Redemption: The Pink Elephant Connection
by James E. McCarthy
© 2016 by James E. McCarthy
ISBN: 978-1-944136-00-0

Ashanti Victoria Publishing
109 Ambersweet Way
Suite 313
Davenport, FL 33897

jamese_mccarthy@yahoo.com
www.jamesemccarthy.com

James E. McCarthy

CPSIA information can be obtained
at www.ICGtesting.com
Printed in the USA
LVOW06*2314281217
561162LV00012B/41/P